THE
GUILTY
ONE

Also available by Bill Schweigart

The Devil's Colony
Northwoods
The Beast of Barcroft
Slipping the Cable
Women and Children First (with James Patterson)

THE
GUILTY
ONE

A NOVEL

BILL SCHWEIGART

CROOKED
LANE

NEW YORK

Copyright © 2023 by Bill Schweigart

Published in the United States by Crooked Lane Books, an imprint of The Quick Brown Fox & Company LLC.

Crooked Lane Books and its logo are trademarks of The Quick Brown Fox & Company LLC.

Library of Congress Catalog-in-Publication data available upon request.

ISBN (hardcover): 978-1-63910-246-4
ISBN (ebook): 978-1-63910-247-1

Cover design by Nicole Lecht

Printed in the United States.

www.crookedlanebooks.com

Crooked Lane Books
34 West 27th St., 10th Floor
New York, NY 10001

First Edition: March 2023

10 9 8 7 6 5 4 3 2 1

To Kate, my love, and Sidney, my world.
I'm grateful for you every day.

1

Six months ago

THE MASSIVE TWEAKER spun Patrol Officer Callum "Cal" Farrell round and round on Duke Street. It was like riding a
frothing, tattooed carousel, thought Cal.

Then, *I don't belong here.*

It was an odd thing to think, even for this situation, which was
plenty odd already. Cal had been called to a convenience store on
the long avenue that ran east–west toward Old Town Alexandria,
where a large, shirtless vagrant called Tiny had posted by the front
door to harass the owner, unnerve patrons, and generally make a
nuisance of himself. It was hot—an unbearably sticky day for July
in Northern Virginia, which was a harbinger of an unbearably hot
and sticky summer ahead—and Cal's mood was sour. The sun
seemed to have leached the blue from the sky and the air was dis-
torted around the tires and hoods of the cars idling along Duke,
which Cal caught in flashes as Tiny whipped him around.

Up close, Tiny's head was massive, made even more so by
a wild mane of dirty—very dirty—blond hair that exploded
from his head and chin, flowed outward, and pooled around
his shoulders. It gave his head a triangular shape and put Cal
in mind of an erupting volcano. Maybe it was the heat. But

the eyes at the center of the volcano weren't filled with rage, but rather fear and confusion. *God knows what he really sees*, thought Cal as he spun around. Beyond Tiny's leonine head and impressive shoulders, Cal saw snatches of their surroundings. *Convenience store. Takeout barbecue joint. Lines of cars. The supermarket across Duke. Used tire store. Convenience store again. Takeout barbecue . . .*

This was not as fun as it looked.

Still, Cal enjoyed being a cop for the most part, which is why the stray *I don't belong here* was so unbidden, like it was a signal from someone else that his brain's Wi-Fi had intercepted. His father had been a cop, and Cal liked helping people, and patrolling a patch of territory to keep the peace, but he knew he would *love* being a detective, and this was the path to get there. Along the path there were obstacles and hazards: dragons, rolling boulders, raging rivers, or like today, a shirtless giant who smelled like boiling vinegar.

But the path was the path.

Cal had hoped to talk some sense into the giant—Cal was hot, Tiny was hot, all of Old Town was hot—so maybe he'd just buy a couple of slushies or ice cream sandwiches and talk Tiny into wandering off to find a nice patch of shade. Tiny was probably just loitering by the entrance to get the occasional blast of air conditioning. But as soon as he pulled into the small parking lot, he saw that Tiny was having an episode. Yelling at customers, yelling at no one, yelling at himself, then laughing uproariously at a joke for one. He knew Tiny was battling mental illness, and at the moment he was losing.

And he was drinking from a forty, so Cal added alcohol to the list of aggravating factors.

The man's head was clearly in the clouds, teetering on a very rickety psychological ladder.

Tiny cursed Cal before he had fully exited his patrol car. Alexandria's policy was one-officer units. There were pros and cons to this. Two-officer units meant you had backup sitting right next to you, but the administrators argued it cut the number of beats a shift could cover in half . . . and that it was paying two officers to do the job of one. As in most other domains, money won the day over safety. Most days, Cal just enjoyed the solitude.

Today was not most days.

The large man rushed him, thrusting his hands out toward Cal's chest, but Cal managed to snag one of Tiny's gigantic arms and twist it enough to get a single cuff on, but the man's wrists were slick with perspiration and Cal's maneuver was not the smooth and seamless one he'd executed time and time again, which is how he found himself clinging to one loop of his handcuffs while the other was clamped around the giant's wrist, who now whirled Cal around as if the vagrant was Thor, and six-foot-tall Callum Farrell was nothing more than his enchanted mallet.

Then, unbidden: *I don't belong here.*

He didn't quite know what particular *here* his mind was referring to. Here, as in at the end of a pair of swinging cuffs, trying to hold onto this unmerry-go-round before the centrifugal force hurled him into busy Duke Street? Here, in uniform on such a punishingly humid day? Here, in the uniform at all? Cal didn't have much time to ponder it, as a second patrol car arrived during one of his sweeps. He had to gain positive control of the situation quickly before one of two things happened: it escalated dangerously or he died of embarrassment.

Plus all of this spinning was beginning to make him sick.

Cal got his feet under him, slowing the man's momentum. When the tweaker's arm met with resistance after swinging freely, it threw him off balance for a moment. Cal planted his feet then, and with all of his strength jerked the man's arm downward, pulling the giant toward him. At the same time, he drove his knee into the giant's thigh, striking the long nerve that ran the length of his leg. As juiced as he was, Tiny still yelped and fell like a redwood, his leg numb. As he toppled, Cal launched himself onto the man-mountain, riding him all the way down. They had barely bounced off the pavement when Cal wrenched the man's free arm into the waiting, empty cuff with a blessed *click*.

Christ, it wasn't even ten AM yet.

Rivulets of sweat poured from them both, and after their brief wrestling match, Cal realized the man's ripe body odor was now his ripe body odor. Even cuffed, the man rolled back and forth. Cal scrambled to stay on top and not get pinned. It was like some sweaty logrolling competition.

"Damn it, man," Cal said through gritted teeth. "I was going to buy you an ice cream cone."

Tiny stopped rolling. He stared up at Cal, blinking.

"Mint chocolate chip?" he muttered.

Cal exhaled. "Sure, big guy."

With Tiny suddenly docile, Cal took a beat to look around. The steady stream of traffic on Duke had stopped to watch the show. Among the gawkers was Patrol Officer Jimmy Vance, who exited his patrol car at a leisurely pace. Vance wore a wolfish grin and a high and tight haircut. The July sun gleamed off the shorn sides of his head and the lenses of his wraparound shades.

Why did it have to be Vance?

Jimmy Vance, aka Super-Cop. With his hair and shades, he resembled Iceman from *Top Gun*, which likely would have pleased Vance to no end had Cal actually told him, which he would not. Invoking *Top Gun* would only make Vance stronger, thought Cal. The man was at the top of their class at the academy, was in peak physical condition, and sharp as a tack. He was also Axe Body Spray in human form. Worse, Cal got the uneasy feeling he was a little *too* locked on, which Cal sensed might become a problem down the line.

Vance offered a slow clap as he approached.

"I applaud your commitment."

"What?" said Cal, exhausted and irritated. Tiny was now wavering on mint chocolate chip and muttering alternatives to himself.

"Pairs figure skating. Practicing in this heat?"

"Cute."

"Oh no, it's you two who are cute. But I think if he's going to spin you around, he should get to put on the police officer costume. But you have a couple of years to work out the kinks before the next Winter Olympics . . ."

With Vance's help, they lifted the man and folded him into the back of the cruiser. No sooner was the man-mountain secure than a long tone emanated from the radio. Tiny ranted over it, now adamant about black cherry.

Vance leaned into the passenger side window of Cal's cruiser and smacked the clear plastic partition to the back seat with the flat of his hand.

"Shut up, you."

This quieted Tiny down long enough for Cal and Vance to catch the tail end of the tone, which lasted several seconds and overrode any radio chatter. The long tone was designed to get everyone's attention.

". . . multiple gunshots heard in 1800 block of Duke Street. Three callers."

"Three callers," said Vance. Cal knew what he meant. One caller could be nothing. A car backfiring, an air-conditioning unit falling onto a sidewalk. Two callers was more serious. But three?

Even in the heat, Cal felt a sudden chill.

"Five callers," added the dispatcher.

2

Now

DETECTIVE CAL FARRELL saw the body dangling from the tree by chance on his early morning run. He didn't realize what he saw at first. When it dawned on him, it was like a blow, knocking him backward. He scraped his palms on the cold asphalt trail before scrabbling back to his feet.

He'd taken up running again since that Very Hot Day. That was how he and his counselor referred to it without saying it outright. His visits with Dr. Julia Mohr, the department's psychologist, had been mandatory.

He would've gone anyway.

He had been relatively fine in the immediate aftermath of the Very Hot Day, but he had read enough to know that there was a grace period before the bill came due, so he knew to get ahead of it. But he couldn't outrun it. And sure enough, all of the requisite emotions revealed themselves like clockwork, so much so that he thought it was a self-fulfilling prophecy. Loss of interest in everything. Wanting nothing more than to sleep and being unable to. General fatigue, punctuated by adrenaline dumps and feelings of panic. The feeling of being underwater or living in a black-and-white movie with the sound turned down. An abject feeling of emptiness, and not having the energy or even the desire to want to fill himself again.

His only persistent emotions were guilt, feelings of worthlessness, or a lack of emotion altogether.

Dr. Julia Mohr was a wry woman who actually went through the checklist with him. Oddly, he mustered more energy for their appointments than just about anything else. He even told her so. He was afraid he was performing and that she might think he was always this "up."

"Like cleaning before a maid shows up," said Julia with a laugh. "Happens all the time. Which reminds me, what's the general state of your house these days?"

He lived alone in a small bungalow in the Del Ray neighborhood of Alexandria, just north of Old Town.

"Untidy."

"Was that a preexisting condition?"

"Negative."

She made a notation in her pad.

"So predictable," said Cal.

"That's good."

"The fact that you can set your watch by how fucked up I am is good?"

"*God, yes.* You're what we refer to in the business as *refreshingly* fucked up," said Julia, laughing. She was not at all what he had expected when he was ordered to meet with her following the Very Hot Day. He pictured a dour elder in a tweed jacket who reacted to Cal's disclosures with a restrained "ah" or "hm." But Dr. Julia was animated and her face was incredibly expressive. Her smile ranged from an impish smirk to a wide, toothy beam. The dark curls of her shag shook loose when she laughed, and she laughed a lot. Her eyes could go wide one moment and burrow into him the next. Her entire face was fluid and captivating.

She was also tough. She had to be if she cracked the shells of the hard cases in the department. She somehow managed to make him comfortable and keep him off guard.

"Thanks?" he said.

"Look, you're one of the few guys here who have chosen to be proactive. Do you have any idea how many of your colleagues have to be brought here kicking and screaming? They wait until they become full-blown alcoholics or abuse their families or get so depressed their reaction time suffers and some dirtbag gets the drop on them on the street. And when they finally do come to my office, they consider it some sort of personal failure of their manhood. Most bristle or balk at the slightest personal question. Which reminds me, how's your sex life?"

Cal balked at the personal question, but after her speech, he felt compelled to be transparent. Had she maneuvered him into that? Was she giving him a performance too? Even if she was, at least she was encouraging. In her own way. He decided to stick with transparency.

"Imaginary."

"Sex drive?"

"Less in Drive, more like in Park."

"Clever."

"Thanks. I'll need a nap after that."

"Have you always used humor as a shield?"

"Only when questions feel like swords."

She smirked and made a note. "Sleep still restless?"

He motioned as if making a check mark with an invisible pen.

"Come on," she said.

"I'll crash hard, then after a couple of hours I'll just be up. I remember getting dumped once in high school and it was kind of like that."

"Like being heartbroken," said Julia, "minus the girl."

There is a girl, thought Cal. But it wasn't like that. Not exactly.

On and on went the checklist, with Dr. Julia naming indicators of depression and Cal confirming or denying them. She expressed her approval or incongruous delight at the timely emergence of a new manifestation. It was nice to know he wasn't crazy, or was at least crazy in an obvious, predictable way.

She put her pad to the side and looked at him. It was near the end of their session. "The blackouts?"

"Is it a blackout if it happens when you're asleep?"

"Very philosophical. How about we stick to life's answerable questions."

Cal shook his head. "No incidents in a good long while."

Dr. Julia nodded sagely, made a note. "The feelings of worthlessness? That you don't belong here?"

He met her eye. "We both know medication isn't going to change that."

That high school heartbreak was a bit of a revelation, though. He thought about it more that night. It seemed so silly and trivial now that he had once gotten himself twisted into such knots over a girl. He remembered how he turned the corner then: running. He'd been on the soccer team, but the breakup was during the off-season, so he hadn't been exercising as he should have been. It had been the perfect storm, everything set up to allow for maximum wallowing. But he laced up his running shoes, put one foot in front of the other, and began to sweat the heartache out with forward motion.

He vowed to do the same again. The morning after that session with Dr. Julia, he went for an early morning run before work. Waking before dawn was easy when you weren't sleeping anyway, and the Mount Vernon Trail paralleled the Potomac River, offering scenic vistas. It felt good to move. But after a half mile, tears welled unexpectedly in his eyes. Fortunately, it was still dark and none of the other predawn runners saw him swiping at his face. He felt feverish, as if his muscles were sapped of strength, so he walked the rest of the way. The next day, he promised himself he'd try to work up to a full mile. As the medication accumulated in his system, he accumulated more sleep and more miles. After a few weeks, he felt as if he was pulling out of a downward spiral and leveling off.

The pre-shift runs became a ritual, which is how he came to be on the Mount Vernon Trail at dawn on a Tuesday morning, running south toward Old Town. To the east, a wooded bluff sloped down to the Potomac. To the west, there was a sliver of green with a copse of oak trees, where in the largest tree hung a dead body.

Hallucination had never been a symptom Cal had ticked off on Dr. Julia's checklist. Was he still ahead of the curve?

He stared up into the tree's canopy and blinked twice.

He realized with a guilty relief that the body was real.

3

Then

THEY WERE THE first on scene.

Cal followed Vance east on Duke Street, their lights flashing and sirens blaring, parting the sea of cars in front of them. He tried to listen to new information from the dispatcher, but his passenger in the back seat thrashed and yelled, suddenly coherent, and Cal missed most of it.

"Man, let me out! Come on, man, let me out!"

Tiny may have missed most of the content, but the tension in the dispatcher's normally detached voice made the vagrant more nervous than any words he may have actually heard. It unsettled Cal too. The dispatcher's voice was usually low and even, a fixed, stationary presence on the radio, but now it sounded a little faster, a little higher, as if the voice itself was becoming unmoored and floating away. Cal pictured the dispatcher holding a huge bouquet of black balloons, being slowly lifted off the ground.

". . . repeat, multiple gunshots. Possible active shooter situation. Twelve calls."

Suddenly, he heard Vance's voice boom on the radio. "Units 232 and 235 responding. Hold Vance and Farrell en route!"

It was official. Even though he had responded without hesitation, not even pausing long enough to release Tiny, and was now speeding down the center lane of Duke Street toward the source of the shots, it was hearing his own name spoken aloud that made it real. It was a kind of roll call, and his name was now inextricably linked to whatever was unfolding blocks away. And whatever it was he was hurtling toward already felt big. Large enough to have its own gravity, drawing him in before he was fully aware of it. Large enough to become a tentpole in his life, an event by which he would measure other events, by where it fell on his personal chronology, before and after. His first kiss. Getting sworn into the Navy. Graduating from the police academy. The death of his father.

This very hot day, whatever it may bring.

"This is Officer Farrell. I have a mental health crisis in the back seat."

"Kick them loose," said the dispatcher. There was a pause, then "Twenty callers."

He did not have time to dwell on his thoughts, and couldn't articulate them until later, because Vance screeched to a halt in front of him. They had arrived in less than a minute.

4

Now

MOST PEOPLE NEVER look up these days. Heads buried in their phones, their navels, anywhere but up. But Cal did. In the Navy, his chief taught him a little meteorology and how to read clouds for weather. The calm of cirrocumulus clouds, like tiny fish scales high up in the sky, or the massive gray anvil of a cumulonimbus, promising a storm.

Keep a weather eye out, his chief had schooled him.

The body was high up. Impossibly high up, in fact. Standing beneath it, he had to arch his back to see it, and the lyrics to "Rock-a-Bye Baby" popped into his head unbidden.

When the bough breaks
The cradle will fall,
And down will come baby,
Cradle and all.

Standing on the dark trail in the predawn, staring up and trying to focus on the body gave him a momentary feeling of vertigo. He had felt this before, and he didn't like it. He shook his head roughly and after a moment the sensation passed.

For someone with his head in the clouds already, the sudden difference in a tree he had passed every day for months immediately drew his eye. It wasn't a conscious decision. Cal simply registered a fullness in the barren crown.

If he had clocked it, others would too.

He didn't have his police radio to call it in. He pulled his phone from his pocket and dialed 911 like anyone else.

"This is Detective Cal Farrell, Badge 901. I'd like to report a body. I'm on the Mount Vernon Trail—on the trail—and there's a body hanging from a tree."

He looked around and tried to triangulate precisely where he was from landmarks. He had left his home in Del Ray, running east, until he merged with the Mount Vernon Trail and headed south. If he kept running along the trail, which paralleled the Potomac River, he would eventually end at George Washington's colonial estate several miles away. But his normal morning run was just a dip into Old Town, giving him a view of the river, the trees, and some monuments on his way back.

"I'm just south of Slaters Lane, but north of Tide Lock Park. There's the old coal plant overlooking the river and I'm south of that. There's a trail entrance at Third and Fairfax. Park there, leave an officer to tape it off, and walk north. Have someone tape off Slaters Lane too, and head south. I'll be waiting. I'm in running gear."

He gazed up into the tree again.

"And bring a serious ladder."

From his vantage beneath the tree, he had an impressive view. Beside the tree was the trail, and beside the trail was a steep slope down to the river's edge. He could see a wide stretch of the Potomac. To the north, a plane was taking off from Washington National Airport, and beyond that, the red aircraft warning lights at the top of the Washington Monument and the illuminated dome of the Capitol Building were visible in the predawn.

He looked to the south, in the direction he had been running. It was the middle of winter and there were few leaves on the trees. From Cal's approach, the body's back was to him. From its extreme height and in the dim morning light, Cal could not tell if

the victim—he had already classified it as a victim in his mind—
was male or female. He pulled his phone from his pocket again,
angled it up, and took a photo, then zoomed in on it. It wasn't
helpful. The victim could be a woman or a man with long hair,
but the head and torso were obscured, and the photo was dark and
grainy when magnified.

What was so striking was the height. The victim was sixty,
maybe seventy feet in the air. There were plenty of sturdy, eas-
ier-to-reach branches to choose from, so the height seemed sig-
nificant, a message. Had it been in spring or summer, the victim
would have been invisible, obscured by leaves.

Cal passed directly beneath the body, heading slightly down-
hill. He looked back in its direction.

The victim appeared to be dressed in baggy jeans and a heavy
coat. If it were later in the day and the sunlight was rich and
golden, perhaps the colors of the clothes would provide a clue, but
as it was, at this hour, the day was overcast, and the lifeless body,
drenched in shadow, may as well have been rendered in black and
white.

While he waited for officers to arrive, Cal couldn't take his
eyes off the victim. The weather was chilly but with no wind, and
blessedly, the body neither twisted nor twirled from its suspension.
It remained completely still, facing Old Town. Cal looked toward
Old Town as well, wondering if its southerly orientation was just
how the victim came to rest or if that was by design as well. From
that height, the person would be able to see the trail winding down
to the coastline, the parks and promenades of the waterfront, the
historic buildings of Old Town, the Ferris wheel at National Har-
bor across the river, and the Woodrow Wilson Bridge beyond.
He wondered how far one might see downriver on a clear day. He
wondered about all of the things one might be able to see from
that height. But the body in the tree would have been long dead
by the time it reached that vantage.

It was early January. Cal had been eager to put last year, with
its Very Hot Day, behind him. He could not think of a worse
omen for the year ahead.

5

Then

THOUGH THE CONVENIENCE store was less than two miles away from the scene, it may as well have been a different town. Gas stations and quick oil change shops gave way to engineering firms. Vape shops became organic grocers and single office tax preparers bloomed into investment brokerages. This commercial center was the last stop before Old Town's cobblestone streets and tony colonial homes, its art galleries and esoteric boutiques and tourists dining along the waterfront. When Cal normally drove east along this corridor, he sensed the money amassing like storm clouds over the Potomac on a summer afternoon.

Cal stood on the brakes in front of a brick and stone office building on a half-acre lot. The building was nestled among other structures of similar size and similar façades, giving the entire block a homogeneous feel. Had Cal not been there before, he would have needed to search for the address. Or follow the gunshots. He leaped from the cruiser. Tiny moaned from the back seat.

"Oh God, man! Lemme out. Please!"

Cal would have cut the man loose anyway, no matter what dispatch said. Tiny was already pretty scrambled, and Cal didn't think a long sit in the back of a car on a ninety-plus degree day with 100 percent humidity would improve his mental state. Not to mention, Cal didn't know how many gunmen were in the building and if one might slip past or overcome law enforcement to make it onto the street.

Tiny would be a sitting duck.

Without breaking stride, Cal yanked Tiny's door open on his way out of the vehicle. There was no time to uncuff the man-mountain, so Cal jammed the key into the man's front pocket. He'd have to figure out the rest on his own.

Rain check on the ice cream, thought Cal. If I survive.

"Go."

Vance had parked first and had a short head start. He didn't wait for Cal and Cal didn't blame him. The other officer was doing what he was trained to do—run toward the gunfire in an active shooter situation. Prior to Columbine, the protocol had been to set a perimeter and wait for SWAT. Following Columbine, it was go, go, go. Do not wait for backup. Every second could be another life taken. Another victim hiding in a closet or under a desk or a bathroom stall with their feet drawn up. *Go.* Do not wait for backup. *Go.* Ignore the wounded crying out or crawling toward you. EMS would take care of them. *Go.* Your job was to press onward, no matter what. Run toward the threat and neutralize it as quickly as possible. *Go.*

Go. Go. Go.

Cal bolted for the glass front doors, which reflected the sun back at him. It was like a wall of pure light. Vance was almost there.

No sooner had Vance pushed into the revolving door than several sharp pops riddled the façade. Cal dove behind a planter and heard the shrieking behind him on the street. He glanced around and saw passersby hiding, ducking behind cars or mailboxes or running flat out with their heads down. Cal came up with his weapon and threw his arms over the planter. Over his front sight he saw that large sections of the gleaming façade were gone, revealing darkness framed by the jagged teeth of the remaining glass.

And the still form of Officer Jimmy Vance, tangled in the revolving door and spilling out onto the pavement.

6

Now

THE FIRST TWO officers rounded the bend of the trail from the south. They were rookies, but to be fair, Cal wasn't much older than they were. He studied their expressions when they first caught sight of the victim, dangling by its neck. He could tell which of them had never seen a body before. One marveled at the height and tried to puzzle out the logistics of it. The other simply gaped, reckoning with the simple fact that a dead body was presented before him in a tree. If he was to remain police, he would see all manner of terrible things befall the human body—gruesome car accidents, trees crushing children's bedrooms during storms, forgotten elderly people expiring in their homes and ripening enough to alert the neighbors—and they would carry those images forever.

And then there were the murdered ones.

You never forget your first, he thought.

The officers murmured to each other in low, respectful voices, but did not speak to him unless directly questioned. They stood together in a small knot, keeping largely quiet. He asked if they had set the perimeter, they answered in the affirmative. More officers arrived from the north and the knot swelled. Gone was the customary gallows humor, perhaps because it may as well have been an actual gallows.

From the south, he heard a familiar voice.

"What have you gotten yourself into this time, Farrell?" said Detective Adam Massey.

Why did it have to be Massey?

The detective was tall and gregarious, with a great reputation. He and his old partner had caught a man who was responsible for a series of shootings dating back a decade. It made the detective a star, and he wore it well. He practically shone. It had the unintended consequence of making everyone look dimmer by comparison. Standing next to Massey, Cal felt like a black hole.

He watched the uniforms watch Massey, studying his movements, hoping to learn something. Massey's presence had the exact opposite effect on the men than Cal's. Their shoulders relaxed, their smiles came easier.

"Out for a run," said Cal. "And I noticed this."

"What are the odds?" said Detective Stacy Porter.

Porter was far more circumspect, and looked at everyone with suspicion or disdain. Or maybe it was just him, thought Cal. Cal looked at her and she looked back, unfazed.

Massey gazed upward, hands on his hips, and blew an appreciative whistle. "I'll be damned," said Massey. "How the hell do you suppose they got all the way up there?"

Porter looked around, saw the abundance of trees and their wide selection of available, lower branches. "If the vic was trying to off themself, they had a hell of a lot of easier options."

"It's deliberate," said Cal. "The placement, the height. Someone is trying to say something."

"That they're Spider-Man?" said Porter.

Massey laughed, but nudged Cal. "Don't listen to her. She hasn't had her coffee yet. You have dispatch call the RCPA?"

Cal nodded. The dispatcher informed him they had alerted the city's Department of Recreation, Parks and Cultural Activities.

"Well, this is going to take a while," griped Porter.

More uniforms arrived to maintain a cordon, but broke position to get a glimpse of the dead body in the high tree. Finally, after another thirty minutes, Cal heard the diesel-fueled laboring of a heavy machine. A few seconds later, a vehicle unlike any he had seen before rounded the bend. It looked like a hodgepodge of different vehicles, as if it hadn't made up its mind what it wanted to be yet. It had log-skidder style tires and a large plow on the front. It also had an operator cab seated atop the rear, with a large, telescoping boom. At the end of the boom was a basket, large enough for a single person. Cal absentmindedly wondered if the thing could also transform into a robot. The all-terrain tree trimmer just barely navigated the narrow stretch of winding trail.

Cal also wondered if the party responsible for the body's placement knew how difficult this evolution would be.

The operator told them the boom could extend to seventy feet. This was met with nervous looks between Massey and Porter, but ultimately Massey drew the short straw because he was taller and able to get better pictures if the boom couldn't reach.

"Take my picture," he told Porter. "This is one for the scrapbook."

"Scrapbook," smirked Porter. "Sure."

There was a small buzz that ran through the knots of officers as Massey donned a hard hat and climbed aboard. By the looks on their faces, some uniforms thought it might be a fun ride under different circumstances. Cal saw others shake their heads. *No fucking way.*

The operator shifted some gears, there was a whir, and Massey was slowly, inexorably lifted toward the body.

7

Then

CAL NEVER HEARD the familiar report of Vance's weapon, a Glock 17, the same as his own. The officer hadn't had time to get a shot off.

From behind the planter, Cal yelled into the radio's microphone clipped to his bulletproof vest that there was an Officer Down and that the Duke Street entrance was not viable and that he was going to attempt to breach the building from the side door on John Carlyle Street. He hadn't even realized this was his plan before he was yelling it into the radio.

In the awful silence following the gunshots, he heard the people on the street rally themselves and begin alighting from their hiding spaces. He did the same and sprinted away from Duke Street onto John Carlyle, a small side street that paralleled the building and opened to John Carlyle Square. It was a small park, just a roundabout with green space and some benches in the center, but he liked driving his cruiser around it in the springtime. The flowers were pretty and it was a nice few seconds of respite from whatever kind of day he was having, whether mundane or horrible. He didn't notice the flowers this time.

He expected more shots to ring out, more glass to shatter, as he ran past the windows. After a few seconds, he found what he was looking for—the John Carlyle Street entrance. It was in the shade, not glowing from the sun's glare as the front had been. He saw inside.

Clear.

He slipped through the door.

He had taken part in an emergency exercise in the building once before, during his first few weeks on the job. He remembered the layout. The front entrance opened directly into a wide foyer with banks of elevators and a receptionist's desk. He inched down one of two narrow corridors that approached the desk from the sides. He reached the end, back pressed to the wall, and was about to whirl into the main lobby when he heard a noise.

Ping.

The elevator.

Cal knew most people instinctively fled from the sound of gunfire via stairwells, not wanting to chance waiting out in the open for an elevator car—or worse, get trapped inside one. Elevators were a sitting duck option in a fight-or-flight scenario. And no one in their right mind would summon a car to go back *up*.

That left only one person. The shooter.

Cal took a deep breath, blew half of it out and stepped away from the wall. He whirled around and leaned out, visualizing a man with a semiautomatic rifle, ready to squeeze out as many rounds as it took to put him down. But the lobby was empty, save for Vance at the other end, still tangled in the revolving door. From this vantage, out of the blinding sun now, Cal could better see the effects of the rifle on his fellow officer.

He wished he hadn't.

A bulletproof vest could only do so much, and nothing at all for the face.

Cal pulled his gaze away from his fallen comrade to above the elevators, looking to see the floor where it settled. It landed on the fourth. He heard sirens now, lots of them, in the distance. The Alexandria Police Department, Fire Department, and Emergency

Medical Services would soon descend en masse. In moments he would no longer be alone. *Finally*, he thought, but he knew it had probably been less than ninety seconds since everything went to hell.

The gunshots resumed. Muffled and faint, but unmistakable. Single shots now. Deliberate. Four floors up.

He bolted for the stairwell, pinching the microphone on his vest once more as he went.

8

Now

Detective Lavaar Sydnor rounded the bend from the south just as the basket lifted into the sky. He carried two cups of coffee and a blue jacket draped over one arm. Twenty years Cal's senior and deep into middle age, he had lost the fight to creeping baldness and decided to steer into the skid and shave his scalp smooth. He wore a dark, thick mustache over the even line of his mouth. His two most common expressions were ambivalence and wariness, and Cal wondered which his partner would wear this morning. When Sydnor saw him in his running shorts, the man just shook his head.

The first call Cal had made, after the switchboard, was to his partner. He filled Sydnor in on his morning and sheepishly asked that the senior detective bring him a jacket. The sweat from his run, now long over, had dried and he was standing around on a cold January morning in shorts. He had not asked for the coffee, and Cal wondered for a moment if it was really for him. Even after six months of partnership in Vice and Narcotics, Sydnor didn't generate a lot of warmth. So Cal was grateful when his partner approached and extended the arm with the coffee and the blue jacket, whatever face the detective made while doing so.

"Playing with your toy trucks now?"

Where Cal was tall and lean, Sydnor was short and compact. With most people, Cal saw his height as an advantage, but he felt gangly next to his partner, like one of those flapping, inflatable tube men at car dealerships beside Sydnor's coiled steel spring. And Sydnor never missed an opportunity to make Cal feel every bit the rookie detective he was. It wasn't mean-spirited, it was just Sydnor's way. For the first three months of their partnership, Sydnor would call Cal "kid" or "junior" or "youngblood," or pause before saying his name, as if he had temporarily forgotten it. *Good morning there, ah, Farrell.* Worst of all was when he called him "Detective." He didn't say it with any sarcasm or malice, but the formality of it stung a little every time. They had settled into a far better rhythm the past three months, but Cal never fully relaxed around him.

"Something like that," said Cal as he donned the blue jacket with APD in block white letters on the back. He took the coffee. "Thanks."

Sydnor looked up into the canopy and the detective in the basket. "That who I think it is?"

"Yep."

Sydnor grunted.

Massey had been Sydnor's last partner. They had solved the Windlass shootings case together when Sydnor was in Crimes Against Persons, but they split up after that. Sydnor transferred from Violent Crimes to Vice and Narcotics. Cal wondered why on earth his new partner would want to leave CAP, particularly Violent Crimes, or why the Investigations Division would allow such a successful pair to split, but it had allowed Cal to partner with the veteran detective, so he didn't look too closely into the maw of that gift horse. Sydnor himself only offered vague clues about his decision to leave Violent Crimes. Once, Sydnor tapped his head and said, "What goes in doesn't come out." And on another occasion, Sydnor obliquely referenced his old partner, Massey.

"Things run their course," he had said.

"How's that?" asked Cal.

"There are workhorses and there are show ponies."

And that was all Cal could get out of him.

Now Cal followed Sydnor's gaze skyward, where Massey floated above all of them, his arm outstretched like the subject of a fresco. Sydnor smirked. The basket drew alongside the body and Massey reached toward it to take pictures with his phone. The medical examiners had arrived by now as well, and after a few minutes, Massey signaled to the operator to bring him down. When he climbed down from the top of the tree trimmer, he saw Sydnor and walked over.

"Hey, Lavaar," said Massey.

"Backing up Killer Callum here, Syd?" said Porter.

Cal concealed his wince by looking up toward the dangling body. At least Porter said it out loud, to his face. Ribbing him in the way that colleagues do. Not like the others, who stood around in their clusters and mumbled it to each other.

It's what he told himself, even if he didn't believe it for a second.

"What do you say there, uh, Adam?"

A tiny squall of hurt passed over Massey's face, there and gone in an instant. Cal stifled a smirk. Sydnor and Massey had been partners for ten years, and with Sydnor's trademark pause, it was like that decade had never happened. It was a shot, a tiny one, but it had found its mark.

Sydnor nodded at Massey's phone, not even bothering to acknowledge Porter. Cal usually tried to smooth over Sydnor's abrupt, rougher edges in conversations with peers, but this time he reveled in the awkwardness.

"You going to share with the rest of the class?" asked Sydnor.

"Sure, Lavaar, sure," said Massey.

Massey keyed his phone and the four detectives huddled and looked at the screen. There were an assortment of different angles and shots—gouges on the branches, the taut rope, and close-ups on parts of the body—until finally, there were a series of pictures of the swollen, empurpled face.

Cal felt sick.

"I know him," he said.

9

Then

CAL TOOK THE stairs three and at a time. At the landing of the fourth floor, he pushed the door open and sighted over his weapon. He moved down the corridor, identical to the lobby's floor plan, until he reached the banks of elevators. Once more, he swung into the lobby. There was no sign of the gunman.

Only those he had left in his wake.

Two people had made an unsuccessful break for it. A man was sprawled face down in the center of the lobby. A woman on her side, red hair obscuring a pale face, lay just outside the glass double doors of her office suite. Both of them so close to making it to the stairwells, to getting out. Now their blood soaked into the carpet in dark blooms, slowly spreading as if reaching toward each other.

Cal felt his stomach rise to his throat, but swallowed it back down again.

He heard another gunshot. Loud, immediate. Close, coming from somewhere inside the suite ahead. He bolted for the glass doors of the suite, casting a last glance at the bodies splayed on the floor. No signs of life, but unable to stop even if there were.

Damn him, thought Cal. *God damn him.*

He grasped the handle of the glass door and pulled.

Locked.

If he smashed it, he would alert the gunman. Didn't matter. Better to draw attention to himself and away from any survivors still left in the suite. He found his expandable baton on his belt and flicked his wrist. It telescoped with a satisfying *shing*. Etched on the doors was a stylized ATMA, and beside it in smaller, block letters, American Tooling and Machining Association. He reared back and aimed for the center of logo when someone seized him from behind.

10

Now

"THAT'S TINY," SAID Cal.

It was bad enough standing there in running shorts and a jacket, while everyone else was in their suits or uniforms, but now the three other detectives went from scrutinizing Massey's phone to scrutinizing him.

"Homeless," continued Cal. "Liked to hang out on Duke Street. I had a run-in with him when I was on patrol . . ."

He realized then that his last run-in with Tiny was on that Very Hot Day. Cal hadn't seen him since. After that, Cal had transferred from the Field Operations Division to the Criminal Investigations Division, a promotion designed to be ceremonial, but instead caused resentment among many of his peers. He supposed he didn't blame them. It was too much too fast, and specious besides. Whispers of "Killer Callum" followed him around the department, except for those mornings when dead men hung in trees and his fellow detectives didn't bother to whisper it. It all fueled Cal's burgeoning impostor syndrome, another bit of emotional fallout to contend with.

Cal cleared his throat. "Just before ATMA."

Massey glanced at Cal. He understood the reference. They all did. To Cal's relief, Massey moved past it quickly. "Tiny?" he said, then gave an appreciative grunt at the irony. "Close up, he's a big specimen."

"How the fuck did he get up there?" asked Sydnor.

Massey swiped the phone a few times.

The pictures went from Tiny to the tree. There were gouges in the outer bark at intervals, and a few shots revealing flashes of the pale, new wood beneath. Up near the crown and the branch where Tiny was suspended were deep grooves in a foot-like pattern.

"Some kind of shoe?" mumbled Massey, looking at Sydnor instead of his own partner. Old habits die hard, thought Cal.

"Crampons maybe," interjected Porter.

Sydnor looked at her with mild alarm. "Crampons? Like tampons?" said Sydnor. Cal had to stifle a grin at his partner's confusion at the term.

"Never been ice climbing, I take it," said Porter.

"Or in the ladies aisle," ribbed Massey.

"Whatever," said Sydnor. He marched over to the tree. It was a wide trunk just off the trail. The tree was on a grade and woods rose up and away. Sydnor approached it from the trail, then climbed the grade to circle it, stepping gingerly over the brush and bramble, until he was on the side of the trunk hidden from the trail. He scanned the trunk until he found what he was looking for.

"Here," said Sydnor. "Hand me your phone, Mass."

Massey handed it over and Sydnor took more pictures, while Massey, Porter, and Cal waited on the trail. Sydnor came out from behind the tree and handed Massey's phone to Porter instead, now with additional pictures of deep grooves.

"What's that tell you?" he asked.

"More footprints," said Porter. "Climbed the tree from the covered side. The suspect did not want to risk being spotted."

Massey peered up to the canopy and the basket, now containing one of the medical examiners, and shook his head in amazement. "Talk about a high degree of difficulty."

"One hell of a flex," said Sydnor.

It wasn't just the difficulty, thought Cal. He remembered his morning run, the light fog parting to reveal a dead man. He remembered the shock, the dreamlike unreality of it, and that momentary feeling of vertigo it produced. He didn't know if, under similar circumstances, the other three detectives would have had a similar reaction if they happened upon a body in a tree.

The suspect didn't want to spotted, thought Cal, and yet . . .

"He wanted to be *seen*."

11

Then

As PART OF a boarding team in the Navy, Cal had to investigate a mostly sunken boat in the Straits of Hormuz. It appeared to be a sailboat, masts shattered, so it was possible someone needed assistance, but more likely someone had once needed assistance long ago. Now the boat was mostly submerged, with barely a foot of freeboard bobbing above the surface, and a hazard to navigation.

It was night and the destroyer dispatched a zodiac to zip across the flat sea to investigate. Cal loved that part. Getting off the ship even for a few moments and skimming the waves in a smaller craft. The speed of it, the wind in his hair. A sip of freedom. Soon they were alongside the sailboat, and he alone clambered aboard. It was a small boat and any more than him might capsize it.

He peered into the open hatch.

There was nothing to see in the flooded compartment but black water, darker than the night around them. Then Cal saw a head of hair, swirling back and forth. The spotlight from the destroyer, so powerful moments ago, was now just a silver thread in the dark behind him. Everything beyond it was black. He had been buoyed by the late-night joyride moments before; now a sense of disquiet fell over him like a shroud. He pulled a flashlight from his belt and shone it inside. The hair resolved into the frayed ends of a rope. In the darkness, those snaking, swirling coils had resembled the hair of a siren, beckoning him forward, into that tight compartment, where she might ensnare him, pull him down into the deep, and swallow him whole. He half expected an eye to appear out of the dark water.

He crouched over the open hatch, thinking of a fish trap coming loose from its float, sinking to the bottom of the sea. Dead fish inside luring new fish in an endless cycle.

He signaled for the zodiac to pick him up.

In the morning, the gunners mates used the sailboat for target practice and sent it to the bottom of the Gulf, and Cal made a point of watching it go down.

Standing at the doors to the office suite, it was like he was staring into those hypnotic ropes once again. Only this time, an eye did find him, peering through a tangle of auburn hair, matted with perspiration. The redhead clutched his pant leg with a bloody hand, her face creased with pain. Both eyes found him now and said without words *Do not pass me by.*

My God, he thought. *She's still alive.*

He knew he was supposed to keep moving. It was protocol to *go*, but she held his eye. Despite her pain, he saw her determination. It was like she was on a deserted island and he was a ship on the horizon. He saw the signal fire, the waving of her arms, heard her frantic yelling, all in that piercing gaze.

Please do not pass me by.

He surveyed her body, trying to ascertain her wounds. She was doubled over, but he couldn't tell if she had been shot in the stomach or the back. He didn't want to risk moving her, but at the same time, they were incredibly exposed in the elevator bank. In a wide swath between two sets of double glass doors, with no cover or concealment.

"I'm Cal," he said quietly. "What's your name?"

"Hea—Heather," she panted.

"Heather, help is on the way."

"Don't . . . go."

It was the first moment he had stopped to think since hearing that long tone over the radio and the report of shots fired. Since then, he had been swept along by training, by momentum, by adrenaline. By gravity. It was a natural instinct to want to get her out of there, far more of a human impulse than running toward the sound of gunfire. No one would judge him, not really. SWAT was seconds behind him and they would find this animal and put him down. Cal would eat shit, maybe lose his job, but he could escape with a single life saved. One point snatched from the final tally of stolen lives. She might live.

And in time, maybe he could learn to live with himself.

He grabbed her hand. "You're going to be fine—"

Another gunshot. Ahead. Somewhere on the floor, behind those glass doors.

He stared at the glass doors, his own face now contorted with pain. Every second could bring another shot. Each shot meant another life. Another Heather. He had to press on.

When he looked back at her, she looked different. Resigned. She released his hand and reached for her neck. She made a wrenching motion. In her bloody, trembling hand, she clutched a lanyard. At the end of the lanyard dangled the electronic badge for the door.

It was the bravest thing he had ever seen in his life.

"In black," she said through gritted teeth. "Like you."

"Heather, I'll be back. I promise."

"Go," she said.

12

Now

I T WAS DIFFICULT to preserve evidence seventy feet in the air.

"All this crampon shit is real fascinating and all," said Sydnor, "but how the hell are you going to get him down?"

Massey was lead detective and was running the scene, so he walked over to speak to the operator of the all-terrain vehicle, who made a call. If it had been a more conventional scene, Cal would have gotten the side-eye for lingering, but he was a witness. Even though they had gleaned everything they could from him in sixty seconds—what he saw and when he saw it—he stuck around anyway. He was a detective after all, even if he felt childish standing around in his running gear. At least he had the Alexandra PD jacket now. Plus, Sydnor was here. Massey had too much respect for his old partner to tell them to move along, and everyone else would have been too afraid to.

Also, this was *different*. A truly bizarre crime scene that none of them had any context for. This was not a robbery or a stabbing or a shooting. There were no other witnesses, shell casings, blood spatter, or burnt tire tracks. Just a man in a tree. It was like some morbid fairy tale with a boogeyman. They all sensed without acknowledging it that they'd be talking about this in bars for the rest of their lives. Like a macabre fish story, except instead of the size of the fish growing in the retelling, it would be Tiny's altitude. *I'm telling you, he was a hundred feet up. Two hundred . . .*

Everyone was out of their depth. *Or height*, Cal corrected himself silently. No one would admit it, but they were not about to turn away an extra pair of eyes or two.

Except Porter.

"Don't let us keep you from the rest of your day," she said.

"It's no trouble," said Sydnor sweetly.

"Stacy," said Massey, and nodded his head to the side. Stacy followed him over, away from the other detectives and the knots of patrol officers.

Massey spoke quietly enough that Cal couldn't hear what he was saying, but he heard Porter's response.

"It's not your old partner I have a fucking problem with, Mass."

Could this be any more awkward? thought Cal. He was a newly minted Vice detective at a murder scene—that he discovered—where one of the lead detectives clearly did not want him around.

Sydnor looked up at the body again and whistled. "You alright?"

"Well, this morning's run was not my personal best."

Sydnor, still craning his neck, grunted. "That's what you get for running anyway."

Fifteen minutes later, a pair of men marched up the trail from the south with hard hats, long coils of rope slung over their shoulders, and harnesses that wrapped around their waists and legs. The men introduced themselves as Mitchell Quinn and Jake Hilliard, arborists for the city.

Quinn was short and ropy, with muscular, blocky shoulders and forearms nearly as large as his biceps. Cal noticed the tips of tattoos poking from the collar of his T-shirt, perhaps the wing of a bird or a mythological creature. Hilliard was taller and leaner, with facial hair somewhere between a few days unshaven and an actual beard, giving his face an out-of-focus appearance. It made Cal want to blink the longer he looked at the man. The smaller arborist, Quinn, looked uneasy, glancing up at the strange sight of the dead man. If it was unusual for the cops, Cal could only imagine how it appeared to civilians.

Massey explained to the arborists the necessity of preserving as much of the scene as possible, which meant getting Tiny down without additional trauma to the body and saving the branch he was hanging by. "I'm sorry to put you in this position," he said, "but I'd like to keep from cutting the rope. I'd prefer to keep it all intact—the branch, the rope, and the victim. Can you cut the branch and secure the body so that it doesn't, you know . . ."

Massey made a whistling sound that started high and ended low as he pointed to the ground.

The men nodded.

"And keep your eyes open when you're up there," said Porter. "Take a picture of anything out of place. Anything at all."

"Like what?" said Quinn.

"Piece of fabric from torn clothes, cigarette butt, who knows. Mass, give him your phone?"

"My phone?"

"You already have the other pictures on it."

Massey made a face, but handed it over. He made the whistling sound again. "Same goes for my phone. Can you handle this?"

"Yeah," said Quinn, clearing his throat. Then louder, psyching himself up. "Yeah."

Surrounded by the detectives and patrol officers and other city workers, the arborist did not want to be the one who couldn't do his job, even if the job at hand was awful.

Cal knew how he felt.

13

Then

WITH THE FAINTEST click of the double doors, Cal was inside. He panned in every direction, the office suite focused over his Glock 17's front sight. Down both ends of the corridor, he saw fallen bodies, with attendant haloes of blood. But the shooter was deeper into the office suite.

He was in a terrible position. He was in the open—in the middle of a long corridor that appeared to connect two quadrants full of cubicles, offices, and conference rooms. Zero cover, unless he retreated back outside to the elevator banks.

A shooting gallery.

He stepped backward, still scanning down both ends of the corridor. He reached into a pouch on his vest and removed a small notepad. With the same hand, he opened the double doors again and slid the pad into the gap, keeping the doors from latching closed.

He swallowed and keyed the microphone receiver clipped to his vest. He whispered, "This is Officer Farrell. The shooter is somewhere in the northern suite on the fourth floor. Company name is ATMA. Repeat, A-T-M-A on floor number *four*. I've propped the doors open."

Every nerve ending in Cal's body felt as if it was on fire, screaming to scoop Heather up and get the hell out of there. But if Heather was brave enough to give him her badge, he was damn sure going to press on.

"The woman at the entrance is alive and needs immediate medical attention. Her name is Heather."

He wasn't clear whether to go right or left down the corridor, but he had to make a decision, and he didn't want the report of another gunshot to lead the way. There had been too many already.

He noticed the bloody boot prints then and followed them to the right.

14

Now

Tʜᴇ ᴀʀʙᴏʀɪsᴛ ᴠᴏᴍɪᴛᴇᴅ from seventy feet in the air. It made a showering sound as it hit the asphalt trail. Cops scattered, cursing. The arborist at the base of the tree yelled up, "Mitch!"

Mitchell Quinn called down, "He shit himself, Jake!"

Minutes before, Cal had watched the two-man team's preparations with interest. It became apparent quickly that Quinn would be the climber, while Hilliard would be the ground man, taking station at the base of the tree. Quinn tossed a throw line, placed his ascent rope, then scaled the tree with surprising quickness. The arborist then set up a workstation in the crown, alongside the branch to be trimmed, and began constructing a block rigging system. Once the branch was cut, the branch and the body would free-fall for a moment before being caught by the block, Hilliard explained, but he assured the detectives his partner was the best arborist in the city and would control the descent of the "load." Hilliard installed the pull and guide ropes and prepared the chainsaw to be hoisted. Quinn had been setting up the block rigging system above, affixing ropes to the branch and the ripening dead man, when he showered the trail.

"Should've warned him about that," said Massey, shaking his head.

"Once he comes down, let's take a look at his spurs," said Porter, out of earshot of Hilliard. "Measure his feet. Just in case. Anchor man too."

"I don't know," said Sydnor, peering into the canopy. "Spider-Man's puke was pretty convincing."

"Could be nerves," said Massey, smiling.

"Maybe," conceded Sydnor.

After the commotion caused by the spontaneous waterfall, the two men settled into a rhythm. Quinn finished his system of ropes and pulleys, calling down estimates of the weight of the entire load—Tiny and the branch—and Hilliard wrapped the ropes a few more times around a friction cylinder. When they were ready, the chainsaw rose into the air. There was its telltale growl overhead, and then suddenly, the branch was cut, the load free. The chainsaw's buzzing ceased. The victim and the trimmed branch lowered, both graceful and gruesome, as if coming down from a trapeze in a musical.

Except it was silent. No one said a word as the man called Tiny's feet touched the ground.

15

Then

CAL DIDN'T STOP to ponder the shooter's path, but he knew the killer had begun on the fourth floor. There had been no forced entry on the double doors. No shattered glass, no smashed card reader. So he was a disgruntled employee, or a pissed-off vendor or customer, or an abusive boyfriend or husband of a worker at ATMA. Whoever he was, he had access. It wasn't random. Well, the killing had been random. Once it started, it would be indiscriminate, but the selection of the target almost always had a purpose in these situations.

So the rampage began here.

Then the shooter tried to leave—perhaps to flee, perhaps to continue his spree along Duke Street—but he encountered resistance. Vance, Cal, sirens in the distance . . . so he summoned the elevator. Decided to retreat to what he knew and where he had the upper hand—ATMA.

Cal saw two sets of footprints, one bright and stark heading out toward the double doors, and then fainter, heading back in. Cal glanced behind him—he left no such prints. This information told him that the shooter had walked away from a lot of blood, and had now returned to it.

This tactical knowledge was helpful. It grounded Cal in the moment and fended off the rising cacophony in his head. He fought off thoughts of Vance, of the victims in the fourth-floor lobby, of the look on Heather's face. He fought tunnel vision, tunnel hearing. If he stopped to think, if he pondered the enormity of the situation for even a moment, it would overwhelm him at best. At worst, it would get him killed. Either way, he wouldn't be any good to anyone.

He breathed deeply. The edges of his vision expanded. He drew another deep breath and the rushing in his ears subsided too.

He followed the bloody footprints to the end of the hall and a big open bay, maybe a quarter of the entire floor. There was a maze of cubicles and offices along the walls. The shooter could be lying in wait in any of them, but he saw the twin tracks of footprints by a room in the corner of the building. One track exiting the room, deep and rich, the other leading back to it, fading.

Cal fought a chill and moved toward it as quietly as possible. A nameplate on the wall indicated it was a conference room. He reminded himself that no one else could hear the hammering of his heart. He had to trust that he was moving stealthily and soundlessly, and not clattering down the hallway.

He paused beside the entrance to the conference room. He heard the sounds of movement from inside. Heavy breathing, the rustle of clothes. The smell of gunpowder was pungent. He took a breath, let it out halfway, and whirled into the threshold, coming face to face with the minotaur at the center of the maze.

CHAPTER

16

Now

Tiny lay on the trail, his feet pointed south toward Old Town Alexandria, his head pointed north toward Arlington and still attached to the branch by the rope. Massey and Porter moved in first, with the medical examiners waiting for their turn to take over. With the body on the ground, the spectacle was over and therefore no more macabre than any other dead body confined to terra firma. Most of the uniforms wandered back to their posts along the trail where the caution tape blocked off the bikers and pedestrians. Cal maintained a respectful distance with Sydnor, until Massey glanced at his old partner and made a slight nod in their direction.

C'mere.

Porter's jaw flared, but she said nothing.

Sydnor started over, but Cal hung back. Sydnor turned to face him.

"You wanted to be murder police. Step lively, junior."

Once upon a time, it had been Cal's dream to be a detective in the Violent Crimes Unit of the CAP Section—Crimes Against Persons. To be an investigator. But that was before he had seen more murder in a single hour of a Very Hot Day than most police saw in a full career. Now he wasn't quite so sure.

"Give me a second," said Cal.

Cal watched Quinn, the climber, complete his descent. When he touched the ground and began coiling his ropes, he wore a sheepish look. "Sorry about the puke," mumbled the arborist.

"Nothing to be sorry about at all," said Cal. "You did great. We appreciate the help."

The arborist looked him up and down, raised an eyebrow at the shorts.

"Out for a run."

"Oh."

"See anything of interest up there?"

"Dude's a fucking amateur."

"How's that?"

Quinn retrieved Massey's phone from his vest and went to the camera roll. There were close-ups of spiked boot prints and two good shots of the boot prints leading up the trunk into the canopy.

"Those are spikes," said the arborist.

"Yeah?"

Quinn lifted each of his shoes off the ground, showing Cal the bottom of his feet. "You don't see me wearing spikes, do you?"

"No . . ."

"Any arborist or climber worth a shit would not use spikes or spurs on a living, healthy tree."

Hilliard joined them. "Some services might if they're pruning, but they're fucking hacks. Call around for a quote."

Quinn continued. "It's like stabbing a tree over and over. It disrupts the flow of nutrients, invites pests . . ."

"So unprofessional," said Hilliard, shaking his head.

"This guy did not give a *fuck* about trees," said Quinn.

"Or people," added Cal.

"Well . . . yeah."

"What else can you tell me other than our killer's disdain for the local flora?"

"These aren't just spikes. They're crampons. Something you fix over your shoe. Not professional spikes or spurs, which have just one spur per foot." Quinn shook his head. "Just tore the shit out of the bark."

"Where can you find them?"

"Online. REI. Sporting goods stores. Anywhere, really."

Cal was hoping for something more distinctive.

He glanced up to where the branch had been moments before, now open sky.

"Professional opinion on how someone got the victim up there?"

"They just hoisted him," said Quinn.

"How?"

"Same as me. Ropes and pulleys. Here . . ." Quinn swiped the screen on Massey's phone again until he found the photos he wanted. Cal studied them. There were more gouges to the tree, less savage than the crampon prints. Smoother, crescent indentations.

"See here?" said Quinn. "Rope burns. And these are where the pulleys dug into the bark."

Cal nodded. "Thanks a lot, guys."

"So," said Hilliard, "can we, like, roll?"

"Let me check with the lead detectives." Cal nodded to another tree that was a safe distance away from the body. "Hang back over there for now."

The men started over toward the tree, and with his back still to the detectives, Cal selected the photos, dropped them into a text and typed in his own phone number. Once they were sent, he deleted the text.

"Farrell!" called Sydnor.

"Coming," said Cal.

17

Then

THERE HAD BEEN indicators.

There were always indicators if one knew where to look, if one cared to look, but for most of his life Vapor had remained invisible.

James Allan Milton was thirty-two years old, but his problems began before he could remember. His father was an erratic presence, a drinker who disappeared for days at a time, and when he was around, beat his son when he was angry. It was clear he didn't really want to be around, so he was angry all the time. No money, not enough jobs, too many immigrants . . . What Milton began to suspect was that his father was just plain old angry, and if he had money in his pocket, or a good job, and no immigrants in sight, he would simply find another reason to be angry.

Sometimes it was a belt, sometimes a switch, but he'd use whatever was handy. Telling someone about his father would require talking to someone, and James had difficulty talking to people. Other children were the worst. They cornered him and beat him too.

There was one bright day he always remembered—his first day in computer lab. When he sat at the glowing monitor and his hands found the keyboard, it was like everything—*everyone*—receded.

Like tunnel vision. It was fascinating, a portal to anywhere beyond his shitty North Carolina town. The best part: computers had their own language, and for some reason he understood it implicitly. It was like a symbiotic relationship, only he didn't have the words for it back then and no one to tell if he had. So he spent all of his time in the lab, figuring out the inner workings of the device and mastering its language before taking his first tentative steps online.

The computer may as well have been a rocket that blasted him out of his hometown. It got him into a college, and he never looked back. He wasn't any more successful with people there, but it didn't matter. He could now interact mainly online. There were message boards where he could actually express himself for a change. He could create multiple personalities if he chose.

After college, he left North Carolina for an IT job in Virginia. At first, it was great. Sure, there were the same shitty people as everywhere else, but he had his own place, an apartment in Landsdowne, on the outskirts of Alexandria. He amassed computers, gaming consoles, gear. He amassed debt amassing those things, but every night after work (and sometimes at work when his helpless coworkers would leave him alone for a goddamn minute), he escaped into his virtual world. In the twenty years since he first explored a computer, a sci-fi utopia had been delivered to him: social media, massively multiplayer online games, even the dark web. With multiple avatars in all of these platforms, he could contact anyone. If he didn't like a politician, he could fuck with them. If he thought an actress was a bitch or should show her tits, he could tell her so. And if it got him blocked, he could just switch to another avatar. His favorite was Vapor. Vapor had real estate on every platform and congealed into his centralized online persona. He had always liked the sound of the word, the idea of it. Something that was invisible, but suffused the air. And with pressure alone it could become liquid.

Plus, it just sounded fucking cool.

Vapor joined quests in fantasy worlds, raiding parties throughout the cosmos, Special Forces operations in the Middle East, all without leaving his couch, all anonymously. He could drop into games and talk to like-minded people through his headset, and shout down anyone who disagreed. Nothing and no one was off limits to Vapor.

While he had been spending more and more time on the dark web instead of the Clearnet, something in the country had changed. Vapor surfaced back to traditional social media and realized the conversation had shifted. Shit he had posted anonymously as Vapor was now commonplace. People were ranting freely about whatever the fuck they wanted, and it made a lot of sense. He was young, white, male, and gifted—smarter than everyone else—so why did he have to ask permission to simply *exist* these days? Why tiptoe around women, minorities, and people who didn't even belong in this fucking country?

He found he was not alone, and was welcomed into entire new communities.

It was like the scene in *The Matrix*. Where he could take the red pill and see the truth or the blue pill and go back to his life. He took the red pill and started to see things as they truly were.

And things were not fair.

His physical world was not commensurate with the glorious life he had built for himself online. James Allan Milton had a supervisor, work hours, bitchy coworkers, but Vapor? Vapor was a god.

He stopped showing up on time, started to leave early. Any idiot could do the work, it was so fucking simple, so why bother keeping office hours? He'd go in when he wanted, if he wanted. Pretty soon, the idea of going in at all seemed like a waste of time.

Barry, his supervisor, disagreed. Which is how he got fired. There was something about porn at work and "problematic" posts on Facebook and Twitter. James must have let it slip to the wrong person that his handle was Vapor, and someone must have connected the dots. He didn't fucking care. Barry was a pussy and it was a shitty job anyway. Still, Vapor needed steady income. He was already in debt and he couldn't bear for his gear to become obsolete.

Fuck them, the voices in his machines told him. The silent, faceless voices in the hidden corners of the internet. *Vapor is a god. Vapor is a hunter. Everyone else was prey.*

And they were right. He had often wondered what it would be like to go on real raiding missions, real hunting parties, real operations. He just needed the right kind of gear. Fortunately, one thing hadn't changed in the country—it was so very easy to get that kind of gear.

* * *

Most of this Cal learned in the aftermath, pieced together through data forensics by the Electronics Investigations Section with a little help from the FBI. The rest Cal wondered about on his many sleepless nights.

On that Very Hot Day, though, he knew none of it. Nothing of James Allan Milton. Nothing of Vapor.

As Cal moved silently through ATMA, the shooter was simply the minotaur at the center of the maze.

When he whirled into that conference room, he realized it wasn't a maze at all.

It was an abattoir.

18

Now

Cal joined Sydnor in the detectives' huddle. From the pictures, Tiny's face had been shrouded in shadow, but distinctive enough to identify. Here on the ground, with the sun now higher in the midmorning sky, Tiny's face was a misshapen mosaic of bright, unnatural colors: sickly yellow, angry red, deep purple.

"Here," said Cal, handing Massey his phone.

"Thanks, Kil—" said Massey, clearing his throat. "Cal. Climbers have anything else to say?"

Cal pretended not to notice the slip, but it stung. "If they have their way, they'd like the suspect to be charged with arboreal assault." He nodded toward the phone now back in its owner's hands. "Photos of the tree, all torn up. Killer likely used ropes and pulleys to hoist him and . . ." he said, nodding toward Porter, "*crampons.*"

It was a peace offering, but for what he still had no clue.

Porter smirked at Sydnor.

The medical examiners moved in and the detectives stepped back. The MEs were kitted up in their white suits and weaving through and around them, hovering over the body. If Cal let his eyes lose focus, they looked like ghosts.

Anything not to look directly into Tiny's face.

Or at Tiny's fingertips, which showed no sign of defensive wounds, or at his throat, where the deep groove of the rope's bite showed darker than the surrounding skin, or even at the branch positioned above his head, with the rope still connecting it to the body by a double knot.

Cal narrowed his eyes.

Double knot.

He took a step closer to the branch. Sydnor stepped out of his way and Cal bent to it. He studied it for a moment, then straightened again and stared out at the Potomac. The sun was now shining on the river directly, and he saw silver flashes through the trees.

He turned back to the climbers. "Quinn!" He waved him over. The arborist did not look happy to approach the body again.

"What are you doing?" sneered Porter, any momentary detente a memory.

"Uh, what?" said Quinn, stopping well short of the body.

"It's okay," said Cal, positioning himself between Quinn and the corpse, sparing the arborist another glance. "What kind of knot is this?"

"That's easy," said Quinn. "Double back figure 8."

"Is that common for climbers?"

"Strong as shit. It's a go-to knot."

It was in the Navy too, thought Cal, where he had learned it in basic seamanship.

19

Then

THE NEXT THING Cal remembered, he was in the back of an ambulance. Slowly, his senses returned to him one by one, like coming out of sedation, and he reached out and seized one of the paramedics by the arm.

"What the fuck?"

The paramedic seemed startled. Cal realized his bulletproof vest and weapons belt had been removed and he was stripped down to his undershirt, and he could see his hands and forearms were covered in dried blood.

"*What the fuck!*" he said, shaking the paramedic, who now was screaming as well and calling for his comrades. By the paramedic's reaction, Cal surmised that he must have been docile just a moment before. Cal continued shouting and began trembling until two more paramedics manhandled him down onto the cot in the ambulance. They crowded into the tight space, swarming him, but that only made his panic worse.

They assured him he was safe, instructed him to take deep breaths.

"It's not your blood," they told him.

One paramedic came at him with a needle. He was afraid if the needle punctured his skin, the gaps in his memory, which were fresh, might be paved over forever. Part of him thought that might be a wise idea, but he needed to know. He held up his hands—trying to ignore the blood on them, beneath his fingernails, the flecks of gunpowder—and said, "Okay! Okay."

The paramedics stepped aside altogether when two gruff voices from outside the ambulance asked if there was a problem.

"No problem," called Cal past the paramedics.

It worked. The voices ordered everyone out of the ambulance and the paramedics complied. Two senior officers crowded in and shut the ambulance doors behind them. Cal didn't like the closed doors, but he fought to remain calm. The first was his Patrol Division captain, Captain Andrea Mariano, and her boss, the head of the Field Operations Bureau himself, Deputy Chief Fred Simbulan.

"How are you, Farrell?" asked his captain.

"I'm fine. I think. They said . . . it's not my blood."

"Some of it is," said Simbulan. The deputy chief pointed to a gash on his head. "Medics say you're concussed."

It tracked. He felt dizzy and nauseated. In a fog. A far-off ringing in his ears.

"What do you remember?" asked Captain Mariano.

"I, uh . . ." Cal closed his eyes. "I remember hearing the call on the radio. Vance was with me."

Shit. Vance.

He opened his eyes and searched the faces of his superior officers. His captain didn't quite meet his eye. Deputy Chief Simbulan pressed. "How did it go down with Vance?"

"I had a civilian in cuffs already in the car. I cut him loose. Vance was ahead of me. Went in the front door and . . . I'm so sorry, captain."

"You're not the one who shot him," said Mariano.

"Go on," said Simbulan.

"I ran up John Carlyle to the side entrance, but the shooter had already gone up to four. I took the stairs and . . . accessed the spaces . . ."

The girl. He promised to go back.

"Oh God," said Cal, "the woman." Jesus Christ, he thought, she had told him her name. *What was her name?* "With the red hair. What happened to her?"

"Keep going," said the chief.

"Heather!" he shouted. "Tell me what happened to Heather?"

"Easy, Farrell," said Mariano. "She's in very bad shape, but she made it out. I suspect she's in surgery this second."

"Look, you need to tell us what happened," said the deputy chief. "We don't have much time and we need to get in front of this."

Cal was confused, but continued. "I accessed the suite and I . . . followed the . . ."

Bloody footprints.

He looked at his two superiors, at the sealed door to the ambulance. It was stifling inside. "What do we need to get in front of?"

"Farrell!" said Simbulan.

"Chief," said Mariano, cutting off Simbulan. A look passed between the two senior officers. Whatever it communicated, his captain seemed to win. She said, softer, "Cal, can you help us out here?"

He cleared his throat. "I followed the trail."

"And?" she said.

"I remember . . ."

Taking a breath, letting it half out. His uniform shirt soaked through beneath his vest, his undershirt soaked through beneath that. The oppressive heat and humidity in the blinding sun outside, now all of that perspiration cooling in the heavy air conditioning and dim fluorescence of the office suite, already causing a chill at the threshold. Counting to three, then whirling around, plunging forward, his weapon pushed forward . . .

"I engaged." He looked into the face of his captain, then his deputy bureau chief. "Didn't I?"

20

Now

THE MEs WERE swarming over the body and there was nothing left for the bystander detectives to do, so Sydnor drove
Cal to his house in the Del Ray neighborhood of Alexandria.

"How are you holding up?" Sydnor asked from the driver's
seat, without looking over. It was an awkward question, delivered
tersely enough that it may as well have communicated *do not reply*.
He remembered riding in his father's pickup truck as a kid, and
his dad uncomfortably saying in a monotone voice, "Well, you're
getting to that age where you're going to have questions about, you
know, sex, so you can go ahead and ask."

Cal did have a question. "Someone at school said 'oral sex.'
What's that mean?"

Cal's father cleared his throat. "Mouth."

"What about it?"

Cal's father winced. "Jesus Christ, son, ain't you ever heard of
a blow job?"

And that was the sum total of his birds-and-bees talk from his
father. And Sydnor, in his gruff, no-nonsense manner, with a thick
crust concealing a deep well of love and affection—hopefully—
reminded Cal of his father. That generation went right at a problem,

kicking in the door with guns blazing . . . unless it was something deeply personal, then they snuck around back or approached it from the side, warily, if they engaged at all.

Cal and Sydnor's most comfortable lexicon was gallows humor, the darker or more inappropriate the better, so Cal answered with a perfunctory "Fine," then tacked away from the fraught topic of how he was holding up. "You know the media is going to call the killer The Hangman."

Sydnor glanced over at him.

"Too soon?" said Cal.

The body was still on the trail, so it was entirely too soon. Sydnor broke at that. Cal loved making Sydnor laugh—it was like the sun bursting through the clouds for a moment on a dark day. And it had been a very dark day.

Humor as a shield, thought Cal, and the morning had offered plenty of reasons to need a shield.

Still, when the laughter stopped, Cal felt rotten for making a joke at Tiny's expense. A homeless man, an unwell man, who had been brutally murdered. Cal considered what he was becoming, what was left of the man who had existed before that Very Hot Day, and wondered, in the balance of things, if being a detective was worth the pieces of himself he had traded away. For a moment, he felt like he was back at sea and had fallen overboard on a moonless, starless night. Black above, black below, suspended in darkness. He had been treading water since spotting the body. Since last summer really. And God help him, in that moment, Sydnor's laugh was a pinprick of light on the horizon. He would add the joke to his running tally of things to feel guilty about later.

CHAPTER

21

Then

THAT NIGHT, AFTER getting cleared by the doctor and debriefed exhaustively by Captain Mariano, Deputy Chief Simbulan, and even Chief of Police Miriam Ravelle herself—Cal surrendered his weapon. He was to go on administrative leave pending all necessary reviews—from Chief Ravelle, from Internal Affairs, from the Commonwealth attorney—but it was all perfunctory, they assured him with tight smiles.

The doctors went over every inch of him. He would be half-drained of blood to test for HIV, hepatitis, and anything else he might have been exposed to in the bloodbath of ATMA's conference room. The doctors advised him against sexual intercourse while he waited for the results, and he stated flatly that wasn't going to be a problem.

What worried him was that only Captain Mariano really met his eye, and she wore a pained look on her face. It would help if he could remember for himself just what had happened once he entered that conference room, but he couldn't—it was a void. One of the doctors spoke to him sweetly, as if he was a young boy.

"Think of your brain like a circuit breaker. If there's excess current from an overload—horror or trauma—it protects the circuit. It interrupts the flow and resets. Maybe those memories will come back, maybe they won't. And if they won't, that's your brain protecting itself. That might not be the worst thing."

Cal didn't like that answer. He needed to *know*.

An officer drove him home late that night, while another followed behind in his car. Alone, he stood in his shower long after scrubbing away the remaining blood crusted in his fingernails, the hair on his arms, his eyebrows.

He had no idea what he was supposed to do next.

The doctors, his superiors, everyone told him to *rest*. He stretched out on the bed in his bungalow. His body was certainly tired enough, and it felt like his thoughts had to pass through a medium of dark water instead of instantaneous electrical impulses.

Cal may not have remembered the particulars, but it didn't protect him from the facts.

Seven dead.

Five men and women who, that very morning, had gone to work in an office building in Alexandria. One fellow officer. And the shooter himself. And now they were gone. And whether he remembered them or not, he had seen every last one of them.

He very clearly remembered Vance. And the dead man in the elevator lobby with . . .

He sat up in bed. He looked over at the alarm clock. It was early in the morning of the next day, but he didn't think it would matter. He put on a pair of jeans and a polo shirt and drove the three miles east to Inova Alexandria Hospital. He realized at the information counter that he didn't know Heather's last name.

"She was a victim of the mass shooting yesterday."

"Are you family?" asked the staff member.

He didn't want to explain. He didn't like playing the hardass, but it was the path of least resistance. He pulled his badge from his pocket, looked the staffer in the eye, and said, "I found her."

"Of course," said the staffer. "Heather Hayes. She's in the Intensive Care Unit."

Cal followed the signs to ICU. He pulled the same trick on the nurses at the station. They were filling him in when a man the same age as Cal passed by. His eyes were red and puffy.

"You're asking about Heather," said the man. "Who are you?"

"I . . . I'm a police officer. I was one of the responders. My name is Cal Farrell." He offered his hand.

The man reached out slowly for it and took it, not even shaking it, just holding it. "You were there?" said the man.

Cal nodded, not trusting his voice.

The man tugged him forward, not releasing the hand. "Come with me."

He led Cal around the corner, still holding his hand, to an alcove where several teary people were gathered. The man cleared his throat.

"Everyone," he said, "this is Officer Farrell. He was there today. This is the officer they spoke about during the press conference . . ."

Press conference? No one had told him about any press conference.

"He saved Heather," said the man. "*Cal stopped Milton.*"

"Wait," said Cal, but it was too late. Everyone was on their feet and moving toward him. He was enveloped by Heather's tearful loved ones—family, friends, coworkers—each grabbing him, clinging to him, sobbing into his shirt.

Cal tried to protest, but it was no use. They didn't want to hear it. No one wanted to hear it, and the more he protested, the more they thought it was false modesty. He wanted to shout *I don't remember*, but the last thing he wanted to do was frighten anyone more than they were already frightened. And it wasn't about him. As Heather's friends and family swarmed him, he searched out the man who was responsible for this huddle, the one who had made the announcement. The man stood a few feet away and a few inches shorter than Cal. He was clean-cut and handsome. The man looked to have had a haircut recently—an expensive one— and wore stylish shoes. Even in the midst of grief, the man looked pressed and put together. Cal felt rumpled and wrung out.

"I'm Heather's boyfriend Jason. Jason Blye," said the man, smiling now, his eyes shining with fresh tears. "And you're my new best friend."

22

Now

CAL FIGURED DISCOVERING a dead body—a murder victim in particular, and garishly staged at that—was a pretty definitive sign it was going to be an all-time shit day. He could win the Powerball, but it would always be the day he found that dead guy in the tree.

A dead guy he knew.

He was running very late now, but he hopped into the shower to rinse the dried sweat from his interrupted run and to warm himself under the hot water. As he dried off, he remembered he had plans that evening. Drinks with the crew. He began running through excuses in his brain for why he couldn't make it, including the truth.

He allowed himself the fantasy of bailing out while he shaved, but as his day began to pick up momentum with every article of clothing or piece of equipment he donned, his commitments began to reassert themselves. As tired as he was, as foul as his mood would be, and as much as he wanted to, he couldn't cancel. He found a tie, already tied, and poked his head through and tightened the knot around his collar as he thought, *They'd never let me live it down.* He slipped on his shoulder holster and picked up his father's penknife, small and slender, from his bedside table. It was something he'd fished out of his father's cigar box when he was a kid, and his father, rather than yelling at him for snooping, let him keep it. He'd taken to carrying it after he died. As he slid it into his pocket, he thought, *Just one drink and I'll cut out.*

First, he'd have to make it through his day.

He drove himself to Alexandria Police Headquarters on Wheeler, just south of Duke Street and west of Old Town, the historic center of Alexandria. It was four stories of brick and glass, topped with a pitched roof that gave the modern building a jaunty, almost aerodynamic appearance. Seeing the large, replica Alexandria Police Department badge on the front usually put a lopsided grin on Cal's face. The building also housed a state-of-the-art criminal investigations laboratory, emergency communications center, and space for 500 law enforcement officers. Despite the hazy circumstances of his promotion, Cal was proud to call a desk in such a building his own.

But not today. He was too lost in the events of the morning to notice the open plaza in the middle of the small green campus, his favorite feature, or the airy public atrium of the entrance that provided natural daylight for every floor.

The only thing that snapped him out of his daze was the feeling that someone was watching him. He glanced up to the lounge area on the second floor and discovered he was correct. Dr. Julia, the department psychologist, stared down at him, clearly waiting.

She didn't look happy.

23

Then

JASON SET UP a rotation, cycling through friends to keep watch over Heather. Cal found himself on the list. Her parents were flying in from out west but would not arrive until the next day.

"Look, I could use the help," Jason told him. There were friends who were weeping, who needed comforting themselves, and that wasn't much help for Heather. Jason needed order, which Cal understood. A plan. For Heather. Cal had a feeling it was more for Jason, which he supposed was normal too.

But Cal didn't really know what normal felt like anymore. He was numb, and Jason and the rest of Heather's friends mistook his numbness for quiet strength or stoicism or whatever, so he was pressed into service. But it gave him something to do. A way to get out of his own head.

He ducked out and got coffee and donuts for everyone. The grieving friends. The nurses at the station. The doctors. The paramedics who brought her in. Even the people at the information desk who pointed him to the ICU. Enough for the entire hospital—dozens and dozens of donuts and cardboard jugs of coffee. It cost hundreds of dollars and took several trips back and forth to his car. It was something to do.

If he sat in a chair in that pocket of grieving, hysterical people, he might start crying too. And if he started, he might never stop.

That wouldn't do. Not right now. It was not about him. It was about Heather.

She had survived the initial trauma and blood loss, but she had far more to contend with. Surgeons consulted the family, and information filtered through to the rest of the gathered friends and family in somber whispers. Phrases like "upper motor neuron injury" and "sacral spinal segments had been spared." To Cal's concussed brain, it might as well have been a foreign language.

"What does it all mean?" he asked Jason.

"It means a wheelchair."

Jason ran the show, but he began to show signs of wear as well. Cal, still numb, acted as his lieutenant. He just fell into it. Cal had been given time off—he didn't remember how long, but it didn't matter—and his whole world had become the hospital. He continued bringing food. He gave rides to family members from the hospital to their hotels. He avoided his Del Ray house, did not call in to work. He was self-aware enough to know that it wasn't all altruism, that he was not dealing with what had happened, but the hospital was a place he could *do* something, and the job wasn't finished, so he stayed. No one questioned his presence. Everyone was grateful to have an extra pair of helping hands.

He watched friends and family come and go like the tide, got accustomed to everyone's rhythms. Who showed up before work, who came after. When family members took breaks to eat or get coffee. Most, at some point, fell into his arms sobbing, thanking him, so very grateful. He wanted to tell them he had failed to come back for her, that he did not scoop her up in his arms and stride out the front door with her, that he did not stop the bad guy in time. Not even close.

That she survived not because of him, but despite him.

Her father, a short man who could barely get the words out, just patted his cheek. "You were there," he said, before breaking down completely.

Days passed. Heather was moved from ICU, but still in a medically induced coma. More visitors came and went.

A portrait began to form of the woman at the center of it all. Cal "met" Heather under the most gruesome circumstances possible, and they had only exchanged a handful of words. She had asked that he not leave her, but she knew he had to, and even though she was bleeding out, she gave him her badge, knowing what it meant. One way or the other, he would not be coming back for her. In that instant, he saw the resignation in her eyes. And she gave him her badge anyway. It was far more than his badge had done for her.

That was all he really knew about her. Yet it told him everything.

Still, he enjoyed hearing details about who she was. She had a loud laugh, like a startling bird call. She wasn't just open and friendly, but a natural leader. Whenever someone joined or left their office, she organized the welcome and farewell happy hours. She had backpacked through Europe, and wanted to retrace her steps. She loved to dance and sing. The more he heard, the more he liked her.

One morning, days later, Jason was coming apart. Cal could see it—he had barely left Heather's bedside.

Cal pulled him aside.

"You're going too hard. You need a nap and a shower. Let me drive you home."

Jason looked around the alcove. It was empty at that hour, just the two of them. "I can't . . ."

"You have to take care of yourself." Cal knew that was rich coming from him, but his hypocrisy didn't make the advice any less sound. "You're no good to her or anyone if you pass out from exhaustion."

"'Put on your own oxygen mask before the kids,' you mean," said Jason with an exhausted chuckle.

"Good advice at any altitude."

Jason stared at him then, his eyes coming into focus. "I don't know what I did to deserve you, Farrell, but you're a gift from the gods."

Cal shook his head. "Beat it. She won't be alone, I promise."

"I'll just be a couple of hours."

"*Go.*"

Jason left and Cal took a seat in Heather's room in the pre-dawn. With everyone else gone, he was suddenly very self-conscious. What business did he have to be there? What right? He was a stranger in a dark corner of this poor woman's room. But he didn't want her to be alone. She had already been as alone as one could be in that elevator lobby.

He pulled his chair alongside her bed and closed his eyes.

He dozed for just a second.

When he awoke, Heather was staring at him.

24

Now

"Cal," Julia called down to him. She recovered with a bright smile, but he had seen her furrowed brow clearly, if only for a second.

She held two coffee cups and gently shook one, luring him upstairs.

He sighed and climbed the stairs to the lounge.

"In the neighborhood?" he said.

"I mean, I could play that game if you'd like, but my poker face is for shit."

"Who called you?"

"Who didn't?" she said with her bright laugh.

"I'm fine."

"We can talk in my office, if you'd prefer."

He glanced around. Detectives and uniforms passed through the entrance below. More peered out from the internal windows of the upper floors. Still more walked along the open corridors that overlooked the atrium and the lounge. He was in a fishbowl.

"No need."

"No need because you're too tough and manly to talk or because you're secure and enlightened enough to have a conversation with the police psychologist out in the open."

"Which one gets me the coffee?"

"Option B."

"Then out in the open it is."

She smiled and handed him the coffee.

They settled into a pair of lounge chairs across from each other. "You didn't return my calls this morning. A girl could take it personally."

Dr. Julia's manner was always bright and intense, punctuated at times with wicked humor that veered, occasionally, toward the inappropriate. She was a few years older than he was, and it put him in mind of a cool, older girl from high school who he shared a class with as a freshman. Overly familiar, even flirty at times. Then again, Cal didn't much trust his own judgment these days, particularly regarding women.

"You are by far the strangest psychologist I've ever met."

"Have you been meeting other psychologists?" she said, pressing her hand to her heart. He laughed, and so did she, and when he was sufficiently softened up, she said, "Seriously, I can make room for you today."

"I'm okay."

"I think we should resume our old schedule."

"I'm a detective, Julia. I'm going to bump up against the odd body now and again. Comes with the territory."

"You're a Vice and Narcotics detective, not Violent Crimes. And from what I heard, it was a very odd body indeed."

"I'm better. Really."

"Really?"

"Sleeping better."

Technically it was true. His nights consisted of a series of cat-naps, but that was better than the extreme insomnia he had suffered in the immediate aftermath of that Very Hot Day.

"No blackouts, no lost time?"

He wanted to find a witty retort, but he was growing frustrated in the fishbowl. He just wanted the conversation over.

"Not that I know of."

She broke into a smile then, the relief on her face obvious.

"That's good, that's good," she said, leaning back in her chair. "Reached out to your family?"

"Had Christmas dinner with them." He didn't mention that it ended in a three-way shouting match, but he didn't need to.

"That good, huh?"

They had barely finished their meal before his mother and sister ganged up on him for staying with the department. Again.

If Meredith Farrell was displeased, she did not keep it a secret from her children. It had been true with Cal's father, Sean. And now, it seemed, he inherited her same displeasure.

Cal's parents had met on opposite ends of a case years ago, but their mutual attraction overpowered their sparring. They learned they actually shared similar values, then became allies, then more. But after years of watching the job age him and eat away at the edges of his soul, Meredith gave Sean an ultimatum. He had enough years to retire, so it was his family or the force. As stubborn as his wife, he refused to leave at first, so they separated. Cal ran interference for both of them. It was a bluff—Sean knew it, Meredith knew it, and Cal knew it—a game of marital chicken that would last a month or two at most, right up until Sean dropped dead of a massive heart attack, alone in an apartment off of King Street.

Sometimes, the worst thing in the world was to be right.

His mother could forgive neither herself nor his father. Cal was already long down the path of following in his father's footsteps when he died, but she gave her son the same ultimatum. But Cal proved to be just as obstinate as both of his parents. And though she had tripled her efforts after that Very Hot Day, he would be damned if he would let James Allan Milton chase him away from doing what he loved. Or admit that his mother was right.

As summer turned to autumn, they retreated to their neutral corners again. There was too much pain and anger just beneath the surface, and visits usually ended with arguments. She didn't want to watch him destroy himself and he was tired of explaining that he wasn't. Christmas had been no better. Meredith called him pigheaded, a glutton for punishment. "Just like your father," spat his mother.

His older sister, Cassie, who had flown in from California with her husband and two kids, slammed her hands down on the table. "Well, that's a Merry Fucking Christmas in the books."

Cal left early.

He looked at Dr. Julia now and offered a tight smile. "I made the minimum payment and they're off my back for at least a month."

"Are you getting out there more? Socializing?"

He nodded. "Plans tonight in fact." Abbreviated plans he was going to abandon at the earliest possible moment, but still.

She made an impressed face.

"And still running," he added. He cleared his throat and looked around the fishbowl. "Obviously."

"Which is what you were doing this morning when you found that body."

He nodded.

"What are you going to do now?"

"Change my route for starters."

"Cal."

"It's not the first dead body I've seen, Julia."

"I'm well aware. But I don't want this to set you back. Tell me what happened when you saw it. Did you have the spins? Be honest."

Cal looked around again, sighed.

"It was dawn, barely any light, and I looked up in the tree and saw him. It took my eyes a second to adjust. To even believe what I was seeing."

"How did you know to look?"

"What do you mean?"

"Word is, he was really high up. Like, *really* high."

"He was. Probably seventy feet. It was crazy."

"So how did you see it? When I'm running, I usually look at my own shuffling feet."

"And wish you weren't running?"

"Exactly."

"Well, there you go. I keep a weather eye out."

Dr. Julia cocked her head at him.

"It's a nautical thing. Anyway, there's a slight dip in the trail from the north, before the tree, so I was running up and out of it. And there's no leaves on the trees right now, so a two hundred and fifty pound dangling silhouette kind of draws the eye." He was irritated by the line of questioning and his tone said so.

"Understood," she said. "And your reaction?"

"Vision telescoped a bit. Felt wobbly for just a moment, but got my breathing under control quickly and called it in. Lasted less than thirty seconds."

She glared at him, as if trying to pry the truth from his skull with her eyes.

He raised his right hand. "Want me to swear on the DSM?" In Dr. Julia's circles, the *Diagnostic and Statistical Manual of Mental Disorders*, or DSM, carried more weight than the Bible.

"You're still funny."

"It's more convincing when you actually laugh."

That made her laugh, but it faded quickly. "I'd like you to start seeing me again. Regularly."

He made a face and drew a deep breath in order to issue a lengthy protest when she held up her hands.

"Again, I'm well aware this wasn't your first dead body. That's precisely the problem. You've seen *too many*. And more garish and grisly than anyone has seen on the entire force."

He sat back, took it in. He looked at her sideways, still irritated, but said nothing.

"I'm trying to help," she said.

"I understand."

"No, you don't." She leaned in. "You need to stay ahead of this."

Something in her voice got his attention. "Why?"

He leaned forward too, his elbows on his knees. A part of him recognized that their faces were closer than they'd ever been before, but a much larger part needed to hear what she said next.

"I wasn't joking when I said, 'Who hasn't called me?' I received multiple calls this morning about your presence at the scene. Up and down the chain, side to side. Some concerned for you, some concerned by you. Not everyone here has your best interests at heart, Cal."

He could imagine Detective Stacy Porter making such a call about "Killer Callum." Would Massey? Was the detective's gregarious façade just that? A bullshit front? Then again, it could have been any number of the uniforms, whispering in their tight clusters off to the side. Jesus Christ, would Sydnor? Would his own partner drop a dime on him? Sydnor had asked him how he was doing, but he could have placed a call to Julia if he was genuinely worried. Cal didn't think so, but Sydnor was inscrutable enough that he couldn't be sure.

So not everyone had his best interests at heart. This was not news. Not since that Very Hot Day, and the promotion that followed.

He leaned in further until their faces were inches apart.

"And what about you, Julia?"

He noticed her cheeks redden. At the proximity or the question, he didn't know, but she was quick to answer.

"I'm always rooting for you. You're thoughtful, empathetic, conscientious. In times like these, the department needs you. You're one of the good ones, Detective Farrell."

He leaned back and took it in. And he couldn't help but notice that when he leaned in, when he pried, her shields went up. *Detective Farrell*, she said. But that hardly mattered. She was an ally.

When he looked at her again, she was looking around the atrium this time. After her survey, their eyes met.

"Don't give them a chance to screw you, Cal."

Cal nodded. But who exactly was *them*?

25

Then

"SHE LIGHTS UP a room," Jason had told him. "I know every-one says that. When something bad happens to a woman, it's what everyone says. But she does, she really does. She's incandescent."

Right now, it felt like her gaze was burning two holes into Cal. He had been dozing, and when he opened his eyes, she was staring at him. He bolted upright. She looked pale and small, wrung out. He stood then and yelled for a nurse.

Her gaze softened then. Like a storm passing. What he had mistaken for rage or anger or recrimination was just intense con-centration. There was a ton of drugs in her system and though her eyes were open, she was not yet all there.

Then she smiled and it was like the sun came out.

Cal felt such relief he sank back into the chair. He couldn't help but smile back.

"You came back," she slurred.

She opened her hand and he took it. She gave it a small squeeze.

Cal hung his head and started to weep. It was like a dam bursting. He tried to stop—who was *he* to cry in front of *her?*— but the more he tried the harder it was to stop. He put his head on the side of her bed and his shoulders shook and he said, "I'm so sorry," over and over. When he lifted his head again, she was still watching him. With great effort, she lifted her arm and moved her fingers toward his face. She touched two fingers to his knotted forehead. She pressed then, into him, swirling the creased skin in two tight rotations.

Relax.

She smiled again and despite himself, he burst out laughing.

Incandescent, he thought.

CHAPTER

26

Now

CAL WONDERED HOW the investigation into Tiny's death was going as he pulled up to the condo in Fairlington, a quiet, tree-lined neighborhood of brick townhomes and condominiums bisected by I-395, with Alexandria to the south and Arlington to the north. What were Massey and Porter doing this very minute? Waiting on the medical examiner's findings? Canvassing the local shelters and churches? Interviewing associates and possible witnesses? Cal had only discovered Tiny that morning, but knowing Massey—or at least his reputation—they might even have a suspect in an interview room already.

Cal put his car in park and let his head loll against the headrest. He'd come straight from headquarters, not allowing himself to go home first. Once inside his bungalow, he knew too well the gravitational pull of his couch would be irresistible. If his friends knew the morning he had, they would happily allow him to retreat to his couch. A dead man in a tree was bad enough, but a dead man that he had a run-in with on that Very Hot Day? They would send him straight home, do not pass Go, do not collect $200. But he didn't want to invoke that day, not with this crowd.

It's not too late to make another excuse, he thought. *Cat in a tree . . .*

"Suck it up, Farrell," he said.

He considered leaving his blazer in the car, but then his weapon would be visible and that would look super douche-y. Despite what he'd been through, Cal wasn't the type to carry his weapon off duty. If he was going to the mall or the movies, maybe. But he wasn't one of those guys to take a weapon to the supermarket or out on a date, if he ever landed one. He wasn't a "gun bunny" before, and he'd be damned if he'd let James Allan Milton turn him into one. That monster had changed him enough as it was.

So he got out of the car and ran his hands over his blazer, hoping to smooth some of the wrinkles. *Get in, get out, and you'll be reunited with your couch in no time . . .*

He pressed a number on the callbox and heard a buzz, followed by the front door's deadbolt unlatching. There were a few doors in the lobby and he heard raucous sounds and high-pitched laughter behind one on the right. Before he reached it, the door swung wide and the man who lived there beamed.

"Keep it down, ladies," said Jason Blye, "someone called the cops!"

A cheer came up behind him as he opened the door wider to reveal four young women, all drinking and clearly having a good time. Jason pulled him into a bear hug, and over his shoulder, Cal watched Heather raise her eyebrow. Cal met her eye as Jason clapped him roughly on the back.

When Jason released him, Heather had wheeled her chair into the center of the living room, next in the queue to collect a hug. She was dressed for a night on the town, in a tight dress with a unique print that looked like flowers. She wore an open sweater over it, but the dress's V neck revealed the creamy skin of her chest, and her long red hair cascaded around her strong shoulders. He scarcely had time to register those details before her bright smile demanded his full attention.

"Hey," he managed.

"That's all I get?"

"Ha," laughed Cal, recovering. He bent over and she leaned up and they embraced. She smelled like a spring flower he couldn't quite place. She gave him a good squeeze and made a low, satisfied growl mid-hug that he always secretly enjoyed. Heather gave the best hugs.

"What do you think?" she asked, spreading her arms.

"I, uh, great dress. Are those flowers?" He leaned closer and saw that they were sharks. "Oh wow."

Their faces were close again, and when he looked from the dress to her face, he saw that her smile had turned into a satisfied smirk.

"Farewell and adieu to you fair Spanish ladies . . ." she sang softly as she rotated her chair away.

When he straightened, he noticed there were three other similarly attired ladies that he should probably greet as well.

Heather introduced them all as Jason went to the refrigerator to get Cal a beer. Two Cal recognized from the hospital, but one he had never met before. She was introduced as Carly, a very attractive brunette in a merlot midi dress with a floral print.

As he retrieved the beer, Jason stood behind Carly and mouthed, *"Single."* He pointed at Carly from behind and his eyes were wide and his pantomiming was so ridiculously over the top it would have been comical if it didn't make Cal feel so lousy.

Shit. This is why they had been so damn insistent that I show.

Cal gave Jason a pained smile; he was still mouthing *SING! GUL!*—and practically hopping from foot to foot.

Cal glared at him. *I got it.*

Jason gave him a silent thumbs up. He came around Carly finally and handed Cal his beer, then bolted to the other side of the island as if it had been a grenade. Now it was just the two of them.

"So," said Carly, "you're a detective?"

"Yes." Cal struggled for something witty or intriguing to say. Carly was beautiful, and her eyes were wide and hopeful. "Guilty as charged."

"I'm a bit of a true crime nut. *48 Hours, Dateline* . . . pretty much any show that says 'Friends say she lit up a room,' I'm there."

Cal glanced at Heather.

"Do you have lots of interesting cases?" asked Carly.

"Oh, it's not like what you see on TV. No aha moments. Mostly just people being shitty to each other, plus paperwork."

"That doesn't sound as fun."

"Your intuition is correct," he said. "You'd make a fine detective. Hey, are you looking for a job?"

She laughed and it lifted his spirits. Just a bit.

"I think you're being modest." Carly leaned in and lowered her voice. "It's amazing what you did that day."

Cal's spirits plunged again.

27

Then

CAL WAS SUMMONED to Chief of Police Ravelle's office at Alexandria PD's headquarters. He spent more time in a patrol car than at headquarters, and never on the chief of police's floor. Just another bizarre entry in a surreal week. He had surrendered his weapon, per protocol, and had been given leave. Not as punishment, they assured him.

He tried to puzzle out the gap in his memory, but the more he tried to visualize the ATMA conference room, the more fortified it became, like a bricklayer adding another layer of bricks and mortar. It was maddening. The news didn't help either, blaring the death toll constantly and interviewing witnesses who did not provide him with anything he didn't already know. He remembered Heather, the bloody footprints . . . then nothing. The conference room where he confronted James Allan Milton was locked tight.

However frustrated he felt, he knew the City of Alexandria was faring worse. The shooting dominated news coverage. Even in the shadow of Washington, DC, where the news cycle turned over daily, sometimes hourly, the shootings captured DC media for an entire week. It was relentless. Alexandria was a little jewel—a charming historic port city in the shadow of the Nation's Capital—and it had been shattered.

Now he was back in uniform for the first time since that day, waiting in the chief of police's anteroom with Captain Mariano. His boss leaned over and said quietly, "Thanks again for coming, Farrell."

Cal found it an odd thing to say. Then again, everything seemed out of kilter these days. Like the world was carrying on, but he was on a seven-second delay.

"Didn't have much of a choice," he said.

"I suppose not. But no worries, alright? You'll be great."

I usually don't worry until people tell me not to worry, he wanted to tell her. Instead, he asked, "Do I need my union rep?"

Before the captain could answer, the administrative assistant said, "The chief will see you now," and buzzed them in. They rose and Cal realized at that moment he was missing his handcuffs. He put his hand over the empty pouch to conceal it as he passed the assistant, as if she'd notice. He made a mental note to get another pair. It'd come out of his annual uniform allowance, but he doubted he'd be given too much shit for it, considering.

When he entered the chief's spacious office, he discovered a meeting already in progress. Several men and women were seated at a large conference table. He was astounded to see Mayor Schleicher among them, sitting next to Chief Ravelle. The room went quiet as Cal entered.

"Officer Farrell," said Chief Ravelle, "please join us."

She stood and crossed the expansive room to usher Cal in as if he didn't know how to use his own legs. It was a fair assumption, he thought. She led him to the vacant seat at the elbow of the mayor. Beside him was Mariano. Ravelle claimed her seat across from Cal, and beside her was Deputy Chief Simbulan, who sat stone-faced. The assortment of suits, some of whom Cal recognized, were denizens of City Hall, who he saw once in a while in passing at police headquarters.

The mayor shook Cal's hand, thanked him for his bravery and service, and rattled off the names of the assemblage: *City council, city attorney, communications and public information officer, various liaisons and special assistants . . .* Cal nodded at them all in greeting, forgot all of their names immediately, and wondered if he was dreaming.

It seemed like the entirety of the city government and the PD brass were seated at the table. If a gunman came in right now, he could wipe out the entire leadership structure of Alexandria, decapitating a city. Thoughts like this came to him more frequently now.

The day before, Dr. Julia and Captain Mariano gently shared with him the general details of what had transpired in ATMA's conference room. As Cal suspected, it was where the carnage began and, after killing Vance, where the shooter returned for a last stand. But when Cal entered, James Allan Milton took his own life. There was more to it than that, but the city had so far kept the more garish details out of the press.

But it was simply a story told to him. It was like trying to recollect someone else's memory. Everything between standing at the conference room's threshold to waking up bloodied in the ambulance was still walled off in his psyche, an impenetrable black box. Dr. Julia likened it to squeezing a baseball bat too hard. Loosen your grip, she told him, and you'll have a better chance of connecting.

Regardless, it didn't change the math. All Cal knew was that, in the end, he hadn't saved a single life.

He tried hard not to physically shake his head to clear the imagery, and focused on Mayor Schleicher's words, who was in mid-speech.

". . . you know more than anyone, the city is in shock. It's grieving. It's going to take a long time for its wounds to heal and it's our job to . . . to stitch things up as best we can. To *triage*, if you will, the collective trauma to the city."

Cal nodded, hoping no one noticed him gritting his teeth. The extended metaphor was too on the nose, and it was not helping.

"Bob?" said the mayor.

A well-dressed man at the other end of the table spoke up, someone far too well dressed and polished for a city official. He was more put together than the mayor himself. "Officer Farrell, my name is Robert Conway. I've been contracted by Mayor Schleicher and the city. My expertise is crisis communications. I wish I'd been brought on board sooner because time is so crucial and early errors can compound an already terrible situation, as I'm sure you can imagine, but I'm here now." He offered a toothy smile and everyone else followed suit.

Cal didn't smile.

"If I may be so blunt," continued Conway, "the city needs a win."

Cal said nothing.

From what he had gleaned in the news and from the statements he had read, both on and off the record, the city kept the precise details of the horror of the scene—of that conference room—from the public. As his own mind had done with him. The talking point had been that by the time the Alexandria Police Department had arrived, meaning Cal himself, whose name had not been released, everyone in the conference room was *incapable of life.*

It didn't begin to describe the carnage, and yet the terseness of it said it all. *Incapable of life.* It let everyone fill in the blanks. Cal still had plenty of blanks, but he was beginning to remember the blood, what seemed like a lake of it.

For a moment, Cal tried to pierce the veil of his own memory, when he realized Conway was still talking. Words words words.

". . . *narrative.*"

"I'm sorry?" said Cal.

Conway was smiling again and his hand was in the air, floating with each word as if he were placing them on an invisible marquee. *"Hero cop single-handedly stops carnage."*

The cobwebs fell away. It finally fell into place why he was there. He looked at the mayor, the chief of police, then to Captain Mariano and said, "I—I don't think it was like that."

"It was," Mariano said quietly.

"But I don't even remember what happened."

Mayor Schleicher spoke. "I've received personal assurances the Commonwealth's formal review will be greatly expedited. As will Internal Affairs', isn't that right, Chief?"

"I don't understand . . . ," said Cal.

The chief of police leaned forward, teeth clenched. "You heard Mayor Schleicher," said Ravelle. "The city is grieving. And it's our job to help it heal. You don't want to let the City of Alexandria down, do you, Officer Farrell?"

"Of course not, but—"

"Then *Hero cop single-handedly stops carnage.*"

The mayor stood suddenly and half the table rose in response. Cal was still reeling.

"Then it's settled." Schleicher thrust out his hand. "It's an honor to meet you . . ."

When Cal shook his hand, the mayor seized his forearm in a firm grip and smiled toward the other end of the table.

". . . *Detective* Farrell," said the mayor.

"What?" said Cal, following his gaze to Conway, and the photographer now over his shoulder. Before he could think *Where did he come from?* it was too late. The city already had its narrative and now it had a photo to go along with it.

28

Now

*A*MAZING WHAT *I did that day, you say? Getting there too late? Watching Vance die? Practically stepping over Heather only to* not *save her friends and coworkers? Amazing. Sure, that's the word I'd use, Carly.*

Carly stood there, smiling, expectant. Over her shoulder, he saw Heather, who was laughing, dressed to the nines, and surrounded by her friends, ready for a carefree night out on the town. And Jason, who he now wanted to strangle.

"Funny story, though," said Cal, desperate to change the subject. "That's not how I met Jason."

"What?" she said, looking confused. "I thought—"

"No, I busted him."

"What?" guffawed Carly. "Stop it."

"Oh yeah, total sleaze. I'm Vice and Narcotics and he's one of my confidential informants."

She was cracking up enough that Jason felt it safe to wander back.

"You two seem to be getting along . . ."

"I was just telling Carly how we met," said Cal, giving Jason an icy smile. "When I busted you for drugs."

Jason looked solemn and held up his hands in surrender. "I was set up."

"Caught him crossing the border into Alexandria," said Cal. "Ninety balloons of heroin in his rectum."

"After the first ten you stop counting, but if you're going to do a job, do it right, Mama always said."

"I always thought it was strange. That was a lot of work for a six-block drive."

"It's not work if you love what you do."

"Oh my God, you two," said Carly, laughing as she rejoined the other ladies.

Jason turned his back to the knot of women and gave Cal an exaggerated excited face. He looked like a mime. "Check you out with the banter," he whispered. "She totally loves you!"

"I should put a boot in your ass," said Cal through clenched teeth. "How about a heads up next time you're trying to set me up. With a true crime junkie no less."

"Mea culpa," said Jason, putting his hands up. "But you'd prefer someone who doesn't like what you do? And besides, if I told you I was trying to set you up would you have come at all? Be honest."

He looked over Jason's shoulder, where Heather was holding court, her smile wide, her eyes twinkling.

Lighting up the room.

"It's a busy time, is all. I'm still trying to find a rhythm with the job."

"We never see you. And when we do, it's bite-sized, man. It's not fair."

Cal sighed. "I'm here, aren't I?"

Jason clapped him on the shoulder. "Attaboy."

They eventually moved outside. The light was already fading. Heather had an accessible van, but she was drinking, so Carly volunteered to drive.

"What's the plan for tonight?" asked Jason.

"Dinner," said Carly. "Then karaoke at RockIt Grill. Dancing . . ."

Heather looked away, then over her shoulder at the men and batted her eyelids. "Hot girl shit . . ."

"Are you sure you don't need an escort by a policeman and an upright citizen?" asked Jason.

As Jason chatted with her friends, Heather flung her arms in the air beside Cal, threw her head back, closed her eyes and smiled. Her hair tumbled loose. She looked like she was waiting for another embrace. Or a kiss. His heart raced. *What the hell?* he thought.

He was pondering what to do when she said, "A hand, kind sir."

"Oh, of course."

He bent and scooped her out of her chair.

"A girl could get used to this service," she said.

A chorus of catcalls arose from the sidewalk. "Farrell, you're making me look bad!" called Jason.

Jason collapsed her chair and loaded it into the back of Carly's SUV, still lobbying to tag along, as Cal rounded the front of the vehicle, Heather in his arms.

"Alone at last," she said.

"Are you flirting with me, Ms. Hayes?" he said.

Their eyes met. Heather didn't look away. She smiled.

"Some detective."

By now, all the women were in the vehicle and Jason stood beside Cal.

"Last chance," said Jason. "Do you really want to leave us two manly specimens unsupervised?"

"We'll take our chances, babe," said Heather.

Jason began to sing softly. *"Never mind, I'll find someone like you . . ."*

"Oh shit, he's breaking out the Adele. Start the car, Carly."

"I wish nothing but the best for you two . . ."

All of the girls were laughing. "Bye, Jason. Bye, Cal . . ."

As the car sped away, Jason ran into the middle of the street, bellowing after it, *"Don't forget me, I beg!"* When the car rounded the corner, the women's laughter trailing the vehicle, he returned to Cal on the sidewalk.

He gave Cal a dark look.

"I can see right through you, Farrell, you're so fucking transparent."

"What?" said Cal, wondering if there was a residual blush on his face.

"You were about to say 'I've had a day, I'm just going to bounce.'"

"I did have a day."

"You always have a day. And yet you still need to eat. So we're having dinner. And—*gasp*—a drink. Maybe even two. In an establishment where other humans congregate. And I'm driving, so you can't roll out."

Cal looked at his shoes for a moment. Jason was a good friend, maybe his best these days. He had allowed most of his friends to drift after becoming a cop. Then there was the death of his father, the Very Hot Day, and now playing catch-up as a new detective. There just didn't seem to be the time to maintain his relationships. The truth was that the thought of calling an old friend and filling them in on his past couple of years seemed exhausting. Too daunting to go into and too overwhelming to dump on an old high school pal or a Navy buddy.

He wasn't much of a joiner anyway, he told himself.

But there was Jason. Had they met under different circumstances, he doubted they'd even be friends. Cal had been raised by a cop father and a lawyer mother with blue-collar sensibilities. Jason came from real money. Something to do with computers on his father's side, and the skills were hereditary. And Jason was cultured. He ran the network at the Alexandria History Museum because he liked to, not because he needed to make a living. Cal, on the other hand, was decidedly uncultured, and his first remedy when his laptop malfunctioned was to blow on the keyboard.

It would have been so easy to resent Jason . . . if he weren't so goddamned nice. And ironically, their shared trauma made it easier to be around him than others. It required zero explanation.

Cal sighed. "Fine."

"Outstanding!" As they walked toward Jason's SUV, Jason added, "Hey, how'd you know about the balloons?"

"Don't make me laugh, Blye. I'm still mad at you."

"You'll get over it. Carly's hot, dude. And I'm telling you, she digs you. "

They found a sports bar in Arlington where soccer played, and they sat beneath a flat screen that broadcasted a La Liga match. Real Madrid was demolishing Valencia, but Cal didn't care. The passing of the ball back and forth along Real Madrid's side was so graceful as to be hypnotic, and it relaxed him. Jason was right, this was what he needed. And Jason was easy to hang out with. He did most of the talking. When he asked about Cal's day, Cal kept it noncommittal. He didn't need to pollute Jason's mind with the garbage he had seen that morning. Jason, like himself, had already seen too much.

Cal was as relaxed as he was going to get when he made it home, his mood lifted from the depths of the morning. As he climbed into bed for another unsuccessful night of sleep, a low hum ran through his body. He realized he had been wrong. It wouldn't be the day marked by finding a dead man he knew in a tree, nor even the day Julia told him he had unseen enemies lurking throughout the Alexandria PD.

He would remember it as the day he finally held Heather in his arms.

29

Then

CAL REMEMBERED IT as the day she smiled. That drugged but incandescent smile was like the sun breaking through the clouds on a stormy day, but it also had an effect similar to a fever breaking. He realized his vigils had been more selfish than selfless. She was not some sleeping beauty and he was no prince. Their lives had briefly entangled, but his role in her story was over. It was time to let her move on. That day she woke from her multiple surgeries and smiled at him was his last visit.

Until Jason called.

"Heather wants to talk."

Before Cal could answer, Jason added, "In person."

Cal may have made up his mind, but he found himself unable to deny a direct request. Within the hour, he found himself back in the hospital. Jason met him with a hug in the cafeteria, then led him to a new room on a new floor, one Cal hoped was a reflection of a less precarious state. Jason patted him on the back and beckoned him onward. Cal took a deep breath and entered, bracing himself for what he might find.

It was like stepping into a kaleidoscope. Gone were the soothing but drab beiges and grays of her previous room. The walls

were covered with prints of pink sand beaches and blue moun-
tains. Someone had taken apart a calendar and hung the photos
of each dazzling month in Heather's eyeline. Cal saw February in
Rome. June in Versailles. October in Santorini. There were fabric
wall hangings and dozens of postcards and crayon drawings from
children. Vases spilling with bright flowers covered every surface.
He ventured a step further and peered overhead. A massive poster
of Van Gogh's *Starry Night* was taped to the ceiling.

At the center of it all was Heather. It was so bright and startling that he almost didn't notice the machines behind her, which,
he supposed, was the point. Upon closer inspection, she looked
to be in the center of a spider's web of surgical tubing, though
this time—alert and waiting and propped on several pillows—
she looked more like the spider than a fly. She wore an emerald
pashmina, her hair was brushed, and the color in her face had
returned.

He had never approached a throne before, but he imagined
this felt close. Her eyes were fixed on him, like she was about to
render judgment. He fought the urge to kneel.

"I've decided we should be friends," said Heather.

Cal nodded. "Decided to approve my application?"

She shrugged. The tubes lifted with her shoulders. "There
were openings."

It was the verbal equivalent of a suspect disarming him and
pointing his own weapon back at him before he could blink.

So much for light and breezy, he thought.

"They tell me I'm never going to walk again," she stated.

He didn't know what to say to that. And he hadn't been
around the last few days to receive the latest prognosis, but his gut
reaction was to push back. "Hey, maybe . . ."

She shook her head, cutting him off. The tubes swayed.

"Rule number one, friends don't bullshit each other."

Cal swallowed whatever he was going to say. After a moment,
he met her gaze and nodded.

"Ever heard of the Stockdale Paradox?" she asked.

"Can't say I have."

"My father's an army veteran. Big reader, history buff." She smiled. "Real tough guy, but I'm a daddy's girl."

Cal had met him. The man had been inconsolable, and stayed that way during most of Cal's time there. Whatever he had been, this had broken him.

"Admiral Stockdale was a pilot during Vietnam. He was shot down, and as his plane was going down, he said to himself, 'I will be a prisoner of war for at least five years.' It was seven total. An interviewer later asked him who lived and who died in the POW camps, and he said it was the optimists who died. They thought they'd be free by Thanksgiving. Thanksgiving would come and go and they'd think they'd be free by Christmas. And Christmas would come and go, and they'd think they'd be free by Easter. And Easter would come and go and they'd die of a broken heart."

Cal had already seen this woman nearly bleed out before him. Now he was watching her spirit bleed out too. She had called him here to bear witness. And he deserved it. He stared at his feet for a moment, but when he forced himself to meet her eye again, she surprised him.

"The Stockdale Paradox is the radical acceptance of the worst parts of your current reality, but having absolute confidence you're going to prevail in the end."

Her eyes were alive. Her cheeks were flushed. She radiated power from the center of her web.

He cleared his throat, found it hard to speak. "That's a good paradox."

"It's my favorite paradox," she said, smiling now. "That and jumbo shrimp."

He smiled too.

"I heard you got promoted," she said.

He blushed, his cheeks pink with shame. "Yeah, I don't think I'm going to accept."

"I thought it was a done deal."

They had ambushed him with his very own dream, but it felt all wrong.

"I'm thinking about another line of work."

"But why?"

Why? he thought, incredulous. He forced himself not to point at her legs or blurt something about the sudden openings in her friend group or the horror that floated just outside his grasp but kept him up every night. Then he saw her bite her lip to keep from smiling. The laughter exploded out of him. Once he broke, she finally laughed, the tubes dancing around her. They laughed so hard a nurse ducked her head in and made a face that made them laugh harder.

When their laughter finally subsided and they caught their breath, she fixed that intense gaze on him once more.

"Hey, I'll prevail if you will."

It was then that Cal realized he was the fly all along.

30

Now

DISCOVERING TINY STIRRED everything up again, which, Cal thought, probably accounted for the brawl inside headquarters.

Despite months of whispers, guilt, sleepless nights, and days filled with impostor syndrome, Cal did his best to move forward. And then he found Tiny. The man's real name, Cal learned, was Wylie Gilbert. Finding Gilbert was bad enough—it would haunt anyone—but this new horrible scene had dredged up Cal's previous horrors as well. The Very Hot Day was like silt along a river bottom, and suddenly it was kicked up all over again and everything was cloudy. Cal felt like he was underwater and blind.

Sleep worsened. His days were a fog, the silt never quite settling. He tried a new route along the trail, heading north toward Arlington instead of south toward Old Town, but part of the comfort of running was the routine, and he couldn't quite find a rhythm. He timed his route wrong, and was late for work. Paperwork that he usually completed on autopilot now took him twice as long. He misplaced his pen. He tapped his jacket pockets and opened his drawer to find another one.

He nearly sprang from his seat. Fortunately, Sydnor was off getting coffee and hadn't seen Cal's reaction. He looked around the bay to see if anyone else had noticed. Satisfied no one was watching him, he peered into his drawer.

Sitting on top of the usual detritus was a pair of handcuffs. It would have been perfectly normal except for the bow, red and shiny.

He glared around the bay again, his jaw set. He waited for someone to meet his eye, to reveal themselves. The hum of the detectives' bay continued unabated. No one noticed him.

He took the handcuffs from the drawer, ripped off the bow, and threw it in the plastic garbage pail by his desk. He scoured the drawer for a note or another clue, but there was nothing else. Just the cuffs.

The implication was clear: they were his old pair. Or supposed to represent his old pair. He appreciated pranks or gallows humor among his friends as much as anyone, except he didn't have friends here. The closest he had was Sydnor, and this wasn't his style. And it wasn't funny. Not to Cal.

Not everyone here has your best interests at heart, Cal.

He dropped the cuffs back into the drawer and slammed it closed. That turned a few heads, but his murderous expression did not invite inquiries.

He walked to the cantina. No one was in there. He paced for a minute and took some deep breaths. Once he settled down, he realized he had forgotten to eat again. He spied a bag of pretzels in the vending machine. He fed the machine its due, but the pretzels got snagged on the coils and hung, pinned between the dispenser and the plastic window. He patted the window a few times, but the pretzels remained suspended in place, out of reach.

"Come on . . ."

He smacked his palm on the side of the machine. Nothing.

Cal saw red. He saw a crimson-colored bow.

He planted his feet and dropped his shoulder. He pressed into the machine, using his weight to raise it off its front legs an inch, then let it drop. The machine rattled and the floor shook.

The pretzels still floated maddeningly out of reach.

"God *damn* it."

"Whoa. Easy there . . ."

Cal snapped out of it. He had been too wrapped up in his assault and battery of the vending machine to notice the two uniforms passing by the cantina. It was Adelphia and Maddox. He had gone through the academy with Adelphia. They weren't friends—the cop always struck Cal as kind of an asshole—but they had been friendly enough.

"Let's get out of here before Killer Callum shoots it," Adelphia muttered to Maddox. But Cal caught it.

Apparently the friendly days were over.

Cal didn't register closing the distance. He grabbed Adelphia by the arm and spun him around. "What the fuck did you just say?"

Adelphia's hands were fast and Cal's reaction was slow. As quickly as he had rushed Adelphia, Adelphia had shoved him in the chest. Cal blinked. He found himself on the floor, on his hands and feet as if crab-walking.

But all the sudden movement got his blood flowing enough to clear his head. He launched forward again, hauling back his balled fist. Adelphia prepared for the swing. At the last moment, Cal dropped his shoulder and went low instead, slamming Adelphia into the wall. Cal felt the collision throughout his body. The plaques and framed photographs danced along the wall. It felt good.

Let's see you how you like it.

"*Whoa whoa whoa!*" yelled Maddox. "*Hey!*"

Adelphia was trying to throw punches, but Cal was close in and they were tangled together. Cal gripped the other cop's vest tightly, then stepped away, opening the distance between them. Adelphia was able to land a jab, but he was still off balance. Rather than hitting him back, Cal, still grasping the vest with both hands, flung Adelphia into the opposite wall with all his might. Adelphia, now totally off balance, hit the wall horizontally. He went down, but would be up again in a moment. Cal wasn't quite sure what to do next. He hadn't really thought that far ahead. Before he could make up his mind, Maddox tackled him.

When Cal got to his feet, he noticed three more uniforms trying to restrain a red-faced, frothing Adelphia. There was shouting, but Cal barely heard it. For a split second, he didn't remember what was happening. *What the hell is Adelphia so mad about?* He saw the cracked frames and broken glass along the floor. Maddox and someone else were holding Cal back, but the fight had drained out of him. Exhaustion flowed in to take its place.

You fucking idiot, he thought.

"You fucking idiot," said Sydnor.

Cal looked over. His partner had him by the arm and was speaking low, his teeth clenched. "Why are you giving them *ammunition*?"

Sydnor yanked Cal down the hallway as Adelphia rained threats and insults down on him.

"I don't care, you fucking psycho," yelled Adelphia. "You and me! I'll be waiting, bitch!"

Sydnor pushed him into a conference room.

"Jesus Christ, I do *not* need this . . ." The older detective seethed and paced in the room. "I definitely do not need this unmitigated bullshit."

Cal's adrenaline was fading and he was coming to his senses. It sucked knowing your peers didn't trust you or believe you had earned your shield, but he never considered how bad it was to be Killer Callum's partner. He imagined it was like being ordered to take your little brother with you everywhere you went, if your little brother picked his nose or stank or had been at the center of a bloodbath and everyone thought he was a fucking psycho.

"I'm sorry . . ."

"What did they say to you?"

"They called me . . . you know what they called me."

"So?"

"They said I was going to shoot the vending machine."

"Were you?"

"Statistically speaking, people are four times more likely to get killed by a vending machine than a shark—"

Sydnor rubbed his forehead and squeezed his eyes shut. "Please tell me you weren't pointing your weapon at a fucking vending machine."

"Of course not. I was just rocking it."

"Why the hell did you even do that?"

"It stole my mini-pretzels. And yes, saying it out loud just now does makes it sound kind of frivolous."

"Why not just put another dollar in, dumbass? Hit the mini-pretzels again, and you might luck out and get two."

"Lavaar, do I strike you as a particularly lucky person?"

Sydnor grunted. "You know you're going to eat shit over this."

"Well then, I'm going to get my mini-pretzels to help me get rid of the taste. Come on, I could use backup."

"You can't be serious."

"I don't want Adelphia to get them."

Cal stood beside the doorway and swept his arm in an "after you" gesture.

Sydnor passed through the door shaking his head.

"Also, can I borrow a dollar?" asked Cal.

CHAPTER

31

HER NAME WAS Hayley Driscoll, early thirties, a program analyst in one of the thousands of contracting firms that ringed
the Nation's Capital. She was jogging and wearing leggings, a running top, and a hoodie. Being February in Alexandria, it had been
cold, but she was a creature of habit, friends told the police, so she
would have powered through her run that night, taking the same
route she always did.

Friends said she had had a rough breakup a year before. She
had been on a particularly difficult contract, working for a task-
master of a client. It was a federal agency in flux, and the agency
head was paranoid, trying to build an empire, and rode the contract staff like rented mules: impossible deadlines, late nights, no-
notice travel. It was stressful. The schedule was unforgiving, and
Hayley's routines had been shaken. Meals made at home became
quick lunches out, and she put on weight. Her friends had always
described her as a go-getter, a leader, indomitable. She took the
extra weight in stride—it was only temporary—until she found
out her boyfriend, an analyst with the same company, had been
sleeping with another coworker. Someone younger and fresh who
would fall for his line of bullshit, who would not yet realize that
he was one of thousands, perhaps millions of contractors inside
the Beltway who introduced themselves as "consultants." They

proffered their business cards and wore fashionably long coats over their suits in winter, but they consulted on nothing. They went to meetings and wrote reports and created spreadsheets, but they held no sway unless they had an opportunity to burrow into the federal system themselves and perhaps, over time, get senior enough to find their own contractors to abuse.

Hayley broke the chain. She quit. It wasn't the long hours or even the humiliation of the infidelity. Her friends said she took a hard look at her life and didn't like what she saw. She took a pay cut to work for Volunteers of Alexandria, a faith-based non-profit working with vulnerable populations. She cut her hair. She began working out—running—and soon shed the extra weight she had put on, and then some. She got ripped. She made jewelry for her friends and sold pieces on Etsy. She was looking into getting a dog. She was at the tail end of a total reinvention, her friends had remarked. A butterfly fresh out of its chrysalis, spreading her wings and getting ready to fly.

Valentine's Day was a week away, and she had heard from those same friends that the young analyst her ex had slept with had moved on to someone new. "Too bad, so sad," she laughed. Even with her new life, she wasn't above posting a couple of thirst traps of her new body where her ex might see them.

"Eat your heart out . . ."

The end of her favorite running route led her to a narrow lane that cut between Duke Street and Jamieson Avenue. Pinched between a building on one side and a low ravine on the other, the footpath looked darker than usual that night. It didn't faze her. She was close to home and this was her final push. She had come so far. She wasn't about to stop now. She smiled as she poured on the speed.

32

THE MURDER RATE in Alexandria, relative to its neighbor Washington, DC, was low—single digits annually—and Cal heard about them all. Some of the victims had been on his radar: in his Vice and Narcotics files, an associate or family member of someone in a case he had worked, in the wrong life or brushing too close to it. Some he had no experience with at all. Sudden explosions of domestic violence, shocking and senseless. But all were sad, all a failing mark of some sort against the city. The previous year, of course, had been an exception. The number of homicides last year more than doubled the previous year thanks to a single Very Hot Day, but that was a statistical anomaly. "In a macro sense," the Public Affairs folks intoned, the homicide rate in the City of Alexandria remained low.

And the unsolved homicide rate was even lower.

Tiny beat the odds in the worst way. A month after Cal had discovered him, Massey and Porter were no closer to identifying who had killed Wylie Gilbert and strung him high in a tree on the Mount Vernon Trail.

Cal had been interviewed again, but there were no solid leads, or at least none that the investigators were willing to share with a detective from another division. He had to rely on Sydnor to get whatever scant information he could, but Lavaar wasn't keen to stick his nose into his ex-partner's case and doubted Massey would give him the full picture anyway, knowing it would be shared.

So Cal resumed regular meetings with Julia, but he convinced her that fresh, gruesome nightmares of hanging men had not supplanted the old, reliable nightmares from ATMA, so they both cautiously agreed it was progress, and their meetings faded again from regular to semi-regular. He tried to put Wylie Gilbert out of his mind as best he could. He continued running, but changed his normal route along the trail, away from Alexandria and toward Arlington, rather than passing beneath the same tree day after day.

Until the next body was found.

It was February, and the victim was different in almost every way from Tiny. Instead of a man high in a tree on the lonely Mount Vernon Trail, it was a woman in a low ravine that cut through Old Town. Instead of hung, she was slashed. And instead of happening upon it personally, Cal heard about it through normal channels. Some details he heard through scuttlebutt, but most he had read in profiles and interviews with her friends and family like everyone else. Cal couldn't help noting the disparity in the media coverage between Tiny's death months earlier and the killing of a young, pretty, and likable woman. A life is a life, thought Cal, and a murder is a murder. There should be no difference, but he was realistic. With no friends or family to keep him there, Wylie Gilbert's murder was noted in the *Alexandria Times* and the local online Patch. Hayley Driscoll had been in the *Washington Post* every day since she was found. It wasn't fair, but as Sydnor was fond of saying, "Fare is what you pay to get on a bus."

Nothing about the homicides was similar. If anything, they were opposite.

Deliberately so, thought Cal.

It wasn't too much to believe that two killers were operating in DC or Northern Virginia perhaps, but Alexandria?

He mentioned it to Sydnor on their way to the courthouse.

Sydnor grunted in return. The older detective had a day of testifying for the prosecuting attorney on myriad cases ranging from drug possession to lewd sex acts in public, and Cal was tagging along to watch and learn, as he did every week. Apprehending criminals was half the job; the other half was putting them away, and court days offered the chance to close the loop. Still, they were a pain in the ass, and Sydnor's mood reflected it. But there seemed to be an even deeper reluctance to address the Hayley Driscoll case with Cal.

"Don't go chasing waterfalls," the older detective said.

"Are you seriously quoting TLC right now?"

"Lot of wisdom in that, junior."

"So in this case, sticking to the rivers and lakes that I'm used to is Vice and Narcotics and never sharing information?"

"There's sharing information and then there's gossip. Speculation. Loose lips sink ships."

"There's educated guesses, hypotheses, profiling . . ."

Sydnor shook his head. His hands rested on the steering wheel, but he lifted one to jab the air. "If I had a case that had any bearing whatsoever on Massey's case, any helpful information, you bet your ass I'd put my chocolate in his peanut butter. Seeing as how we do not have any helpful information, then we are tourists."

"I'm not advocating sticking our nose in."

"Our nose? Keep my nose out your mouth."

"Fine, my nose. You're not even the least bit curious? What if there's a serial killer operating in Alexandria?"

"If, if, if. If my aunt had balls, she'd be my uncle."

"Not necessarily. Maybe she's just your aunt with balls. Have you ever considered asking her how she'd like to be addressed?"

Sydnor shook his head. Cal waited for his daily *I do not understand your generation*, but Sydnor didn't take the bait.

"The capacity to cram bad shit into your head is not unlimited, Cal. And the worse it is, the more it sticks. You're going to need that space for your own work. And there will be cases, ones on your own plate, that will haunt you." His partner looked him full in the eye, then turned back toward the windshield. "You've already got ghosts. No sense looking for more."

Every now and then, Sydnor would drop a golden nugget. They were rare, and when Cal heard one, he always picked it up, held it to the sun, and squinted at it with one eye, before tucking it into his pocket, adding it to his collection, and modifying his views or behavior accordingly.

Later, he wished he'd listened.

33

I T WAS LIKE falling down a well.

The shortcut of Hooff's Run was probably four hundred feet long. Orbs of light from lampposts dotted the path at intervals, except for a stretch at the halfway point, where Cal now stood. Beneath him, he could hear the faintest burble of the stream, barely more than a trickle. He peered over the railing, into the ravine, and a dank smell arose. A century's worth of stormwater had flowed through here after heavy rains. He'd loved playing in such ravines when he was a kid, trying to catch minnows and hopping from tiny island to tiny island, always failing to keep his shoes and socks dry.

The path doglegged. The adjacent building rose up six or so stories on one side, and on the other a riot of trees along the ravine's bank spread their canopies over the trail, creating a tunnel. Humans and nature unwittingly collaborated to create a perfect snare, thought Cal. He hadn't read the report, but he knew that this was where the killer, concealed in shadow, would have waited for Hayley Driscoll.

It's what he would have done.

Ultimately, the tug of the site had proven too much for Cal. He had to see it for himself. Though he tried not to think about it, Hooff's Run was a mere two blocks from the site of the Very

Hot Day, and the fact that he was still here and not a plaque on the wall in Alexandria PD headquarters like Vance or confined to a wheelchair like Heather was a cosmic coin toss.

And to him, that luck incurred a tax.

Which is why he put the lights and sounds of Duke Street behind him and walked into the swallowing darkness ahead of him, hoping to see what he might see.

Cal moved forward slowly, letting his eyes adjust. He didn't want to use his flashlight yet, or even the light of his phone. He needed to get his night vision. After several minutes, the contours of what he was looking for materialized, and when its shape emerged, he caught his breath.

Ahead, before exiting the trail, was a brick arch bridge. It spanned the stream below, its hollow maybe twenty feet across. From Cal's vantage on the bike path the large barrel vault resembled the cave of a troll who snatched children.

With a shudder, he realized he wasn't far off.

All he had heard was that she was found at the mouth of the bridge, in the stream, at a spot a couple of inches deep, a place shallow enough that the feeble current couldn't move her. With his eyes fully adjusted, he took a deep breath and decided to get on with what he came here to do, why he had brought old tennis shoes in his car. He climbed over the railing of the bike path, where the stream was closest, and dropped onto an earthen ledge topped with dead grass. He sat himself down on the ledge, pushed himself forward, and let his long legs drop down onto the bank. His feet crunched into the mixture of sand, grass, and stones. The icy water seeped through the bottom of his sneakers, soaking his socks. He picked his way into the center of the stream, island hopping as he had when he was a child, until he was square with the black hole.

The vault of the bridge loomed over him, dread soaked. No light from Duke Street reached him, and it was so dark within the vault the void appeared solid. He was in a cold sweat and his heart beat wildly, arrhythmically.

What the fuck am I doing? he thought.

Paying your tax, a sterner voice answered.

Just ahead, the vault let out a cool breath, like a tomb. The troll beckoning him onward, into its maw. Gooseflesh erupted on his neck.

He switched on his flashlight with the red lens. Crimson light flooded the vault ahead, clear through the other side. It was a trick from his shipboard days. Before assuming the watch, one had to take a round of the ship to inspect stations throughout the vessel: the bridge, the engine room, the small boats. Before setting off on a round, he would fumble his way to the flight deck and wait for the stars to reveal themselves. Once he could discern the Milky Way, he would switch on his penlight and begin. Incandescent light destroyed night vision, but red light worked just fine.

And it would not be as conspicuous from above.

The crimson light brought temporary relief, but the darkness beyond its edges seemed even darker now and the water looked like blood. He had to stop himself from swinging his flashlight wildly at every shifting shadow, every rustle from every nighttime critter in the brush.

At the vault's entrance, the rank smell sharpened, yet it was cleaner inside than he expected. There was no floor, just the stream, so there was no grass, no garbage, and no rats. No hanging moss from overhead. Just the light flow of water, smooth brick, and graffiti, some of it even preceded by the @ symbol so admirers could find the taggers on Twitter. He took the requisite pictures, but figured the killer was too smart to literally sign his work. He walked through the tunnel and emerged on the other side, to the south face of the bridge. The darkness slackened and his chest relaxed a little. The waterway both widened and deepened, so he turned back. He was halfway through the vault when his phone rang. He nearly jumped with fright.

"Hey, sugardip," said Jason. He could hear music and laughter in the background. "A couple of us are having drinks at Evening Star. Come on out."

"Can't tonight, in the middle of something."

"And I was in the middle of a Rocket League tournament with money on the line, but here I am. And by here I mean Del Ray."

"Sorry, I'm working a case."

"You're echoing. Are you in a bathroom? Is 'working a case' a euphemism for taking a shit?"

"I'm not taking a shit, Jason."

"Come on. We're practically in your backyard. I can't make this any easier for you."

"I'm far from my backyard right now."

An exasperated sigh, then a loud, *"Fine."*

"Tomorrow night," said Cal. "Happy hour. Wherever you want."

"Holding you to it. Enjoy your shit."

He slid the phone back into his pocket and exhaled. That was what he needed, a tug from the real world. He had ventured into the cave under the bridge and he had emerged again, safe. He took a deep breath. He wasn't a child in a fairy tale, he was a detective. He put eyes on the scene, as Hayley Driscoll had seen it, as the killer had seen it, and he thought he had worked out where it had happened, and how. Gone were the other detectives whispering *Killer Callum*, gone were the macabre presents left in his desk, gone was any second guessing. He was *here*. On the trail of something, narrowing the gap between crime and criminal, and narrowing the gap between who Cal was and who he thought he could be.

He placed his hands on the concrete ledge and pushed himself onto it. From there, he vaulted back over the railing onto the bike path at its darkest point. He shone his flashlight against the wall of the building. There had been a sequence of lampposts, then nothing. But he found what he was looking for. A lantern, affixed to the hotel wall, at the interval where the next orb of light should have been. He imagined the bulb had been shattered in advance. Violent Crimes would have collected the shards and dusted for prints. There would be none.

It's where he would have surprised Hayley Driscoll, rendered her unconscious before she could scream. Then it was a matter of hoisting her—quickly—over that railing onto the ledge below, out of sight. From there, the killer took his time carving her up.

And when he was finished, rolled her off and into the shallows below, where she would be found at the mouth of the bridge's tunnel.

He remembered Tiny suspended high up in the tree. *When the wind blows, the cradle will rock.* And now he considered Hayley Driscoll. Left at the mouth of a cave out of a nightmare, her hair swaying in the current like the fraying rope in that flooded sailboat compartment years ago.

They were as different as they could be, but the stagings were deliberate. Baroque and extravagant. Ghoulish.

And definitely meant to be seen. In order for the killer to communicate *something*. Cal was convinced of this more than ever as he walked quickly back toward the lights of Duke Street, eager to get off the path.

But what?

34

THE NEXT MORNING, Cal skipped his predawn run. He didn't need it to get his blood flowing. The sun was barely up, but he was already dressed, fortified with coffee, and standing in a parking lot in Alexandria's Landmark-Van Dorn neighborhood. It was an overcast day, with the rising sun merely turning the sky from dark to dim. It put him in mind of last night's scene at Hooff's Run. He couldn't quite shake the image of its nightmare vault, but he shoved those thoughts from his mind. He had a job to do.

Executing his first search warrant.

He had been on search teams before with Sydnor as lead, but this time Cal was the primary investigating officer. Under Sydnor's watchful eye, of course, but it was his show, and as such Cal had to request permission to obtain the warrant from Deputy Chief Simbulan. Cal wrote the affidavit and obtained the warrant from the magistrate. Cal established the ownership, occupancy, and description of the search site. And now it was Cal reiterating the top points of his pre-entry briefing to the scowling search team in the empty corner of a Target parking lot. He didn't know if the team was cold and tired, or just hated him.

A little from Column A, a little from Column B, he thought.

Cal cleared his throat and held up a color photo printed from Facebook, showing a thin, bookish man with salt-and-pepper hair. "Brett Dailey. Fifty-four-year-old white male, no known priors. Lawyer at the Department of Commerce, and by all accounts a solid citizen."

Sydnor coughed into his fist.

"But don't judge a book by its cover," Cal added quickly. "Assume nothing. A woman in the neighborhood called in a tip that her husband had been beaten up, but didn't buy his story that he'd been robbed. For a second time. The husband came clean that he was frequenting an illegal gambling parlor at Mr. Dailey's address."

"Everybody has a side hustle," said Sydnor.

"Like your bird houses, Syd?" asked Art Henderson, the designated uniformed member of the search team. APD directives mandated a uniformed officer be present and be the most visible member of the team. Henderson sported a bushy mustache, and his uniform was exceedingly tight around the middle. The prospects of Henderson's next department-mandated personal fitness evaluation did not look good, thought Cal.

"You could stand a hobby, Hendo," said Sydnor. "You know, besides donuts."

Henderson raised a middle finger. Cal hid his smile before getting the proceedings back on track.

"Surveillance over the past week confirmed people coming and going at all hours of the night. Presently, we believe the residence is empty save for Mr. Dailey and a female companion, identity unknown. Any questions?"

Hard stares. A few head shakes. No questions.

Cal glanced over at Sydnor, who returned a slight nod. "Alright then, let's go. Thanks everyone for coming."

As they got into their vehicle, Sydnor said, "'Thanks everyone for coming?'"

"What? It's cold and early. Just being polite."

"It's their fucking job, junior."

"You catch more flies with honey . . ."

"You catch more flies with a warrant. Let's go already. It's cold and early."

They drove the few blocks to the townhouse subdivision in a convoy, with Cal and Sydnor in the lead unit. The homes themselves were homogeneous, but the main road, and the entire subdivision, was laid out in a wide whorl instead of a straight grid. Each complex had its own parking lot that branched off the main winding road, putting Cal in mind of a pier that stretched into a river. The convoy floated down the river until they pulled into the section where Dailey's home stood. The entire journey took less than two minutes.

They rolled in fast and parked. The surveillance car from the night before radioed that they were in position in the alley behind the row of townhomes, covering the rear exit should Dailey inexplicably choose to make a break for it, hoping to lose himself in the warren of high-fenced yards and narrow alleys that Cal now thought of as tributaries. Fleeing on foot would have surprised Cal, but then again, Dailey didn't look the type to rough up a neighbor either.

Cal and Henderson hustled toward the townhouse's front steps, with Sydnor two steps behind them. The Virginia General Assembly had barred no-knock entries before Cal had made detective, so he had to "knock and announce," alerting occupants to his presence and clearly identifying as law enforcement. It was why Henderson was there, grunting to keep up with Cal's long strides.

Cal took the steps to the front door three at a time. As Henderson summited, Cal cleared his throat to ready his command voice. He'd rehearsed it in his mind many times. The last thing he needed was for his voice to crack in front of everyone. He raised his balled fist to pound on the door, Henderson still climbing, Sydnor in their wake, when the door swung wide.

35

CAL DIDN'T EXPECT this.

In addition to barring no-knock warrants, the Virginia General Assembly had also made severe restrictions to the service of nighttime warrants. Dailey's operation did not appear to be active every night, and the bar was too high to obtain a nighttime warrant. And Simbulan didn't want Cal's first warrant to get kicked back, or have Cal's name be associated with aggressiveness by the magistrates—*My name has enough associations*, thought Cal—so they settled on a sunrise service. Technically daytime, but early enough to keep occupants off balance. Even so, Cal would have to knock and announce . . . and wait. The person, or persons, on the other side of the door could be shuffling toward it, dazed and in boxer shorts, or bracing the stock of twelve gauge against their shoulder.

Schrödinger's warrant service.

What Cal didn't expect was for the door to open before his knuckles could make contact.

"Can I help you?"

In the weak morning light, Brett Dailey's hair had more salt than pepper than his Facebook picture suggested. Arched, imperious eyebrows peeked over horn-rimmed glasses. He wore a cardigan over khakis and loafers, and he looked as if he was about to go to work. In Mr. Rogers Neighborhood.

"*Alexandria Police—*"

Dailey winced. Cal realized he had not turned off his command voice. He cleared his throat again. "We have a warrant to search the premises. We have reason to believe this address is housing illegal gambling activity."

The man's eyes narrowed and his brow sank below the upper rim of his frames. "Here," he said, beckoning for the sheaf of papers in Cal's hand.

Cal handed them over.

The man pulled the glasses down the bridge of his nose and began reading in the doorway.

"Sir?"

"Hm," mumbled Dailey, concentrating on the warrant.

"Step aside, please."

The man complied. Cal entered, with Henderson and Sydnor behind him, followed by the rest of the team, who fanned out into the townhouse. Halfway down the long hallway to the living room at the rear of the house, there was a landing with two sets of stairs, one leading up to the second floor and one leading to the basement. Cal had found the floor plan to this unit on the development's website and included it in his briefing to the search team.

"I'm going to call my lawyer," said Dailey.

Cal heard Sydnor say, "You do that."

Cal surveyed the first floor. He wasn't quite sure what he expected to find in an illegal gambling den, but it wasn't this. The place was spotless. Everything dust free and ninety degree angles. There was a broom and dustpan in the entry, as if they had interrupted Dailey in the midst of tidying up. It looked like the model home a property manager walked potential buyers through.

"There is someone else in the house," said Cal. It was a question that wasn't a question.

"My girlfriend is asleep upstairs. I'll get her."

Henderson was already climbing the stairs. "That won't be necessary, sir," said their designated uniform officer.

"She's a deep sleeper," said Dailey. The first sign of alarm crept into his voice. As if the situation was finally dawning on him. He passed Cal on his way to the stairs, calling out, "Irina, honey . . ."

Cal ignored him. He walked over to Sydnor.

"Basement?" asked Cal.

"You mean if I was running this show, would I begin my search in the discreet, windowless basement?"

"Yeah."

"Indeed. Lead the way—"

Cal was waiting for Sydnor to punctuate it with "junior" or "kid" or "champ" when screams sliced through the house.

36

A SHRIEK, HIGH and bloodthirsty, followed by the startled yell of Henderson. Then twin heavy sounds, the telltale clattering of an object rolling across the floor, then the impact of something large crumpling. Something Henderson-sized. Then hard, charging footfalls heading toward the landing at the top of the stairs.

Sydnor's weapon was drawn and level with the staircase before Cal could even drop his copy of the warrant. He yanked Dailey from the stairs and spun him away. He cleared his Glock 17 from the holster in time to see a woman loom over his front sight like a banshee, still shrieking. Her eyes were wide and her blonde hair streamed behind her and she stormed toward him. If she noticed the two detectives drawing down on her and shouting commands, or the other members of the search team rushing toward the sound of her keening, she didn't acknowledge them. She merely banked left and sprinted past Dailey, standing in the kitchen entrance, and out the front door.

She was also stark naked.

Cal and Syd looked at one another, then at Dailey. The man's shoulders fell, and he exhaled audibly. He removed his glasses and pinched the bridge of his nose.

"You should have let me wake her."

The officers blocking the entrance to the parking lot caught up to the naked woman in a hedge. It was like trying to pull a wildcat out of a briar patch. The woman scratched and hissed and spat before the cuffs went on, then she transferred her energy to bucking and cursing in an Eastern European accent. Cal watched in disbelief from the stoop.

Sydnor appeared at his side.

"How's Hendo?" asked Cal.

"Embarrassed. He swears she was passed out, but she brained him with an empty bottle of Stoli from the nightstand."

Cal looked at the struggling woman and shook his head.

"I'm not hallucinating, am I?"

"Nope. That is one brick shithouse."

Cal smiled at this. It was a term his father had occasionally used to describe a woman who was anatomically gifted to an outlandish degree. Cal had to admit Irina certainly fit the bill, more siren than banshee. In the gray February morning, her skin practically gleamed. Her cheeks and lips were flushed from her mad dash in the cold, and her chest heaved defiantly. A Vargas pinup girl half Dailey's age, but rabid. When the officers finally managed to handcuff her, they held her at arm's length, their hands encircling her elbows.

"Which one do you suppose beat up the neighbor?" Cal deadpanned.

Sydnor broke at this, but groggy neighbors were appearing on their doorsteps. They gawked and fumbled with their cell phones.

"Jesus H. Christ," yelled Sydnor to the officers. "Quit fucking around and get her inside already!" he yelled.

The officers finally marched her up the steps, and Cal held the door open for them. She was Cal's height. She looked as if she might spit on them, but Sydnor gave her a look that appeared to have stopped that thought in its tracks. Instead, she smirked and thrust out her chest as she passed, her breasts even with Sydnor's head.

"Irina, please . . . ," cooed Dailey, trying to soothe her. He murmured that she needed to calm down. She hissed at the man and cursed him in a language Cal did not understand. Whatever the language, it was clear Irina did not like police and wasn't too fond of her boyfriend for letting them into the house. As if he had a choice.

"Officers, I apologize. I'll take her upstairs to get her dressed."

"We're way past apologies, Mr. Dailey. Put her on the couch." The officers released Irina and she plopped onto the deep cushions. Cal sent one officer upstairs with Dailey to get her something to wear, while the other officer tried to keep an eye on her without staring. Cal pulled a throw from the back of the couch and splayed it over her. Irina kicked it away and told him in broken English to fuck all the way off.

Cal met Sydnor in the center of the room. He ran his fingers through his hair. "Unbelievable. What a mess."

"Nah. Head back in the game, kid. It's still your show, so what's next?"

Cal took a deep breath, then said, "Basement."

"Right," said Sydnor.

37

"*AMBITIOUS*," SNEERED SYDNOR. It was the end of a long day, and Cal felt dejected.

They had spent the rest of the morning and into the afternoon processing the scene. After Irina's dramatic escape, arrest, and dressing, Cal and Sydnor descended to the basement. Cal expected to find the telltale signs of illegal gambling—blackout curtains, ashtrays, empty bottles, food wrappers—but there were no windows in the basement and Dailey's fastidious appearance extended to the rest of his home.

The basement was a large, open rectangle that, aside from a bathroom and small storage room, covered the entirety of the townhouse's footprint. The nearest section of the basement had a sitting area with a large sectional couch and matching leather club chairs arranged around a mounted flat-screen television. Jerseys, signed and framed, ran the length of the walls at perfect intervals to the other end of the basement. Along the far wall was a fully stocked bar. In addition to the bottles, autographed footballs, baseballs, and helmets floated in acrylic cases on shelves behind the bar. In the center of the basement stood a large, vintage pool table on an area rug, an island between the sitting area and the bar.

Cal's heart sank. It was pristine. There didn't appear to be a piece of lint present, let alone an illegal gambling operation.

If Sydnor was discouraged, he didn't show it. He said, "Alright, junior, let's have a look."

The other detective ducked into the storage room while Cal did a lap of the open space, glancing at the jerseys on the wall. He passed the pool table. Even the balls were properly racked, the yellow number one at the apex and the eight ball nestled in the middle. He squatted behind the bar to peer inside the cabinets: empty save for more bottles, glasses, and cleaning supplies. He started back to join Sydnor in the storage room when his shoe brushed awkwardly against the area rug. He glanced down and noticed a slight ridged line in the rug, running from the pool table to its fringed edge. Cal bent for a closer look. A power cord, the same tawny color as the carpeting, peeked from beneath the area rug and ran to an outlet, low on the wall. Nothing wrong with that, and perfectly in line with the home's immaculate aesthetic.

Except how many classic pool tables required a power cord?

Sydnor emerged from the storage area. "Found a couple of air purifiers—"

Cal pushed the side of the pool table. It gave slightly, the balls rattling in their rack.

And how many pool tables give with a shove?

"Give me a hand with this." Cal gripped one end of the pool table.

"I'm not about to throw out my back, junior."

"I don't think you're going to."

Sydnor gave him a wary look, but took up station at the other end of the table. He gripped it.

Cal bent his knees and braced his core. "One . . . two . . . *three!*"

They heaved upward.

He'd put too much strength into it. Between the two of them, they'd nearly thrown the table through the ceiling. Balls flew everywhere and clattered about them on the floor, sinking into the carpet. The pool table was hollow, an artful cavity that concealed a squat but gleaming machine beneath. It resembled an arcade table game, its face one long screen. On its sides were panels, with padlocks to keep them sealed. On every panel was a slot to feed dollar bills.

Cal and Sydnor laid the fake pool table on its side. Sydnor whistled.

"I believe this is what you'd call 'jackpot,' Detective."

Cal beamed. The discovery of the machine cut through the morning's gloom and the fiasco of Irina like a double espresso. Even Sydnor couldn't contain a smirk. One side of his lips curled upward and stayed that way. Then Sydnor noticed a bookshelf on the opposite side of the room. He walked over, tugged one end, and it swung like a door. Behind it was a slot machine with eight pay lines. After discovering the eight-liner, Sydnor's smirk broke into a genuine, unmitigated, megawatt smile.

The pair returned to the main level to find that Irina was gone and presumably dressed, on her way to being booked for assaulting Henderson. Dailey was distraught, torn between staying behind to supervise the search team crawling all over his home and being by his girlfriend's side. Sydnor informed him they were making the choice for him. Cal read Dailey his rights. The man deflated. Whatever hope he was clinging to when he scrutinized the warrant, and any that still remained after Irina's reckless flight, floated out in one long exhale.

"Hope you don't mind my saying, but you do not look the type for this," said Sydnor to the man. "How in the world did this fucking happen?"

"How?" Dailey had a far-off look in his eye. After a moment, he snapped out of it. "You saw her, didn't you?"

Sydnor's aberrant smile remained undimmed as they returned to headquarters, while Cal's gloom rushed in like a dirty tide. He feared that news of a naked woman running amok during Killer Callum's first ever warrant execution had already spread through the force—or worse, YouTube—but no one cared.

Headquarters was abuzz with other news.

As Cal and Sydnor had been opening the padlocks on the gaming table, the chief of police was announcing the formation of a task force to swiftly identify and apprehend Hayley Driscoll's killer. With nonstop media coverage and no suspects, the citizens of Alexandria were terrified, and they expressed it as anger. Hooff's Run was in the middle of Old Town—the city's historic district, the heart of tourism, and its economic driver. And following the grief of the previous summer, the public did not have the patience for a drawn-out murder investigation.

Back at his desk, Sydnor didn't even seem to notice. Until Cal floated the idea of volunteering for the task force.

"Ambitious," the detective repeated and shook his head.

"I'm ambitious because I want to help?" asked Cal, annoyed.

"I thought I got partnered with a workhorse, not a show pony."

Cal looked around at the other cubicles. No other detectives were within earshot. "Wanting to do good makes me a show pony? That's horseshit . . ."

"We *are* doing good. You just shut down a gambling den!"

Cal was happy about that, but less so about the impending avalanche of paperwork and weeks of coordinating with the IRS.

"Yeah, and I nearly shot a naked lady in the process."

"'Lady'? Shit, little birdies are still flying around Hendo's dome."

"You know what I mean. Compared to Hayley Driscoll, slot machines seem . . . trivial."

"Listen up, youngblood: A good offense puts butts in seats, but a good defense wins championships. Slow and steady, one foot in front of the other, that's how you make a *real* difference. Not with one flashy goddamn case."

"I don't care that it's flashy. It's an all hands on deck situation. An emergency."

"Opioids are an emergency. Trafficking is an emergency. People losing their money is an emergency. Look, the Driscoll case is a fucking shark attack, okay? Horrific? Sure, but more people die every year from vending machines falling on them. Way more. You said so yourself. But someone gets bitten by a shark . . ." Sydnor raised both hands and shook them.

"Jazz hands?" said Cal.

"*Panic.* It's front page news. It's sensational. Everyone's world gets turned upside down. And sooner or later, everyone's too busy closing the beaches and diverting resources from where they're really needed—vending machines."

"Hey, you want to start arresting vending machines I know exactly where to start." He pushed himself to his feet. "Let's go—"

"Mark my words, wiseass, the whole city is going to lose its damn head and go fishing with dynamite. You and I are going to keep perspective and do our damn jobs."

"Easy for you to say, you already bagged your great white."

Sydnor looked at him.

"We don't always get our man, kid."

"Oh, Killer Callum got his," said Cal ruefully. "After the fact."

Sydnor's jaw flared, but he kept his voice even. "You put pressure on him. You held him to that conference room. If he'd slipped the building . . ." He shook his head. "Terrible as it was, it could have been worse. It can always be worse, Cal. And you don't have to prove shit to nobody."

Just myself, thought Cal, but he didn't bother to say it.

38

Cal felt low the next day. Not suffering from the low-grade, free-floating anxiety that was his baseline these days. And not how he felt on the worst days, as if someone had jumped him, like his heart had been scalded. He was just in a funk. Whatever Sydnor had said, Cal still had his own thoughts about the Driscoll case and the task force.

The organization Hayley Driscoll had worked for, Volunteers of Alexandria, helped the homeless population in Alexandria, and Tiny had surely been there before, or people there had known him. Surely Massey had already made the connection.

Massey, it was said, was considered the best investigator in the department. Having seen Sydnor in action—his intuitive leaps, his feel with people—Cal doubted the conventional wisdom. Lavaar Sydnor's approach was certainly different from Massey's. It was tempting to fit them into a good cop/bad cop dynamic, with Massey's gregarious charm and Sydnor's tight-lipped, acerbic demeanor. Massey made you feel like you were pals, while Sydnor couldn't give a shit. He looked at you like he was vaguely annoyed with your presence until given a reason otherwise.

But something interesting happened with suspects around Sydnor.

People tended to work a little harder to crack his shell. With Massey, suspects and witnesses didn't want to fall out of his warm, expansive glow. With Sydnor, they leaned in, swam upstream, and fought harder to earn his esteem. An appreciative look, a nod of approval, or a kind word meant more when it came so seldom. Which is why Cal usually took his advice. Still, it rankled.

Cal was still a rookie, and he figured Massey and Porter had probably thought of everything Cal had in their first thirty minutes on the case. Any paths in the investigation Cal might have taken were likely already well-trodden, the dirt packed, the vegetation beaten back, and every inch charted for those following far behind like him.

At home, Cal had slipped the tie from around his neck and flopped down on the couch, grasping for the remote to see what La Liga or Premier League soccer matches his DVR had dutifully recorded for him. His phone rang. The screen read "Mom." He didn't have the energy today, so he let it go to voice mail to join the other messages.

After a minute, the phone rang again.

"Come on . . ."

This time the screen flashed "Heather."

He bobbled the phone for a minute, then put it to his ear.

"Hey," he said, "everything alright?"

"That depends," said Heather. "Jason here thinks you were going to blow us off, but I said, 'Not a stand-up guy like Cal Farrell. He'd never do that to me.'"

Cal was on his feet. "No. No, I'm not blowing you off. I was just getting ready."

"Are you watching soccer? Because it sounds like you're watching soccer."

"I'm not watching soccer." At that moment, Lionel Messi threaded through three defenders to score on Manchester City and the announcer bellowed that the Argentinian's foot was like a Stradivarius crossed with a hypodermic needle. Cal glared at the TV like it had just sold him out.

Thanks a lot, Messi.

"Is that so?" said Heather.

"I just have 80,000 people in my living room."

"Virtue on South Union. Thirty minutes."

"Yes, ma'am."

39

CAL'S HEART SANK the moment he spotted them.

It was a mild night for February, a gentle evening instead of a punishing winter's night. Old Town was lined with people up and down King Street, from the looming George Washington Masonic Temple at the western edge of the neighborhood, all the way down the gently sloping thoroughfare to the Potomac's edge. Alexandrians were out in force—singles having drinks, couples out for dinner, families sipping steaming cups of hot cocoa, tourists shopping—somehow still unaware that Hayley Driscoll was murdered one mile from the restaurants, or in spite of it. He wondered if people were altering their evening strolls to glimpse the spot where she had been murdered, to tell friends *I was just there!* The notion gave him a heartsick, exhausted feeling. Then he thought, *Hadn't I done the same thing?*

He was rationalizing it away when he entered Virtue Feed and Grain and saw that Jason and Heather had secured a corner table.

With Carly.

It didn't take a detective to realize he had been set up. No other friends, no extended crew meeting for drinks.

As far as ambushes go, there were worse. Carly looked stunning. Where Heather's hair was long and fiery red, Carly's hair had been cut short in a cute shag since Cal had last seen her.

And where Heather's skin was like alabaster, smooth and celestial, Carly was deeply tanned, as if returning from somewhere tropical instead of Alexandria in February. She looked like she had stepped out of a travel brochure or off the cover of a summer boating catalog. Cal should have been overjoyed—she was clearly here of her own volition, part of the operation, and from their last brief exchange, he remembered her as lighthearted and charming. For the life of him, he couldn't think of a single reason why he shouldn't be delighted by her other than the fact that she wasn't Heather.

Heather saw him before the others. Cal shot her a hard look that communicated how he felt about surprises, and she smiled like the cat who swallowed the canary.

Cal took a deep breath and approached the table, summoning what scant energy he had. Jason whirled and gave him a big hug, punctuated by loud slaps on the back. It was his own fault, Cal admitted to himself. Perhaps the hug would be less violently exuberant if he had shown up more frequently.

"Pay up," said Heather. "Come on."

"That's only because *you* called him," protested Jason. "He always blows *me* off."

She made a gesture that said *hand it over*. Jason pulled a twenty dollar bill from his pocket. Everyone was laughing freely—they were already a drink or two in, Cal noted—when he bent down to give Heather an awkward hug. She looked fantastic as well, dressed in knee-high boots, jeans, and an oversized burgundy sweater that fell off one shoulder. She gave him a squeeze, made that little growl, and he moved on. He didn't quite know if he should hug Carly or not, but she stood and threw her arms wide, so he supposed he didn't have a choice. She wrapped him as fully as Jason, and he had to admit, it felt nice.

Cal sat down next to Jason and ordered a lager. He smiled, and tried to conceal his ever-present exhaustion.

Keep it bright, he thought.

"We were just talking about that poor girl," said Heather.

"Not even a fucking mile from here," said Jason.

"Are there any leads?" asked Carly.

Just when he thought his heart couldn't sink any lower, a chamber opened up beneath it. Not only was it a stealth double date, but now they were pumping him for information. He glanced at Heather. It'd be one thing if he was on the task force and could offer a firm but regretful "Guys, you know I can't comment on an ongoing investigation . . ." Something that would shut down their inquiry while simultaneously communicating that he possessed oceans of secret knowledge and was not as fucking useless as he felt at that very moment.

He took a pull from his lager, trying to formulate a clever response.

"I know jack shit."

"Really?" asked Carly, disappointed.

"Really." He put down his beer and held up left hand. "I'm Vice and Narcotics, in Operations," he said, then held up his right hand, far apart from his left, "Murder is Crimes Against Persons, in Violent Crimes. Whole other section."

"But I thought there was a task force . . . ," said Carly.

"Being run out of CAP. And they're very tight-lipped."

Before Hayley Driscoll was found, Cal found a pretense to wander through Crimes Against Persons, past Massey's desk, to see if the detective might share any information on Tiny. *Oh, hey there, Farrell, seeing as how you're the one who found him and you just happened by* . . . But Massey was out and Porter gave him a scalding look as he passed. Hayley Driscoll only increased CAP's pucker factor, and tourists snooping around the section were persona non grata. He resigned himself to the fact that his chances of getting a friendly update on Tiny were slim, and one on Hayley Driscoll were absolute zero.

"Is there anything you can tell us?" asked Heather.

He thought of Hayley Driscoll's crime scene, the dark maw of the bridge. He thought of Tiny dangling high up in the air. He thought of goblins scaling trees with ease and trolls living just under the city's nose.

"Don't go out alone after dark."

It felt like a shroud descended over the table. Everyone was quiet until Jason finally muttered, "Jesus Christ, that's some real Jack the Ripper shit."

"Sorry. It's not a very satisfying answer, I know," said Cal. "But just in case."

"Is that the Alexandria Police Department's official line?" asked Heather, her smirk returning.

"Not yet," said Cal.

"Wait," said Carly. "You're in Vice, right?"

"And Narcotics, yes."

"You always hear about serial killers—"

Cal held his hands up. "I didn't say anything about a serial killer . . ."

"Objection overruled," said Jason, "Please answer the question."

"Permission to treat the witness as hostile," said Carly with a wicked smile and a raised eyebrow.

Well, thought Cal.

"Please proceed, Counselor," said Jason.

"I'm just saying," said Carly, raising an eyebrow, "suppose it was a serial killer. Don't they always work up to it? And sometimes they start with working girls, right?"

Everyone at the table stared at her.

"What?" she said. "I listen to a lot of murder podcasts."

Cal leaned forward, putting his elbows on the table, and glared at her. A plan blossomed in his mind. He broke into a wide smile, as devilish as hers had been. "I knew you'd make a fine detective . . ."

40

CAL WATCHED THE woman from a parking lot across the street from her motel. Her name was Honey and she was perfect. He could tell by the way she carried herself. She wasn't green and she wasn't trafficked. She'd been around. She knew people. But right now, she was all alone.

Or at least she would be soon enough.

Carly had been correct. Serial killers often preyed on the vulnerable and the isolated. In the case of Hayley Driscoll, she was literally alone on a dark path. In the case of Wylie "Tiny" Gilbert, he was adrift from the rest of society, without a solid support network of friends or family, a home, financial resources, or access to the medication that may have kept him from attacking Cal last summer. Both had been easy to pick off from the rest of the herd. Also vulnerable and isolated?

Sex workers.

Thank you, Carly. Carly who was smart, funny, and into true crime.

You really do need to pull your head out of your ass and see what's right in front of you, Farrell.

He sipped his coffee and stared up at the prostitute's room. Many sex workers lived on the far edges of society, their loose networks a poor shield against danger, and more often the source of it. And by the nature of their work, they eschewed safety in numbers nightly, playing the odds and wandering off to rendez- vous with total strangers. It was entirely possible, perhaps even likely, that an Alexandria-area sex worker had had a run-in with an overzealous john with a blade. He doubted any would make an official report. Regardless, he checked NCIC, the National Crime Information Center database, but came up empty.

So Cal set out to get his own answers.

He waited until Saturday night. Most midnights, he was only functionally awake and too exhausted to do anything, but tonight he was wired. He found Route 1 and drove south, through Old Town, until the tight cobblestone streets of historic homes and upscale shops gave way to boulevards with strip malls, chain res- taurants, and retail super centers. He drove farther still, careful to stay within Alexandria's city limits, and his ostensible jurisdiction. He could get away with asking questions about a case he wasn't a part of in Alexandria, but it would be considerably more difficult explaining himself in Fairfax County.

He pulled into the drive-through of a fast food chain, ordered coffee—"fresh please, I'll wait"—then pulled around to the front and parked. Across Route 1, he had a clear view of a two-story budget motel, the kind with a promenade on the first floor and rooms opening onto a balcony on the second. He and Sydnor had been here before to take part in stings. Route 1, along with I-95, was a popular corridor with both independent sex workers and the serious shitbags—the pimps and traffickers who ran girls back and forth between North Carolina and the big spenders in DC.

"It's not like the old days," Sydnor had lamented when they first partnered, "when you rolled up to certain street corners or lonely, out-of-the-way spots where johns lined up in their cars like a drive-through. Girls got picked up at one end of the line and dropped off after, and we scooped 'em all up." It was noisy, rau- cous, and overt, Sydnor told him, and he didn't have to "investi- gate" so much as bring a net. He sounded wistful.

These days, the script was flipped, schooled Sydnor. Most "cli- ents" used sites like Backpage and other message boards to set up their illicit rendezvous, always adding new levels of difficulty and complexity for the police. To Cal, who grew up with the internet as a fixture of his life, it made sense. Everything was done online. The idea of a john just driving up and happening upon a prostitute seemed almost quaint to him.

However it was arranged, at some point, they have to go analog. So Cal watched and waited.

He checked his watch. It was quarter to one. The adrenaline of making the decision to come here was fading. He pictured himself as someone else might see him—a creepy loner sitting in a deserted fast food parking lot in the middle of the night. The impostor syndrome crept in, like someone slipping into the passenger side of his car.

What exactly did he think he was doing?

He didn't have time to answer his own question. At one AM, a door on the second floor opened, and a middle-aged man with a paunch and a bald spot emerged, looked around carefully, then made a beeline for his car.

Cal was out of the car and jogging across the parking lot by the time the paunchy man found his vehicle. They both approached it at the same time. When the man saw Cal cutting him off in a parking lot in the middle of the night, he froze.

"Oh hey," said Cal, waving his hands as if reading the man's thoughts. "Can I chat with you for a moment?"

"Sorry, buddy," said the man and moved toward his car.

"Oh, okay then." Cal had his phone in his hand and took a picture of the man's license plate.

"What the hell do you think you're doing?" said the paunchy man, getting angry. The man whirled in Cal's direction. Cal took his picture too.

Cal looked at his phone and said, "Perfect, thanks." He began walking back toward his car.

"Why are you taking my picture? Hey, get back here!"

Cal turned around and flashed his badge.

"Well, I'm assuming because of your generally non-helpful demeanor, you're not going to give me your name, so I'm going to run your plate, find your address and contact information, and inform whoever answers the phone of your Saturday night itinerary." He pointed at the ring on the man's finger. "Anyway, enjoy the rest of your weekend, sir."

The paunchy man's eyes went wide and the color drained from his face. He looked small and scared in that moment, and it pleased Cal down to his toes. He was wired again, but it was no longer a nervous energy and it spread evenly throughout his body like a humming, not unlike how he felt at Hooff's Run. The impostor syndrome faded and he felt an energized tranquility. Connections, smiles, jokes . . . everything flowed easier.

Cal had barely turned around when the man screamed, "Wait! Hey, hold up, buddy."

"*Detective.*"

"I'm sorry, I'm sorry. Detective. What do you need?"

"It's simple. You're going to go back up to your friend, knock on the door, and say you forgot your wallet."

He held up his hands in front of him. "No problem, sir."

"Are you sure? Because you seem like you're in a rush to get home. I don't want to put you out."

"It's not putting me out at all. I want to help. *Please.*"

Cal exhaled, pretending to mull it over. "I'm going to need you to really sell it to her, like your life depends on it, because I'm not going to lie, it kind of does."

"I got it, I got it."

The man took off, bounding for the steps. Cal followed after him, not bothering to hide his smile.

41

"I FORGOT MY wallet," said the paunchy man to the door.

The door opened, revealing a woman in thigh-high boots, booty shorts, and a bright red bra that barely contained her free-standing, augmented breasts. A tattoo of a large python curled around her leg and around her waist, its head poised ready to strike, eyes staring out from her abdomen. It was difficult to clock her precise age with the makeup that she had been re-applying when the knock came, but she appeared to be in her thirties.

"*Sure* you did, baby," she said.

Cal stepped into the doorframe, holding up his shield.

"Evening, Miss."

She glanced from the paunchy man to Cal, then back to her client, and her flirtatious mask slipped into a spiteful rictus. "What the *fuck*, Walter . . ."

"*Walter*," said Cal, testing out the name and making the man squirm.

"I did what you asked," said Walter. "Can I go now please?"

"Shove off, Walter."

The paunchy man made a beeline for the stairwell to the ground floor, but paused at the top. "You're not going to do what you said, are you? I mean, I helped."

"Fuck off, Walter," spat Honey.

"Yeah, fuck off, Walter," said Cal. He offered the woman a slight bow then said, "I'm sorry, I didn't get your name."

"Eat shit is my name."

Cal feigned a hurt face. "Come on, we have a lot in common. We both want Walter to fuck off. Let's be friends."

The woman considered this. "Honey."

"A pleasure, Honey. I'm Detective Farrell. May I have a moment of your time, please? I just want to talk."

She looked up and down the balcony. Below, Walter slammed his car door and sped out of the parking lot.

"Then put the fucking badge down and get in here. You made your point. I don't need any static."

"Sorry about that, Honey."

Cal stepped into the motel room. There was a queen-sized bed, the sheets in disarray, and a small table. Cal chose the table and stayed well away from the bed. Now that he was inside the room, he realized how very tired he was. It was too warm and smelled of sex and cheap perfume. The room swayed for just a moment. The coffee hadn't made a dent, it had just been some-thing to occupy his hands while he waited. When the room stead-ied, she was unfastening her bra.

"What are you doing?" he asked.

"Let's just get this over with."

She stopped mid-shimmy, her bra unfastened, but still in place. "You're not looking to shortstop?"

"Is that a working girl term?"

"It's a baseball term."

"I'm more of a soccer fan."

"Pussy," she said. "I hit a solid ball that's just about to make it to the outfield, but the shortstop snags it on the hop and picks me off before I make it to first. I got to get around that shortstop."

"Sports analogies are generally lost on me. Especially at this hour."

"We fucking?"

"No thank you."

"'No thank you,'" she said, refastening her bra. She turned to the sink area by the bathroom to continue reapplying her makeup. She was perfect, he thought again. Outside, he had kept his badge up, and the look in her eyes told him she didn't want to run afoul of her pimp. He wanted someone who knew other pros, someone plugged into a network.

"Have you seen the news about the woman killed in Old Town?"

"Wasn't me," she joked.

"Don't worry."

She continued to face the mirror, but found his eye as she touched up her mascara. "Do I fucking look worried?"

"No," he said. He smiled, then began to laugh. "No, you do not." She was playing tough at the moment. She *was* tough. You didn't stay in the business without being able to handle yourself—to a point—but she smiled back, and for a moment he saw a chink in the armor.

"I have a theory," continued Cal. "You don't jump a woman in the dark, incapacitate her, then begin cutting her up by the side of a ravine half a block from a busy street without practice. Without working your way up to it. It's not the guy's first rodeo."

"And you thought, what exactly? That I might know someone with a knife kink? Pull my hair, put a blade to my throat? Honey does not tolerate that shit."

"No doubt. But maybe you know someone who does. Or a friend who had a run-in with someone who was a little too rough. Something like that. Anything?"

"Jesus Christ, my taxes are paying for this? Could you hand me my bag while you're grasping at straws?"

Cal passed her purse over, then sat there feeling stupid, tired, alien. He looked around the room, wondering how he had gotten here, talking to a half-naked hooker in a motel room with decor from another decade and furniture pocked with cigarette burns. He felt like he was in a dream. He thought of standing at the mouth of the tunnel in total darkness, the cold air blowing through it like an icy breath. He thought of Tiny, high up in the air, in the predawn. He thought of that Very Hot Day, when sound and color were dialed way up, and everything, even the air, was super-saturated. He seemed to be finding himself slipping from reality and into this dreamlike state more and more lately and it worried him. He needed to go home, go to bed. Sleep.

"Hey, you alright?" asked Honey.

"I'm tired." He blew out a breath. "Of people dying."

He sat up straight, looked around as if seeing where he was for the first time, then gave his head a little shake to clear the cobwebs. He put his hands on his knees and pushed himself to his feet. "Sorry to bother you, Honey." He moved toward the door, then stopped.

He pulled a business card from his pocket and left it on the table. "If you do hear of something like that or anything at all you think might help, I'd appreciate it."

"Hold up," she said. "You really just wanted to talk? This wasn't some bullshit premise to fuck? Some weird-ass foreplay?"

"No."

"What's in it for me? If I help."

"Getting a serial killer off the streets? Karma? Patriotism? Do I really have to sell this?"

Honey folded her arms. "It's all about sales, baby."

"Statistically speaking, your chances of getting murdered by this particular person are infinitesimal, so infinitesimally lowered chances of getting murdered by this particular person?"

"What else is in your pocket?"

Cal reached into his pocket and pulled out forty dollars and put it on the table, then held up a finger. "And . . ." He reached into his other pocket and pulled out a third of a pack of wintergreen Lifesavers.

Honey stared off to the side, shaking her head, but he could tell she was trying not to laugh. "You are terrible at this."

"Then help me."

She swiped his business card off the table. "'Detective Cal Farrell.' Is this my get out of jail free card?"

"It's your 'Detective Cal Farrell will advocate to lower any future prostitution charges to trespassing' card."

"And you said serial killer?"

Had he? *Shit.*

"That's just a theory. An off-the-record theory."

She flicked the card under her ruby-painted fingernail as she considered his proposal. "I guess it can't hurt to have a Vice detective owe you a favor . . ."

"Don't forget the Lifesavers."

She smiled, then her smile faded. "There was a girl, a few months back. I heard she got cut. She's out of the business now."

"Do you know her name? How I can find her?"

Honey sat on the bed. She leaned back, her arms behind her, making her pneumatic breasts point skyward. "You look too tired to drive. I could give you the number or that money can get you a few minutes of a massage. You look stressed . . ."

"Are you propositioning an officer of the law, Honey?"

"Just looking out for a friend," she said. "We're friends now, Detective Cal. I have your card and everything."

"You're very sweet, but I think I'll stick with the number."

"Suit yourself," she said, reaching for her phone, "but you ought to have your fucking head examined . . ." Her thumbs flew across her screen, her nails clacking against it. Finally, she propped herself on one arm and held out her phone with the other, making him get up and come closer. He bent down to copy the number, but she moved it closer, making him bend over the bed.

"Very funny," he said.

He copied the name—Daisy—and her number. "I appreciate it."

She shook her hair out behind her, spilling it across the bed. As tired as he was, it reminded him of the swaying movements of a cobra.

"It's past my bedtime," he said.

She sat up then, all business, as if someone had drawn the blinds on a sunny day.

"Then bounce already."

"Aye."

He moved toward the door and put his hand on the knob. Over his shoulder he said, "Be safe, Honey."

"Daisy is legit out of the life, so don't come at her like a fucking cowboy like you did here."

"Discreet. Got it."

"And don't look like such a cop when you walk out. It's bad for business. Skulk the fuck out of here, would you?"

42

CAL SAT IN a 1950s-style diner off of Route 17. He didn't know the name of the town, just that it was on Albemarle Sound near Elizabeth City. Daisy said she was done with Alexandria, so Cal told her he'd meet her in North Carolina instead. He had caught a few hours of sleep, surprisingly deep for him, then woke at dawn, and drove the 240 miles south. There weren't many cars on the road at that hour and he made it in under five hours. He was early, but when eleven AM—the time they agreed on—came and went, he felt foolish.

I don't belong here, the voice in his head told him, not for the first time.

She arrived at 11:20 AM, young and blonde and looking very nervous. Cal, nursing his coffee, raised a finger and she came over.

"You're Detective Cal?"

"Thank you for meeting me. What'll you have?"

"I can't stay. I have to get back to church." She wore jeans and a square neck lace top beneath a boxy, unzipped coat that she did not remove. Her cheeks were red, either from nerves or the biting wind outside. She looked as fresh as a meadow in springtime.

"Are you sure?" he said. He smiled, trying to look as harmless as possible. "Eggs? Burger? Pie?"

She bit her lip, shifting her weight from foot to foot, as if testing them before making a quick escape.

Cal leaned in and spoke in a low, conspiratorial tone. "I'm starving, but I'm going to look like a real knuckle-dragger if I eat in front of you and you don't even have a cup of coffee."

She surveyed the diner once more, exhaled, and gave a small, pained smile in return. "Fine. Coffee."

They ordered, her a coffee and Cal a bacon cheeseburger and French fries. He had eaten like a bird over the past six months, losing weight and muscle from his patrol days, and sometimes he felt like he was haunting his own body. But occasionally, something inside of him would remind him to eat and he became ravenous. It put him in mind of a serpent that goes weeks without eating, then swallows a mammal whole.

Between bites, he tried to put her at ease. "Everything we talk about is off the record, and when we're done, I'm going to get in my car and drive away and you're never going to hear from me again. Thing is, I know something about waking up and thinking you're going to have a normal day, only to have it hit you like a train and knock your whole life off course. I'm sorry you had one of those days. I hate to come to here and dredge it back up. I wouldn't have if I didn't think it could help others."

"Yeah, well, maybe getting your life knocked off course ain't so bad sometimes."

Cal nodded like he understood. "Honey mentioned you were attacked."

"I don't know Honey."

"She heard it secondhand."

"Honey must've heard it from Darla. But Darla was good to me. Gave the money to get stitched up, get me home. Darla must owe Honey a favor, because that's the only reason we're talking."

"Did you come home after the attack?"

"It was the last straw. I mean, how many more signs do you need?" Daisy grimaced and looked into her lap. "You ever hear of Otaku Hunt?"

Cal shook his head.

"It's an augmented reality mobile game," she said. "You use the GPS on your phone to hunt and capture creatures in the game."

"Is that the app where people were wandering into traffic or something?" asked Cal, remembering now. It was a brief but powerful craze that swept the area. People's heads buried in their phones, even more so than usual. Strangers suddenly talking to each other on corners about mystical creatures he'd never heard of, and at least one of them walked in front of a bus, Cal recalled. It was all the rage, and then the fever broke and everyone moved on to the next fad.

She nodded. "There would be downtime sometimes," she said, looking over at the nearest patrons, two tables away. "Which my, um, manager didn't like, but you have to pass the time. And I loved that stuff. Anime, manga. Different worlds, creatures, mythologies. So much more interesting than all this." She gestured at the diner and, Cal presumed, the small town around it, and the endless small towns beyond that.

"One night, last fall, I was with Darla. I remember it had been a hot week, a hot summer, then all of a sudden, it got real windy and it was like it changed seasons overnight. I wasn't dressed for it." She laughed bitterly at this. "We were never really dressed for the weather, I guess."

"Do you remember the date?"

"September 30."

Cal wiped ketchup from his mouth and opened his notepad.

"It was dead," continued Daisy. "No one was around. Maybe the wind chased everyone indoors. I was playing the game, mostly to distract myself from the cold and the boredom. I walked down this narrow street chasing an okami and—"

"Sorry, okami?"

"Ancient wolf creature. The okami are fast and really hard to catch. Very rare and worth lots of points . . ."

Daisy trailed off. She put her elbows on the table and put her head in her hands. Cal didn't know if it was to steady her head or her shaking hands. She collected herself, looked at the other customers to make sure none of them were watching her, then looked at the wall clock. "I should get going."

"Just a few more minutes. Please. What happened next?"

"So I walk down this narrow street, more like an alley. You know how they are in Old Town."

Cal nodded. "Where in Old Town?"

She shook her head. "South of King. East of Patrick. Somewhere in there, I can't remember."

"Close to the river, near where the streets become cobblestones?"

She shook her head, "Not that far down. I remember passing that nice hotel, the Alexandrian, at one point, so a block or two from there? I walk down the alley and it's out of the wind, which was nice. I'm just about to catch the okami and it just disappears. I was so close and now I'm pissed and I mutter, 'Damn it,' or something. And then I hear someone giggle."

The hair on Cal's neck stood on end. He was still jotting down the streets when Daisy stood suddenly.

"I . . . I need to get out of here."

"Wait," said Cal, but she was on her feet and halfway to the door. He grabbed his coat and threw some bills on the table before chasing after her. He skidded to a halt in the gravel parking lot, but she was nowhere in sight, like the legendary wolf in her game. It was cold and a strong wind pulled at him. He still clutched his coat in his hand. She couldn't have been that fast. He was beginning to doubt his own mind, wondering if she had been an apparition, when he heard "Over here."

She was on the side of the restaurant, standing on a patch of grass that sloped toward a ravine that emptied into Albemarle Sound.

"Sorry. Needed some air."

He cleared his throat, tried to conceal his relief that she was still there, still real. In the lee of the diner, she lit a cigarette. He put on his coat and leaned against the wall, facing the creek, and stealing glances at her from the corner of his eye. Her hand was shaking when she lifted her cigarette, and he noticed a large tattoo on the inside of her forearm, half concealed by her rolled-up sleeve. He waited for her to take a few more drags before he asked, "You heard a giggle?"

She nodded, blew out a jet of smoke. "My blood ran cold. Like someone poured ice water down my back. Like my body realized before my brain that I was not alone. I pulled my head out of my phone and there was a man crouching beside a dumpster, in the shadows, feet from me. He whispered, 'Closer.'"

Daisy lit another cigarette and Cal waited.

"I almost walked right past him without even seeing him. Another few feet . . . In the life, the other girls told me to trust my instincts with the customers. If something feels wrong, you just bail. But you're already so, like, immune to the whole thing. Your judgment is already skewed, you know? Had my head not been in that game, I might not have been startled seeing a guy in an alley. It wouldn't have been my first guy in an alley, you know? But I was so engrossed, when I pulled my head out of the game, it was like waking up and I just *reacted*."

"And ran," said Cal.

"It was the first time I felt like myself in a long while. Like Daisy." Her voice cracked as she spoke her own name with affection, perhaps at the idea of a younger, purer version reasserting herself in the crucial seconds. Cal thought of Hayley Driscoll then, and wondered if her killer had whispered something to her as well, or if he had learned his lesson.

"You saved yourself," said Cal.

She looked toward the creek and quickly knuckled away a tear.

"Yeah, after putting myself in the worst possible situation," she laughed bitterly. "Guess I was a shitty working girl."

"That's okay. I'm a shitty detective."

She grunted half a laugh. "I got a few feet away when I felt the sting. Quick, sharp. I mean, I felt it, but it didn't slow me down. My adrenaline dumped, man. I was screaming, running the way I had come, then Darla was there and she was screaming too. She grabbed me and we took off. We were three blocks away when I realized I was bleeding."

"Where'd he get you?"

"Right across the ass." She looked away. "I ain't showing you."

"Don't need to see it. You never reported it." It was a statement, not a question.

"Didn't see the point. An active shooter killed a bunch of folks in Old Town a month or so before. I didn't imagine anyone would give a shit about me, considering."

Cal wanted to protest, but said nothing. A fresh wave of shame washed over him. They stood in silence for a while.

"I have a boyfriend now," she said.

Cal smiled. "That's good."

"There's no hiding the scar, so I told him the bare bones. I was out with a girlfriend, I was attacked, and after that I'd had enough of the big city. It's true enough. He doesn't need to know the . . . context. And I don't want him to."

"He won't hear it from me."

"You think it's the same guy?"

"I don't know. Maybe. It's a theory."

"I want to help, but I'm not blowing up my life to do it. I know it's selfish, but it is what it is. So this is it, yeah?"

"I understand. Do you remember at all what he looked like?"

She shook her head. "It was barely a second. Dark clothes, hoodie. Average height, I suppose."

He wrote it all down.

"Anything else stand out? Any little detail?"

She looked at him, weighed whether she wanted to tell him.

"Anything at all," said Cal.

"His eyes glowed."

She took another drag and her hand was shaking again. Her voice too.

"I didn't see his face because it was dark, but mostly because all I saw were his eyes. They glowed."

"Was he wearing glasses? The reflection—"

"He wasn't wearing glasses," she said firmly. "It was like a cat in headlights. I'll never forget it."

Cal nodded slowly, wrote it down.

She took a final drag and pitched the butt. "I really have to go now."

"Thank you, Daisy," said Cal. He tried to dispel the dread before she set off. He nodded to her forearm. "What's that?"

She tugged her sleeve up, revealing the head of a wolf. "In the actual lore, the wolf spirit either kills you or spares you, depending on the kind of life you lead."

Cal nodded. It was a hell of a reminder. It made him think of any lessons he had salvaged from his own derailing.

Daisy saw his gears turning and smiled ruefully.

"I mean, it's not like I can see my backside every day."

Then she got into her car and drove away.

43

SYDNOR DIDN'T NEED to know, Massey reassured him. The senior detective chose the restaurant, Table Talk, two miles down Duke Street in the direction of Old Town and not in the shopping center directly across the street from headquarters. Their rendezvous would be discreet, which Cal appreciated.

What Cal didn't appreciate was that Table Talk was almost directly across the street from John Carlyle Square, site of the ATMA massacre. Massey, embroiled in two murder investigations and now running a task force, had not considered that. And why would he? Massey was preoccupied with his own nightmare, and Table Talk was a block away from Hooff's Run, the ravine where Hayley Driscoll had been found. Cal got there early and waited, his foot bouncing off the floor. He was about to order coffee when his eye started twitching.

"Now?" Cal muttered to himself. "Seriously?"

It was something that began a month or so after the Very Hot Day. It began as a tightening of the skin around the eye, then a flickering of the muscles. It felt like someone was lightly tugging at his eyelid. He researched it online, and unsurprisingly, it was a sign of not enough sleep, too much caffeine, and, of course, stress.

It was a minor symptom, barely noticeable unless someone leaned in and really studied his face, but the pulsing vision made it feel like there was a blinker inside his head, and it made him incredibly self-conscious when talking to someone. Until then, every other manifestation of his trauma had been invisible—no sleeping, lost time, even his telescoping vision in times of severe stress was a private thing. The only person he had ever mentioned the twitching eye to was Julia when it began in a session. He asked her if she could see it and she said no. He pointed to it, and she left her chair and hovered over him for a moment, bent at the waist, her face close to his, close enough that he could smell her skin cream. A clean smell with a hint of lilac.

"Just barely," she said, shrugging.

It was one of the reasons he'd gotten his ass in gear, off the couch, and began running on the trails again. Within two weeks of getting on a schedule, and in a rhythm, the twitching ceased. He'd forgotten all about it.

Now both eyes were going.

He ordered an iced tea instead of coffee without making eye contact with the waitress.

He was here to share all that he had learned with Massey, and if he was being honest with himself, he hoped to impress the man. Massey was the department's star detective, and he had always been nice to Cal. They'd never had any real conversation more than a passing "Hey, how are you?" But when Porter made him feel like a pariah when Tiny was found, Massey had made a point of being publicly kind. As isolated as he felt since last summer, that alone earned Cal's respect.

And now, here he was, subsisting on a steady diet of too much caffeine, too little sleep, and renewed stress since the discovery of Hayley Driscoll, his foot tapping and the skin beneath his eyes flickering like a light bulb half screwed in, waiting across the street from the site of the Very Hot Day for a clandestine meeting with his partner's ex-partner, a meeting that would make Sydnor furious if he knew about it.

Massey strolled in, gave Cal a huge grin.

Cal stood as he approached, then felt immediately stupid for it. He thrust out his hand and Massey shook it.

"Hey, Farrell."

"Thanks for meeting me."

"Very cloak and dagger," teased Massey.

"Sorry. It's just . . ."

Massey held up his hand. "I love Lavaar like a brother, but God forbid you have a thought in your head that wasn't put there by him. And actually disagreeing with him? No, this is our little secret."

Massey laughed his easygoing laugh, and Cal relaxed. One of his eyes even stopped twitching.

"You get my gift?" he asked, all smiles.

"Gift?" Cal didn't understand at first. Then he remembered.

The handcuffs.

"That was you?"

Cal's jaw flared. He looked to the side to cover his anger and embarrassment. Massey was too keen to miss it.

"I left a note . . ."

"There was no note."

"Seriously?"

Cal shook his head.

"Oh shit, Farrell. I thought you knew. Wylie Gilbert had cuffs in his coat pocket with your prints on them. The ones I left weren't your *actual* cuffs, they're evidence obviously—"

"I told you I tussled with Tiny," said Cal. "I told you that on the trail. It was right before ATMA. I had Gilbert cuffed in my unit and dispatch told me to kick him loose. I tossed him the key and damn sure didn't wait around to get them back."

Massey waved his hands. "Relax, it's all good. I heard it over the radio that day. Like everyone else. Shit, you really didn't get the note? I explained it all and thought you could use a spare. I figured you'd appreciate the laugh. Sorry, man . . ."

Cal thought of Adelphia. Had Massey's anonymous gift not rattled him so that day, Cal wouldn't have lashed out at him. Probably.

Massey had attempted a nice gesture with the cuffs. It was the kind of camaraderie Cal had longed for, especially from an investigator he admired, and now he was biting the man's head off. Cal forced a smile.

"I'm the one who should be sorry. Didn't see the note. Thought someone was fucking with me."

"I assure you, when I'm fucking with someone, I want the credit," said Massey with a laugh. "Now. Your email. It intrigued me."

Cal was certain there was no note. Massey may have left the cuffs, but someone had pilfered the note. Which meant someone might still be fucking with him after all. He tried to put it out of his mind. He needed to reset. "I don't want to stick my nose in, but I had a thought—"

"One that didn't come from Lavaar."

"Ha. Right. I had a thought and I ran it down. I thought it might be helpful."

Cal told him all about Daisy. He skipped some steps, deciding to leave out scouting the Hayley Driscoll crime scene on Thursday night. He implied that he'd gleaned the information from his network, letting Massey believe Honey was a confidential informant.

Massey nodded dutifully in the right places, took it all down in his notebook, but the more Cal talked, the more he lost faith in his own discoveries. Skulking around in the ravine on Thursday, shadowing a prostitute on Saturday, making the long drive on Sunday . . . it all seemed far-fetched and more than a little crazy in the light of day sitting across from Alexandria's star detective.

Massey finally closed his notebook, leaned back in his chair, and stared at him, a curious look on his face. The skin beneath Cal's eye pulsed a nervous tattoo. He was sure Massey could see it clear across the table.

"You know," said Massey, cocking his head, "you don't have to be *on* the task force to be on the task force."

"Syd doesn't want me anywhere near it, officially or otherwise. I don't know, maybe he thinks I can't handle it." He decided to introduce the elephant in the room. "Killer Callum and all that."

Massey waved it off. "I heard the story. The real story." He leaned forward. "I'd dig that motherfucker Milton up and shoot him again too. Nothing to be ashamed of."

For a moment, Cal saw an intensity in Massey's face he hadn't seen before. Just as quickly, the detective settled back in his chair, and Cal recognized how tired Massey really was. For the first time, Massey didn't seem so buoyant, so breezy. Cal saw the exhaustion and felt even more of a kinship with him.

"As for Lavaar," continued Massey, "I love him, but he's set in his ways. We'd still be partners today if he wasn't so damn stubborn. Look, I don't have to have your name on the rolls, until such time as we catch the guy, then we can let everyone know you were a part. But we could use the help. The 'task force' is me and Porter, with one patrol officer on loan who is basically our admin. It's a task force in name only, and as far as leads go, let's just say we have a plethora of dearth."

"I figured you and Porter would've been close to finding . . ."

Massey shook his head.

"The MOs for the two murders are so different that it doesn't even track. One, a man, hung from a tree. Two, a woman, stabbed and . . ."

Cal leaned in. "And?"

"Mutilated."

Cal made a face. He thought of the shattered glass of the bulb, then remembered his impromptu merry-go-round with Tiny.

"Here's what I can't wrap my head around," said Cal. "How did someone overpower a man of Wylie Gilbert's size?"

Massey shook his head. "Tox shows Gilbert had a lake of alcohol in his bloodstream. And flunitrazepam."

Thanks to six months on Vice and Narcotics, Cal knew his substances. Flunitrazepam was a potent benzodiazepine used for preoperative anesthesia, and in some cases, a treatment for severe insomnia. Marketed as Rohypnol, but it was more commonly known as roofies, Mexican Valium, or the forget-me pill, and had more sinister applications. A high enough dose caused anterograde amnesia, lack of muscular control, and loss of consciousness. For a man Tiny's size, the dose would have to be mighty indeed. Sadly, roofies were inexpensive and easy to acquire.

"It was likely slipped into a bottle and offered as a gift by our killer. Tiny was roofied to the gills, then strung up. High tech, if you will, and elaborate. Hayley Driscoll was old school, rock to the head, pitched over the railing, and the killer went to town with a knife. Low tech, frenzied."

A rock, thought Cal. *I knew it.*

"Tiny was homeless," continued Massey. "In and out of different shelters. Local organizations have him in their logs as spending a night here, catching a meal there. One of those organizations was Volunteers of Alexandria."

"Where Hayley Driscoll worked."

Massey leaned back, an impressed grin on his face. "Someone did their homework."

"Come on, it's been all over the news."

"So far, that's the only tangible connection. We're going through the records, interviewing other employees, other volunteers, trying to track down some of the organization's other clients, but that's been a nightmare. Most of them have no fixed address, go by different nicknames, and a lot of them are not as firmly tethered to reality as you and I. We even interviewed Hayley Driscoll's old boyfriend, just for kicks. Her former boss too. We marched right into their office and shook them down, not that we thought for a second they had anything to do with it. It was just good for morale."

"Yours more than theirs, I'm guessing."

"The laughs are few and far between on an investigation like this. Her boss worked her like a dog, and her shitbag ex ran around on her. We rattled the hell out of both of them. Porter was smiling for hours."

Cal tried to picture a smile on Porter, but found he couldn't.

"Look, if you have anything else, any other ideas, theories, anything—it's not a bother. Truly. We can use all the help we can get, on or off the books. And don't worry, I'm the picture of discretion."

"I did think of one other thing that links them."

"Yeah?"

"The staging." Massey made a face. "Different sexes, completely different MOs. But both shocking. Both attention-grabbing in their own way. One too high up in a tree, one in a ravine, practically underground. They're not just different, they're opposite."

"Porter's still not convinced it's the same guy." Massey drummed his fingers on the table. "It's good to hear someone else on the same wavelength."

"Both just feel like a statement to me."

"'Sometimes I'm Spider-Man, sometimes I'm Jack the Ripper'? If you have any more theories about what that statement might be, you have my number."

"Thanks for indulging me, Massey."

Massey stood and this time the senior detective thrust out his hand. "It's Adam. And this could work out for both of us. I get my man and you get some of that bullshit 'Killer Callum' stink off of you."

"Even with your partner?"

"Porter's a great detective, but sometimes she gets an idea in her head and it's like a dog with a bone. Remind you of anyone?"

Cal chuckled.

"Seriously, we should make this a regular thing, case or not," said Massey. "It could be therapy, Hardheaded Partners Anonymous or something." The detective picked up the check and left.

Cal sat for a while longer, waiting for his eye to stop twitching.

CHAPTER

44

CAL ASKED TO stop for coffee and Sydnor didn't argue. They had spent days ferreting out Dailey's under-the-table financial transactions and untangling money laundering schemes with IRS Criminal Investigations to build an airtight case. Cal remembered Irina's naked fury and couldn't believe it was the same investigation. Though it had seemed disastrous on the day, he was almost wistful about the jolt of adrenaline it provided. She had been the only anomaly of an otherwise mind-numbingly tedious financial investigation.

They pulled over at Misha's Coffee House on King Street, several blocks up from City Hall. The café was a stalwart staple of Old Town, catering to old-timers, young hipsters, and everyone in between. There were large glass jars along the counter containing whole beans from around the world, pictures on the walls of people posing on vacation with their Misha's Coffee merch—Misha's clientele was nothing if not loyal—and jazz played from the sound system. It was a place both Cal and Sydnor could agree on.

Cal approached the barista, a striking young woman with braids twisted into a bun, piercings running up both ears, and eyes that could knock a man down. Cal had never seen her before. He would have remembered. She exuded nonchalant cool, and Cal felt incredibly conventional by comparison. *Square. Even my references for being outdated are outdated*, he thought. But when he stepped to the counter she looked him up and down and raised her eyebrow.

Suddenly Cal had no need for coffee.

"Hey," she said, smiling.

Don't say ma'am.

"Morning," he said back. He ordered two City Roasts. She turned to pour and he tried not to notice Sydnor at his elbow, smirking. When she returned with the coffees, she said, "You're that cop, aren't you? The one . . . you know . . ."

It happened occasionally. Getting recognized on the street. Conway, the PR flack, had done his job well. Cal never got used to it.

He gave a quick nod and an awkward smile. He handed over the cash, suddenly eager to complete the transaction, but she held up her hand.

"No, man. One of our regulars worked at ATMA."

"I'm sorry," said Cal.

"Yeah." The barista shook her head. "You going to catch the guy who killed that girl?"

"The task force is working on it."

"Are you on this task force?"

He could practically hear Sydnor's eye-roll behind him.

"Afraid not."

"You should be on it." She looked over at Sydnor. "He should be on it. My man gets the job done."

Sydnor grunted something, plucked his coffee from the counter, and walked off.

Cal jerked his thumb toward his retreating partner.

"He's cranky until he gets his coffee."

"Cranky to the very one dispensing his medicine." She spread her arms wide. "The barista's paradox."

He hoisted his coffee toward her. "Thanks again . . ."

"Nora."

"Thanks, Nora. I'm Cal."

"Stay cool, Cal. And catch that motherfucker, feel me?"

"Yes, ma'am."

Damn it.

All the small tables were taken, but there was a large community table toward the back. Sydnor claimed one end, ignoring the couple sitting at the other end. There was a look like indigestion on his face.

"You bring me here on purpose?" he grumbled.

"You know how the air looks all wavy over a grill in the summer?" Cal swung his leg over the bench seat and sat down. "That's how it looks over your head right now."

"Worry about your own head. And pretty young baristas filling it with nonsense."

It was Cal's turn to get cranky. "The Windlass case made your career. But the very idea of me wanting to catch a killer is nonsense?"

"The Windlass case was nonsense too."

Cal leaned back and squinted at his partner. "What?"

"For three years, Nicholas Windlass knocked on people's doors and when they answered, he shot them on the spot. In broad daylight." He pantomimed knocking on an invisible door with one hand and held an invisible pistol in the other. "Knock knock, bang bang. Mostly housewives, but it was indiscriminate really. We finally caught him based on a survivor's description. Windlass wasn't some criminal mastermind, he was homeless and deranged. Floated around Alexandria for years, under everyone's noses, slipping through every social safety net available."

"What's your point? You did your job."

"I always thought Violent Crimes was the tip of the spear. After Windlass, I realized it was the shit end of the stick. Violent Crimes just cleans up the mess. It doesn't address the root causes."

"But Vice and Narcotics does?"

"Education, community programs, social work—that's the *real* tip of the spear. At least Vice and Narcotics is closer to the heart of the matter than Violent Crimes."

"I appreciate that, Syd. I do. But this is important too." He didn't like concealing his meeting with Massey to his partner. It sat wrong. "I have thoughts and I reached out to Massey."

Sydnor froze, his coffee cup raised halfway to his lips.

"You had thoughts?"

"Occasionally I have original, unsanctioned thoughts that were not provided to me by you, yes."

"And you reached out to Massey."

"Are you just going to repeat everything I say?"

Sydnor stared at him for a moment. Cal met his stare. He prayed for his eye not to twitch. He didn't appreciate being lectured. But beneath the bravado, he didn't need anything else on his conscience.

"You're a grown ass man," said Sydnor finally. "Do what you want. Just remember, don't come crying to me."

"What does that mean?"

Sydnor shrugged. "Let's get moving, junior."

Sydnor stood and headed for the front door. Apparently the conversation was over. Cal caught up to him as he opened the door.

"Seriously," said the senior detective. "You bring me here on purpose?"

"Not today . . ."

Cal turned back toward the counter. Nora saw him and touched two fingers to her brow in a mock salute. He smiled back.

"But I damn sure will tomorrow."

45

CAL JOGGED ALONG the Mount Vernon Trail, running his new northern route toward Arlington when he saw them.

The pair of arborists.

He didn't know if that was their official title, but they were the tree workers the city had called in. Cal fought doing a double-take as he ran past. The men were cutting back the undergrowth along the trail. The shorter of the two—Quinn, Cal remembered—rode a wide deck mower in large rows, keeping the grass trimmed on either side of the trail. He was the one who had drawn the short straw and scaled the tree, coming face to Tiny's swollen, purple face.

The other one—*Hiller? Heller?*—stood on the edge of a bluff choked with bramble. He gripped a weed whacker and swept it back and forth like a scythe. Cal caught a glimpse of his face as he ran past. He looked almost meditative. The man was clean-shaven now, but Cal remembered that day he had had a light beard, which gave his face a fuzzy, out-of-focus look. He also seemed to take things more in stride than Quinn that morning. Then again, his partner lost his breakfast—and whatever was left of the last night's dinner—seventy feet in the air. Not that Cal could blame him.

Within a few strides, Cal was past them. He ran for another minute, then turned around to make his way back to Alexandria, slowing to a jog, then a walk. He found a tree and leaned against it, kicking his heel back and grabbing his ankle to stretch out his quadricep. He gazed over at the two city workers. Quinn had ridden farther off in his wide deck mower, and the taller man had taken a break from his work.

When not sweeping the weed whacker back and forth, the man seemed jittery. He rolled up his sleeves. He shifted his weight from foot to foot. A woman jogged past on the trail, and the arborist stared after her. Finally, he fumbled for a pack of cigarettes, tapped one out, and lit it. Only after a long drag did Cal notice the man's shoulders relax.

"Hey, thanks," called Cal.

The man turned around, surprised but not startled.

"For what?"

Cal pointed to the trim line. "For keeping the wilderness at bay."

The man—*Hellier?*—was appraising Cal with a wary look. He took a long drag on his cigarette. Cal noticed a switchblade tattoo on the man's forearm. The arborist blew out a long jet of smoke.

"Just doing my job."

"Well, some asshole biker came screaming up on me last year and I stepped off the trail to give him room. Right into some poison ivy."

The arborist nodded, clearly uninterested.

"Hey," said Cal, "I'm looking for a career change. You like it?"

"Fresh air. Peace and quiet." The arborist took another drag and stared at Cal. His expression went from wary to cold. "Mostly."

Cal nodded.

"Good to know. See you around."

Cal waved and jogged south.

Hilliard, he thought.

46

C AL TEXTED MASSEY.

> Did you ever look into the arborists?

Ran quick background checks
on their entire department.
Elimination only.

> Was jogging this morning and saw
> them.

Jogging is bad for your health.
Think something's there?

> Don't know. How many people do
> you know can climb a tree like that,
> let alone construct the pulleys?
> Could be all that talk of destroying
> trees was protesting too much. Plus,
> being on hand for taking the body
> down could be a second bite at the
> apple, thrill-wise.

You've thought about this.

Cal felt sheepish and stupid. He was tapping an apology and a pledge to mind his own business, when the three floating bubbles of Massey's response resolved into a single word.

GOOD.

Cal let out a breath he didn't realize he was holding.

We don't have the manpower or the bandwidth. If you have a lead, run it down. Unofficially of course.

I don't want to cross a line.

There's a term I use for a little after hours extra credit.

The response didn't come immediately. Cal texted back.

What's that?

"Detective."

Cal scoured what he could find online, from his phone. He didn't want to use the police computers. He could've run Hilliard's name or license plate and gotten the man's record, if he had one, or anything else he needed to know. But that would have required Cal's log-in, which could be tracked, and this was, as Massey said, extra credit. Cal opted for social media instead. The man had a Facebook account, but it was fallow beyond location updates. The man used it primarily to check in to lunch spots to get deals on sandwiches. Who says a person of interest in multiple murder investigations can't be frugal, thought Cal? All Facebook could tell him was that the man cut coupons instead of women, so Cal had to do some legwork.

Alexandria Public Works was less than a mile from police headquarters. At the end of the day, instead of returning to his apartment, Cal sat at the edge of the government building's parking lot until Hilliard emerged. He had a passing knowledge about Alexandria's Public Works services—he knew it primarily from his days on patrol when they cleaned up roads or shut them down—so he decided to do a little more extra credit while he waited.

He got no further than the department's home page.

"The Public Works Services Division provides maintenance and repairs for all City sewers, streets, sidewalks, and fire hydrants; maintains stream beds, weirs, and stream banks; maintains drainage tunnels, box culverts, and storm water pollution removal facilities; maintains bridges; and conducts snow removal and flood control operations."

Sewers, stream beds, bridges, and tunnels.

Hooff's Run.

Cal looked up. Hilliard emerged from the building and lit a cigarette. Cal put his car in gear to follow him home.

47

CAL SETTLED INTO a new routine: Leave work, catch an hour or two of sleep at home, grab some takeout, and park outside Jake Hilliard's apartment complex off of South Van Dorn Street. Cal never had to wait long after sunset for Hilliard to emerge.

Hilliard was a fellow night owl. The first three nights, the man drove aimlessly around Alexandria as soon as darkness fell, sometimes for hours. He'd stop at 7-Eleven and pick up smokes, candy, energy drinks, or any combination of the three. Cal watched him climb in and out of his car, wander into convenience stores, and stand in parking lots blowing jets of smoke. Hilliard tapped his foot and flicked his thumb against the seams of his jeans. He was a bundle of nerves, looking like he might jump out of his own skin. The more Cal watched, the more he worried how the man was going to release all of that energy. And when.

On the fourth night, Cal was wolfing a burrito in his car outside of Hilliard's complex. Each night watching the arborist, hunger hit like a sledgehammer. He could taste the colors in the food again, and he couldn't put it away fast enough. Was it distraction? Excitement? Because he was doing something of use? It would be a good question for Dr. Julia, but he thought better of it. When he had first mentioned his weight loss to Dr. Julia, she had made a note of it. Now she asked him about it all the time, and the questions put him in mind of his mother, and if he was being honest, he didn't want to think about his mother when he was with Julia.

When Hilliard suddenly left his apartment this night, Cal knew right away something was different. Hilliard strode along the promenade to the stairs with purpose, faster than the jittery amble Cal had become accustomed to. Cal tossed the burrito onto his passenger side seat, where it promptly exploded.

"Nuts," he mumbled as he twisted the key in the ignition.

He followed Hilliard's beater northeast as it made its way toward Old Town. It was well after rush hour, and with the sun down, it only took minutes for Hilliard to reach his destination. The arborist took Wolfe Street until it dead-ended at Roberdeau Park. Cal didn't pull onto the dead-end street, but parked along South Union, which paralleled the river. Cal strolled down Wolfe, framed on each side by tony condominiums. He spotted Hilliard's beater, but not the man himself.

Cal walked into Roberdeau Park.

It was a clear night, and Cal spied Hilliard from behind. The man was halfway down the gravel trail connecting Roberdeau Park to Shipyard Park, another small park constructed to commemorate the city's first shipyards. There wasn't much to it besides the river view—just some green space, streetlamps, and benches. Cal watched Hilliard slump into a bench and stare out over the Potomac.

Cal decided not to follow along the trail. Hilliard would see him plainly and may even recognize him—suspicious enough— but Hilliard would certainly notice Cal doubling back when the man decided to return to his car. Cal decided to backtrack to another park a block back from the river, Windmill Hill Park. It had athletic courts, a playground, and its own riverfront vistas, from which Cal could watch Hilliard from above without detection. Even from across the street, he could see the man's knee bouncing as he stared out over the water, hands plunged into a hoodie. The man Cal had followed for the past few days often drove around aimlessly, but he chose this spot—this spot in Old

Town—for a reason. Cal was sure of it. He was trying to discern that reason when Hilliard rose suddenly and turned to face him.

Cal feared he'd been spotted. He found a nearby bench. He sat down and pretended to tie his shoe, glancing over at Hilliard from the corner of his eye. The man was crossing the street toward him. Just then a young woman walked in front of Cal on the trail and blocked his view of the advancing man. When she passed and he found the arborist again, Cal realized that Hilliard was actually clocking her, not him. Hilliard picked up his pace.

He was trying to cut the distance to the woman.

Cal fiddled with the laces of his other shoe as Hilliard passed not twenty feet from him. As Cal tugged his laces tight, he quickly peered over his shoulder to find the woman again, but she had disappeared into a tunnel.

CHAPTER

48

Cut into the bluff overlooking the river, the Wilkes Street Tunnel was a relic from before the Civil War. Part of the old Orange & Alexandria rail line, it connected the railroad to the waterfront for over one hundred years. The track remained operational until the 1970s, and now sat as a historic transportation landmark and another path for joggers and bikers.

It was also another brick barrel vault, just like the bridge at Hooff's Run.

He recalled the Public Works Services Division's home page.

Sewers, stream beds, bridges, and tunnels.

Cal cursed himself. This whole week, he thought he had been so clever with Hilliard. Watching him night after night, following him to the waterfront, keeping far enough away. But he had been too focused on Hilliard and not on their surroundings. *Tunnel vision*, he thought ruefully. Now Hilliard was tracking a young woman into a dark burrow, where he had home court advantage.

His heart beat in his chest like a horse trying to buck the rest of his body.

Cal dashed to the entrance, his fingers brushing against his weapon. Unlike the bridge at Hooff's Run, made smooth by the flowing water, dead tendrils of Virginia creeper snaked up either side of the tunnel's mouth. It reminded him of a giant cobweb. He considered his options as he passed inside.

There was nowhere to hide in the tunnel. It was not a warren with branching passageways. It was one long shaft, stretching the length of a city block. And Cal was far enough away that if Hilliard slashed at the woman, he might be too late. Better not to catch Hilliard in the act at all, realized Cal, but to prevent it altogether.

He entered the tunnel without bothering to be quiet.

Once inside, he breathed easier. Unlike Hooff's Run, it was not an ideal spot for murder. The tunnel was well lit by lanterns in the overhead archway. It was lighter inside than outside. Even so, Cal's vision telescoped. The long tunnel stretched into oblivion. *Not now*, he thought. He gave his head a violent shake and the dimensions retracted back to normal. He spotted the woman far ahead, nearly ready to emerge from the other end. Hilliard was far enough behind her that he would have to jog for a few seconds to catch her. That would give Cal enough time to shout and give chase.

Cal let his fingers drop from his weapon and recalculated.

He stayed far enough behind to keep from being noticed, but close enough to keep the arborist in view. It was like taking station on another vessel in the Navy—locking in on their course and speed and matching both from his position.

The woman exited the western end of the tunnel. Next, Hilliard did as well. Cal followed, emerging into an open cut trench, still below street level. Great clusters of Virginia creeper spilled over the top of the trench like a brittle waterfall. He saw Hilliard at the top of the grade, turning right onto South Royal Street, still stalking like a bloodhound on a scent.

Just as Cal kept station on Hilliard, Hilliard kept station on the woman. She appeared to backtrack a block. Hilliard mirrored her route without fail. More than a coincidence.

The hair stood on Cal's neck.

The woman turned onto South Fairfax. Hilliard quickened his pace, so as not to lose her. Cal did the same, cautious to hang back while fighting his natural instinct to sprint forward. He took deep, even breaths. He remembered something Dr. Julia had taught him. *Ebb and flow,* he thought on the in breath. *Come and go,* on the out. When Cal rounded the corner onto South Fairfax, he saw Hilliard disappear between two buildings. He looked around the street, searching for the woman, but he didn't see her.

Cal ran.

The alley where Hilliard had disappeared was a small brick path between a large brick building and some residences. It was another dark, hidden passageway, a space between spaces, in the heart of the city. Unlike the tunnel, there were no overhead lights.

This time, Cal pulled his weapon from his holster and held it down by his leg as he crept forward. It was almost full dark along the path between buildings. He squinted, trying to resolve the darkness.

He waited to stumble over a body. Or for a man with a blade to explode from the bushes. He thumbed the safety off and moved his head side to side slightly, almost like a fish, using his sharper peripheral vision, and willing his eyes to adjust more quickly.

The alley widened into a courtyard. He passed a church courtyard, a playground, gardens. He jogged alongside the brick path, on the grass, to muffle his steps as he made up ground. He scanned everything he passed, pausing to listen for movements.

Ebb and flow, come and go.

Ebb and flow, come and go.

He continued forward and found the path again, and it narrowed beside another large brick building. He came to an open iron gate and a low brick wall. Streetlamps illuminated a parking lot. He exhaled, his vision restored. He flipped the safety on and holstered his weapon again.

Still in shadow, he peered around the side of the building. A short set of stairs led down to what appeared to be a basement door. He caught sight of Hilliard disappearing below.

Cal followed.

He descended the stairs and pushed open the door to an underground corridor of the dark building. At the end of the corridor, there was a single rectangle of light and Hilliard moved toward it. As Cal drew closer, he heard muffled voices. He was trying to make them out when the door behind him swung open again. A pair of men entered. Cal realized he was standing in front of a bulletin board and pretended to read it, even in the darkness of the hallway. As the two men passed, one of them called out, "Don't worry, you're in the right place."

Cal followed them toward the rectangle of light. From the doorway, Cal spied a cavernous basement room. There was a small stage at one end. Folding chairs were arranged in a circle instead of facing the stage. The men Cal followed found two empty seats. The woman Hilliard had been trailing was sitting in another. There were a dozen others scattered throughout the room. Hilliard was off to the side, pouring coffee into a Styrofoam cup.

As much as he wanted to, he couldn't go in. He had exchanged words with Hilliard the morning he found Tiny and again jogging on the trail earlier that week. How did the saying go? *Once is happenstance. Twice is coincidence. Three times is enemy action.*

Hilliard would know something was up for sure.

Cal quickly moved past the open doorway and went deeper into the corridor, down to the next door. He tried the knob, found it was unlocked, and ducked inside. He found a switch and the light revealed a smaller room used for storage: band equipment, sorted boxes of donated goods, cleaning supplies, and what Cal was hoping to find—rear access to the stage.

He placed his foot on a wooden stair, and it creaked enough that he stepped back and removed his shoes. Carrying them, he summited the short set of stairs onto the rear of the stage. There was a sliver of light where the curtains didn't fully join. Suddenly, all of the voices raised in unison. With the sudden cover of the noise, he shuffled forward. Cal thought it was a song at first. He dropped to one knee and peered through the slight gap, careful not to ruffle the fabric. He could see and hear the circle clearly now.

It was the Serenity Prayer.

Shit, he thought.

A middle-aged man spoke from the head of the circle. His back was to Cal, so it was harder to make out, but Cal got the gist.

". . . my name is Doug and I'm an alcoholic and your secretary . . ."

For the next two hours, Doug went around the circle of folding chairs, and Cal felt progressively worse. The people in the basement bared their souls. They shared deep, dark secrets. Stories of profound loss and humiliating setbacks. Moments of mundane victory and glimmers of hope.

And Cal was hiding in the dark, eavesdropping. He wanted to get up, to slip away, but he didn't. Part of it was guilt. But he knew the real reason was curiosity. He had surveilled Hilliard for days, and damn him, he wanted to hear what the arborist had to say.

Finally, toward the end, it was Hilliard's turn to speak. He sat directly across the circle from Doug, so he faced the stage. Cal leaned closer to the gap.

"My name's Jake and I'm an alcoholic."

"Hi, Jake," said everyone.

He cleared his throat and continued. "I was working the program, doing my meetings. One day at a time, you know how it is. I had almost three years, a good job with the city, and my own place . . ."

Hilliard took a deep breath and blew it out.

"Then I got an early morning call about a month ago. There was a body in a tree."

Cal's eyelid began to throb. He realized he was balling his fists. His fingernails cut into his palms.

"Me and my partner had to get him down. But we couldn't just cut him down, you know? It was all . . . involved and shit. It was, like, evidence. And there were cops everywhere."

Everyone tried to remain silent, respectful, but Cal heard the murmurs. The other members cast side glances at each other. Cal got the sense that they had heard everything—all manner of ruin—but this was new. Hilliard was living his life, putting one foot in front of the other when a higher power, if one believed in such things, had placed an atrocity in his path.

Diabolus ex Machina. Cal knew how it felt.

Even from across the basement and concealed behind a curtain, Cal couldn't help but notice Hilliard was no longer jittery. Probably because he was finally where he wanted to be all week. Where he needed to be. Everyone settled down and Hilliard continued.

"My partner was the one who had to get up close and personal. I just spotted from the ground. Honestly, I was relieved, but I still feel guilty about it. Who knows how bad that fucked up my partner? Mitch won't talk about it. Still, just fucking being there was more than I could handle. I mean, I was just trying to keep my own shit together. I tried to go away in my head, but I still kept my eyes on Mitch to spot him. I had to watch. I couldn't help but see . . . all of it."

He smiled a rueful smile.

"I was in a bar by lunch. But my sponsor helped get me back on track and I've got three weeks."

There were more murmurs, nods of assent.

Hilliard stood suddenly. "Anyway, I got *this.*"

He rolled up his sleeve to reveal his switchblade tattoo. Cal put his eye to the gap in the curtains.

"I read that knives represent cutting ties with your past. With bad shit, with baggage."

Hilliard's nervous energy was spent, revealing the defiance underneath. He looked everyone in the eye.

"I still see that poor fucking guy every day. And all the dumb shit I've done before that. But I look at this, and I just . . . cut it down. Cut it loose. And I move on. A little bit lighter."

Hilliard took a seat and everyone clapped.

Cal withdrew from the gap. He crossed the stage, descended the short set of stairs, and put his shoes on. He emerged into the corridor and hustled past the open door, where the meeting was ending. In moments, he was back up on the street, filling his lungs with fresh air.

My name is Cal, he thought, *and I'm a fucking asshole.*

49

"I CROSSED A line last night," said Cal.

He leaned back in his chair in Dr. Julia's office. She leaned forward in hers.

"What are we talking about here?"

"I had a suspect I was sure was guilty. I mean, I was *positive* . . ." Cal thought of his pursuit on foot last night through Old Town. His heartbeat racing. The hairs on his neck and arms standing on end. Plunging forward into a dark alley. Driven forward by duty and a fair bit of terror and, if he was being honest with himself, a sense of exhilaration. But he had squeezed facts into his theory about Hilliard like a square peg into a round hole. What had seemed so sure last night was preposterous in the cold light of day. Even dangerous.

To say nothing of the massive invasion of privacy.

"Did you hurt anyone?"

He gave Dr. Julia a hard look for a moment. The question stung, but he supposed it was fair.

She shrugged. "I have to ask."

"No."

He pictured himself as someone might see him last night. Sweaty and jumpy, running around the shadows of Old Town, weapon out, high on his own crazy hunch.

I'm damn lucky I didn't hurt anyone, he thought.

"Tell me again why you think this 'extra credit' with Detective Massey is a good idea."

It wasn't an "I told you so," but it felt close. Not that Dr. Julia would have any compunction about looking him dead in the eye and telling him "I informed you thusly." She would do it with relish. She had before.

"It's kind of like an internship—"

"An unpaid internship."

". . . where I learn the ropes of Violent Crimes. It's what I've always wanted. This way I get to see it in action first."

"At night, after hours. And no one can know."

"You make it sound like a booty call. I'm trying to help him catch a killer."

Dr. Julia smirked. "'Booty call,' Detective Farrell?"

Cal fought a smile. "I don't know why I bother . . ."

Dr. Julia glanced at the clock on the wall and stood. "Well, at the very least you can cross one more suspect off your list."

Cal rose too, their session over. He made for the door. "Great. I narrowed our suspect pool from 159,200 Alexandria residents to 159,199."

"Why are you so sure it's an Alexandria resident?"

He tried to articulate what had been floating around his head for days.

"I figure it's someone who lives here, or lives close, or grew up here. It's not like the bodies were found on King Street. They were off the beaten path. A stretch of trail, a barely noticeable ravine . . . It's someone who really knows his way around."

He patted her doorframe.

"Then again, what the fuck do I know? See you next week."

50

S YDNOR HAD WARNED him not to chase waterfalls, yet Cal had spent his nights creeping on the down low. Cal was pretty sure he was mixing up two different songs, but the ladies of TLC had a lot of wisdom to dispense. Regardless, Sydnor had been right again. So Cal fell back into his normal rhythms: Park his behind on the couch after work, watch soccer, and stay out of trouble.

Except he hated his normal rhythms.

He was restless and wanted to be anywhere but home, but too exhausted to do anything about it. Worst of all, something still itched at the back of his mind, causing him fitful sleep. Like a word on the tip of his tongue that wouldn't let him concentrate.

In the early hours, in the liminal space between asleep and awake, stray thoughts swirled like frantic moths fluttering around his brain—tickling it, agitating it—unable to escape. There was Heather, always Heather, a tickle that never went away. Her long, red hair. Her crooked, knowing smile . . . she was a constant, dull ache.

He thought of the murders. How they had given him something to fixate on besides that Very Hot Day. He thought about the staging. Of their intent, their message. How had Massey put it? *Sometimes I'm Spider-Man, sometimes I'm Jack the Ripper . . .*

He thought of Heather again and the last time he saw her, that double-date ambush with Carly. He really should call

Carly. He remembered the four of them sitting there, having fun, enjoying each other's company and conversation, and Cal thought *maybe it could work*. It wasn't right to keeping thinking about Heather. Jason was his friend, maybe his only real friend besides Heather. And then there was something that Jason had said about the murder of Hayley Driscoll. *That's some real Jack the Ripper shit . . .*

Cal rolled flat onto his back, his eyes wide open.

Jack the Ripper.

That was twice someone had mentioned the infamous killer in the span of a long weekend. Cal tried to remember everything he could about Jack the Ripper—what he had picked up in history classes, a lecture at the police academy, and the cultural flotsam and jetsam of over a hundred years. London, gaslights, butchered hookers . . . and an infamous killer who was never caught.

Perhaps it was time to refresh his memory.

He abandoned his bed to find his laptop and started with Wikipedia. Even if it was crowd-sourced, it would give him a decent overview. He read the entry and learned that some of the murders attributed to Jack the Ripper were in doubt, while others were considered canonical. The agreed-upon slayings all occurred in 1888, in the Whitechapel district of London's impoverished East End. The victims were mostly, if not all, prostitutes. They'd had their throats cut, and with each killing their bodies were progressively more mutilated, including the removal of internal organs. Two of the victims were even killed on the same night, within minutes of each other, which became known as the "double event." The grisly slayings culminated with the November 1888 murder of Mary Kelly, of which there was a horrifying photo. The woman, splayed on her bed in her small room, was butchered beyond human recognition. Cal squinted at the glare of his laptop's screen, trying to ascertain the dead woman's features, but there was no use. When he was able to decipher where her face was supposed to be, his stomach turned. He took several deep breaths and quickly read past the photo.

Suspects over the years ranged from butchers to doctors, even members of the royal family. What struck Cal was the sensation the killer had stirred, in London proper, throughout England, and around the world. And down through the years. The murders in the summer and fall of 1888 had shattered any sense of normalcy. Headlines screamed of *Ghastly Murder* and *Dreadful Mutilation*. Terror gripped Whitechapel, fueled in part by letters from the killer himself.

Or at least attributed to the killer. On several occasions, someone purporting to be the killer sent correspondence to the press and the civilian "vigilance committee" that helped the police. In late September, the Central News Agency received a letter that began with "Dear Boss" and pledged to keep "ripping" prostitutes. The letter was signed "Jack the Ripper," the first time the legendary name appeared. Worse, George Lusk, president of the Mile End Vigilance Committee, received a gruesome package containing half of a human kidney with a note that began with "From Hell," and went on to claim that the author had fried and eaten the other half.

Cal shivered in the air-conditioned chill of his dark bungalow. Most of the notes were later debunked, or were widely believed to be hoaxes, written by the very news agencies that printed them in order to boost the circulation of their papers. But it hardly seemed to have mattered. The provenance of the letters and postcards was beside the point; more than one hundred thirty years later, the macabre legend of Jack the Ripper lived on.

Cal sat back and exhaled. While interesting, he didn't learn anything he thought would help catch Alexandria's killer. He closed his eyes and pictured the summer of 1888. Working girls navigating the narrow alleyways and coal-drenched darkness of Whitechapel, hoisting their plume skirts for quick rendezvous with drunken men just outside the nimbuses of flickering gaslights, unaware one of the strangers from the shadows had darker designs. Not unlike Daisy. He thought of Hayley Driscoll, the shattered lamp, the dark stretch of Hooff's Run.

But not a damn bit of it had anything to do with Tiny, hoisted seventy feet into the air.

Cal sighed. When he opened his eyes, he noticed another intriguing entry under *See also*. He clicked in, and his pulse quickened.

CHAPTER

51

"SPRING-HEELED JACK?" ASKED Massey.

This time they met at Fairlington Pizza, a small pizzeria that sold by the slice in Alexandria's West End, just shy of the Arlington border. It was a straight shot up Quaker Lane, and he could be back at headquarters within ten minutes if Sydnor called. Still, he couldn't help but notice they met farther away from headquarters this time. Massey looked exhausted. The detective was still cheerful, still breezy, but it seemed to take effort. Massey looked paler, which only made the dark circles under his eyes more pronounced. Cal pressed on.

"And the London Monster, yes," said Cal.

"This is your big break in the case?"

"It's more like a unifying theory . . ."

"Alright, alright, start over," said a wary Massey. "And slow down."

Cal took a deep breath and tried to organize his thoughts. The next entry was just another bit of Victorian-era folklore, barely a footnote, but it had caught his eye last night. The next thing he knew, he was plunging down one rabbit hole after another, until weak morning light seeped through his blinds. He showered quickly and fired off the text to Massey asking to meet again.

Now Cal tried to ignore the rhythmic tugging beneath his eyelids and focused on telling the story in as linear a manner as possible.

"The last time we talked, you referenced Jack the Ripper. All I really knew about him was that he was like the Elvis of serial killers or whatever, so I did a little research. But let's stick a pin in Jack for now, and go back fifty years earlier to another Jack."

"Spring Jack."

"Spring-*Heeled* Jack." Cal slid a paper across the table with a black and white printout of an old magazine cover. It featured a drawing of a figure with a demon's head, one leg thrust forward and arms spread high and wide. He wore a scalloped cloak, giving him the appearance of a devilish bat.

Massey looked at it with a raised eyebrow. The corner of his mouth inched up, as if he was anticipating the punch line of a joke. "Is this a comic book?"

"It's the cover of a penny dreadful from over a hundred years ago."

"What's a penny dreadful?"

"Cheap, serialized stories from the UK, back in the day."

"So an old-timey, limey comic book?"

Cal shook his head, fighting to keep his words from tumbling out of his mouth, focusing instead on going slowly. Massey must have noticed his frustration. The detective held up both hands. "Sorry. Go on."

"Thank you. It's a leap, but let me lay it all out."

Massey swept his hand over the table, a magnanimous gesture beckoning Cal to continue.

"The first sightings of Spring-Heeled Jack were around 1837. There was an account of a strange man leaping from an alley to attack a woman, then another of a man leaping in front of a carriage, causing it to lose control, then leaping away and cackling madly. There were more cases, and each one differs in its description. Jack had claws or pale features or burning eyes, resembling a ghost or a devil, and the papers reported all of it, feeding the hysteria."

"Okay . . ."

"I know, it's crazy. I had to stop from snickering myself when I read accounts of swooning women being 'deprived of their senses . . .'"

"Bring me my fainting couch," said Massey in a clipped British accent.

"Exactly. But then I realized I was being unfair. It was a long time ago. People today still believe crazy shit, so why should it be any better a hundred fifty years ago? There was mass hysteria, but eventually, things settled down and Spring-Heeled Jack faded into legend."

"So let me guess, in your unifying theory, you're ascribing Tiny's murder to Spring-Heeled Jack."

Cal held up a finger. "Before we get there, let's travel back in time *another* fifty years."

"Good thing I brought my DeLorean."

"It's 1788. For two years, a man engaged in piquerism."

"Which is?"

"Pricking or stabbing someone with a needle or pin. Or a knife. There were more than fifty reported victims. The press started calling him The Monster, and as you'd expect, everyone freaked out. Vigilantes prowled the city, women wore copper pots over their petticoats, and men even wore "No Monster" lapel pins to show that they were not, in fact, The Monster."

Massey laughed at the sheer naïveté, as did Cal.

"Even the pickpockets got in on the action," Cal continued. "They'd rip someone off, and when they were nabbed, they'd point and scream 'It's The Monster!' then vanish in the melee. Again: mass hysteria."

"I'll give you this, Farrell, you're more fun than my high school history teacher."

"Can you guess where the London Monster did the most stabbing?"

"London?"

"The buttocks."

The half smile slowly faded and Massey's eyes narrowed.

"Last winter, Daisy Wilcox walks down an alley and is slashed on her backside. Have you been in contact with her yet?"

Massey nodded. "She was none too pleased with you, but yes. She said you promised she'd be left alone."

Cal didn't feel great about it, but if there was a connection between her, Tiny, and Hayley Driscoll as he believed, the investigation superseded her desire for privacy. He paused for a moment and remembered what she had said about the slasher's eyes.

It was like a cat in headlights. I'll never forget it.

"Did she mention the eyes?"

"Glowing," said Massey. "You left that tidbit out last time."

"I figured it would sound less crazy coming from her than me."

Massey leaned back in his chair, took a sip of coffee, and pretended to be nonchalant, but Cal knew he had intrigued the detective. "What do you attribute the eyes to? A demon walks among us?"

"Retro-reflective contact lenses."

"Good," smiled Massey. "Just making sure you haven't totally floated off into space on me. One problem though: the glowing eyes was a Spring-Heeled Jack trick, no?"

"It's not an exact science, this."

"And our guy may not be a stickler."

"Fast forward and we find Wylie Gilbert aka Tiny hanging high up in a tree."

"You find." Massey hoisted his coffee mug in Cal's direction. "Credit where credit is due."

"Not just high, though. Impossibly high."

"Clearly not impossibly high."

"But we can agree that it's improbably high? Inordinately high?"

"It was a conversation starter."

"Spring-Heeled Jack is known for making incredible leaps."

"People are going to call you Spring-Heeled Cal for your incredible leaps."

"Better than Killer Callum." Cal kept his face even, but he allowed a little steel into his voice. It even helped with the twitching of his eyelids. Massey regarded him, then nodded slowly.

"Fair enough," said the detective.

Cal held up his thumb. "First, Daisy Wilcox was slashed à la the London Monster. Her attacker had glowing eyes, which does not fit the profile of The Monster; however, without them, the attack would be indistinguishable from other commonplace assaults. In other words, unremarkable. And our man is working awfully hard to be remarkable."

Cal raised his forefinger next. "Second, Tiny is murdered, but displayed at an extraordinary height, reminiscent of Spring-Heeled Jack's distinguishing characteristic."

Cal's middle finger joined his other two. "Third, Hayley Driscoll. Butchered and left at Hooff's Run. I don't know anything beyond what has been reported in the news, but you said she was cut bad."

"À la Jack the Ripper?"

"You tell me."

After a moment, Massey nodded slowly.

"So what's next then?" asked the senior detective.

Cal shook his head. "That's just it. Why haven't you heard of the London Monster or Spring-Heeled Jack? Why didn't I before last night? They were both extremely popular in their day, both were reported widely in the press, both incited mass hysteria."

"The passage of time?"

"That had something to do with it. But a bigger, badder, more prolific Jack came along and eclipsed his predecessors. With actual murders, taunting letters, and even lurid photographic evidence. All with breathless newspaper coverage. The eight hundred pound gorilla, the reigning champion of boogeymen. No one looms quite as large as Jack the Ripper."

"What are you saying?"

"I think Daisy and Tiny were appetizers. And I think Hayley Driscoll was the start of the main course."

CHAPTER

52

THE DOUBLE EVENT came in March.

It had been a lovely weekend in Alexandria, offering a preview of spring, but the temperature plunged late Sunday night, high winds raked the city, and a surprise snow caught the region completely off guard during Monday morning rush hour. School buses were late, stranding shivering children at their stops for hours. Patrol, stretched thin, responded to scores of fender benders across the city. The sudden change was jarring. Overnight, winter had reasserted itself.

Monday morning, as the snow swirled outside, rumors began to swirl inside headquarters. Word circulated that the mayor and his entourage were sequestered in Chief Ravelle's conference room with Massey and Porter. The normally boisterous open bays were unusually quiet. Patrol officers and detectives huddled in pairs and small groups, exchanging what information they could glean in whispers. A low electrical hum ran through the building, the snow forgotten.

Even Sydnor was distracted. He kept looking up from his desk to peer around their bay.

In a low voice, Cal asked, "What the hell is going on?"

"I don't know."

Cal didn't like that answer. Sydnor knew everything. By the look on his partner's face, he didn't like it either.

Cal tried to lighten the mood. He flicked his monitor, indicated the never-ending stream of incident reports. "Sharks and vending machines, right?"

"Yeah," said Sydnor, half listening and craning his neck, surveying their space. "Sharks . . ."

Before lunch, Sydnor's patience reached its limit. "Fuck this," he muttered, rose from his seat, and did a circuit of the detective bays to gather information. Then he disappeared—Cal assumed to linger outside the chief's conference room. Despite his own advice to Cal, Sydnor couldn't help himself. The man sniffed a waterfall. Any other morning, Cal would have smiled at the hypocrisy. After twenty minutes, Sydnor returned and slipped back into his chair with some intel. Another body was discovered over the weekend, but the task force was keeping a tight lid on the details.

"It's a black box," he said. "Just that it's our guy for sure."

Our guy. Can't teach an old dog new tricks, thought Cal. "Media know yet?"

"I saw Beth Naff from the *Post*."

"Here? You're kidding."

"They smell blood in the water. My guess is Public Affairs is promising her an exclusive if she doesn't run with it until the brass are ready. They're probably trying to guilt her with an 'After all the shit the city has been through . . .'"

Sydnor glanced at Cal. It was a slip. "All the shit" encompassed Tiny and Driscoll, and surely the Very Hot Day.

Cal pretended to ignore it. "It'll probably only buy them an hour."

Sydnor grunted. "If that."

53

Patrol officers and detectives crowded around mounted flat screens in the briefing rooms and break rooms of headquarters to watch the local news stations cover the press conference live at City Hall. Cal didn't want to stand shoulder-to-shoulder with his brothers in blue, so he headed outside instead. Winter's tantrum had already passed. The wind subsided, the sun was out again, and rivulets of snow melt ran down the sidewalk. Cal walked far enough away from the building to escape its shadow and searched for the presser on his phone. By the time he found the link to stream the broadcast, it was already underway.

Chief of Police Ravelle stood at a podium emblazoned with the seal of Alexandria: a full-rigged sailing ship and a set of scales. Behind him stood Mayor Schleicher, looking somber to the point of pain. His brow was deeply furrowed and his mouth was an even line. Off to the side was the PR flack, Conway.

The gang's all here, thought Cal.

Ravelle surrendered the podium to Detective Adam Massey as Cal put in earbuds so he could hear better.

". . . for joining us this afternoon," said Massey. The other faces on the dais looked like Schleicher's, pinched in a performatively grave manner, but Massey kept his face open and his chin up. He looked tired, but Cal thought his expression was an open palm compared to the city leadership's closed fist. No resting cop face.

"Two victims were in fact discovered over the weekend, and though they were found in different locations, we believe a connection exists between them."

Two victims.

My God, thought Cal. A double event. He looked around in disbelief.

Reporters fired off questions immediately, not letting him finish his statement. They seized on the word *connection*, asking what it meant. Massey nodded sympathetically and let the furor die down.

A reporter from the *Alexandria Times* stood, her voice the last one to be heard in the clamor.

"How were they killed?"

"We're not releasing that information right now."

"Why so vague, Detective?"

Massey didn't appear bothered by the din. In fact, he looked comfortable.

"I understand it all sounds vague, Moira. But you know how it works. There are certain details I just can't share right now because they are known only to the task force and our killer. Our first priority is the safety and security of the people of Alexandria. We can't afford our tip lines to be flooded with well-meaning citizens who hear two facts and extrapolate."

Cal knew what he meant. Senior citizens who called in because a police sketch showed a suspect in a ballcap and they didn't like the look of their neighbor's lawn guy. Conspiracy theorists who were certain all crime in Alexandria was the work of a shadowy cabal of prominent politicians and lizard people. To say nothing of the pranksters who just wanted to fuck with the police. Even if there was a legitimate lead amid all the calls, there was a haystack's worth of time-wasting horseshit to rake through.

And wasted time only benefited the killer.

Eventually, the podium's microphone, which had captured the shouted questions, now captured murmurs. Massey continued.

"Though it's too soon to confirm, information suggests this weekend's perpetrator is also Hayley Driscoll's killer."

More questions shouted. Once again, it was Moira from the *Times* who had the last word and seized on the phrasing.

"What information?"

Massey took a beat and surveyed the reporters.

"There's been a letter."

54

CAL RECEIVED A text within an hour of the press conference's conclusion, asking him to meet in the parking lot of the George Washington Masonic National Memorial Lodge. Perched atop Shooter's Hill, the memorial—dedicated to the first president and prominent Mason—was a striking 333-foot building and tower that looked like a cross between an obelisk and a lighthouse. It stood sentry at the western edge of Old Town. Cal leaned against his car and let his eyes drift over the rolling green hill, glistening from the now-melted snow. On the hill was a massive symbol of Freemasonry emblazoned in concrete—the Square and Compasses, framing a large "G." It was situated such that the tip of the square pointed directly to King Street, the main avenue of Old Town, and the Potomac River.

Cal saw the appeal of the place. It was quiet and solemn, the lawns were always manicured, and everything was orderly, aligned. There was a grand design behind the building and the site, and it gave the impression that the same orderly design spread to Alexandria itself. Or at least the illusion of it, which, he supposed, was the point. But the grand design never accounted for someone walking into a building laden with weapons of war and killing a half-dozen people, or a mad predator stalking innocent people to hang them or carve them into pieces. Cal considered all of this as he pulled his coat tighter around him and watched Massey's car snake its way up the hill.

The detective stepped out of his vehicle and Cal could see then how stooped and gaunt he appeared. He looked like a completely different man than the one who had commanded the podium not two hours before.

Had he been wearing makeup for the press conference?

As he sidestepped puddles of slush to approach Cal, Massey said, "I think it's time we put a ring on it."

"Come again?"

"It's been an epic fucking shitshow of a weekend. The FBI is sending a profiler. We're losing control. There's only one upshot."

"What's that?"

"I have a pretty decent amateur profiler right here."

"I'm no profiler."

"Then you're incredibly lucky. Your theory, your insight, your hypothesis. Whatever you want to call it is spot on. Two more bodies and a letter, just like you said."

Cal had heard it during the press conference, and even though he was hearing it again face to face, he could still scarcely believe it. Massey pulled his phone from his pocket, swiped at the screen, then handed it to Cal. It was a picture of a letter, taken under the fluorescent lights. Cal even noticed the shadow of Massey's hand holding the phone in the photo.

Rock a bye baby,
Out on a ledge.
A pretty, young lady,
At river's edge.

Two more playthings,
Cheap lipstick and leather.
Carved like turkeys
Birds of a feather.

So many pretty girls
Must pick up the slack

It's all fun and games
For your Old Town Jack.

"Beth Naff from the *Post* is running it within the hour," said Massey. "It's going to get nuts."

Old Town Jack. Cal felt as if the temperature dropped thirty degrees. His eyelid began to twitch.

"Is that blood?" asked Cal.

Massey shook his head. "Red ink."

"But there's a connection to the murders."

"Yeah."

"Are you going to tell me?"

Massey shook his head. "Not here. No more *I'll show you mine if you show me yours.* We need you. All the way in. No more pussyfooting around. We lay this out to Porter, and if we can win her over, the brass'll bite too. They won't countermand both Porter and me."

"Porter? That'll go over well."

"Let me worry about Stacy. Believe it or not, she's fair. If there's something to this, she won't care where it came from."

"I'm more worried about Sydnor. He's made his position clear on all of this."

"He give you the shark attack speech?"

"Sharks are splashy, but vending machines are the real scourge . . ."

"Yeah, well, when was the last time you saw Vending Machine Week on the Discovery Channel? Look, let's get Stacy onside first. If we're all in agreement, and we lay it out for the chief, Lavaar won't have a choice. He'll grumble, but at the end of the day, we all took this job to stop bad guys, and this is the worst I've ever seen. Can you stick around tonight?"

Cal turned away from Massey. He didn't want the detective to see his eyelid dance.

Cal looked out over the steps, down past the lawn with the Masonic crest, toward the buildings of Old Town and the river beyond. It was a dizzying sensation. It struck him that Tiny, from his resting place high in the tree, had faced Old Town and the river as well. It was like they were both searching for the same thing, but coming at it from different angles.

Now Massey was offering Cal a chance to get one step closer to seeing what Tiny saw in the end. Seeing *who* Tiny saw.

There was no choice.

"I can."

55

THE REST OF the day passed like molasses. Cal and Massey shook hands on the hill and Cal tried to go about the remainder of his day with Sydnor. They spent most of it at their desks catching up on mind-numbing paperwork from the gambling ring case. It was the worst kind of day. Several times, he almost blurted to Sydnor about what was about to go down, but he stopped himself. He had promised Massey he'd do it his way. Instead, he tried and failed to concentrate on his casework, until he finally received a text from Massey as Sydnor was packing up for the day.

Patrol Division Interview Room C at 7 pm. No prying eyes.

Cal was relieved. Most everyone would be cleared out by then, and no one would be in the rooms. Sydnor saw the relieved look on his face.

"What's up?" asked his partner.

"Huh?" said Cal. When he looked up, he saw Sydnor staring at him, his brow furrowed.

"You're smiling," said Sydnor.

"Oh," said Cal. He faked a smile. "Girl."

"Double-date girl?"

"We're circling a single date."

"About damn time." He slung his empty lunch pail over his shoulder. "Night, junior."

"Night, Syd."

At 6:55 PM, Cal wound his way to the lower level, looking over his shoulder as he went. He was no longer tired now, just wired. The Criminal Investigations Division took up the second floor of headquarters, and consisted of his own Vice and Narcotics and Massey's Crimes Against Persons. Patrol Division had the entirety of the building's lower level, beneath the first floor where the public entered. Going into an interview room with Massey on his own floor would certainly get back to Syd. But a detective wandering the Patrol Division wouldn't raise eyebrows, and it was possible to slip unseen, or at least unnoticed, into the floor's most out-of-the-way interview room. Massey was waiting for him just outside it, the hallway momentarily deserted.

"Hurry up," said the detective, waving him inside.

Once they were both inside, Massey sighed. "I have to make a quick call. Porter is grabbing us sandwiches. Chill for a minute?"

"Go do your thing. I'm good."

"Thanks."

Cal took a seat. If he could convince Porter that the two murders were not just connected, but a string of assaults that began with Daisy Wilcox, then the door to the investigation he had thus far been viewing through a keyhole would open wide, and perhaps he could help them catch a killer. And, if he was being honest, the case might prove to everyone that he deserved his status as a detective. There was no tougher nut to crack than Porter—a perfect representation of the department's resentment of him—but if he managed it, perhaps he could shed his scarlet letter. His excitement began to get the better of him, and he felt the tightening at the corner of his eyes. The last thing he needed was to be twitching when he saw Porter, so he leaned back in the uncomfortable chair, folded his arms, and took a few deep breaths, as Dr. Julia had taught him.

His breathing grew longer and more even. His heartbeat fell into sync with his breaths. The tension in his neck melted. The chatter in his mind faded. After a few minutes, he looked around, more relaxed, and saw the sparse room as if the for the first time.

A table, three chairs, mirror. No Porter, no Massey. No sandwiches.

He looked at the two-way mirror, then back at the door.

He rose from his chair, made a show of a yawn and a stretch, and was walking around the table when Massey and Porter entered, holding file folders and arguing.

"No you didn't," said Porter, irritated.

"No sandwiches," said Massey. "I told Stacy to order, but she either forgot or just feeds on my disappointment."

"It is delicious," she said in Cal's direction, the first time Cal recalled her speaking to him, or at least around him, without hostility. Maybe there was hope. She addressed Massey. "Let's bang this out so we can all get the fuck out of here and you can eat whatever you want, princess."

Cal smiled, feeling relieved and a bit silly as they all took their seats.

"So," said Porter, reaffixing her scowl, "you're the strange."

Cal narrowed his gaze, not quite understanding.

Massey chimed in. "She's accused me of cheating on her with a silent partner, though I keep telling her she's the only one for me."

Cal smiled again.

Even bickering, Massey and Porter possessed a shorthand, even an affection, that was alien to him. It wasn't that Lavaar Sydnor was aloof with him—he was aloof with *everyone*. Some days passed with barely a grunt from the man. When Sydnor did give an insight on a case or regale Cal with a story from his younger days on the force, it was usually more corrective than reminiscent. Watching Massey and Porter's playful one-upmanship actually made him jealous.

"Catch him up, Porter," said Massey.

She shot Massey a look, like she had swallowed something unpleasant, but she exhaled, resigned. "Turns out there was a connection between Hayley Driscoll and our local Tarzan. Wylie

Gilbert didn't like to spend the night in shelters if he could help it, and there's no records of him doing so at their Old Town location, but Volunteers of Alexandria takes boxed dinners and hot soup to various parks in Alexandria. Common knowledge among the homeless community. They'd show up and stock up, then disappear again into the night. Hayley Driscoll was on that volunteer rotation, and Tiny was apparently a fixture. We don't know what that means, but it possibly places two of our victims at the same time and place, and maybe more than once. Maybe someone else was there too, someone who was jealous or God knows what. We've pored over all of the records, sign-in sheets, anything, trying to deduce a pattern, but that's pretty much what we have. Which is fuck all."

"Farrell may have found another link in the chain," said Massey. He nodded at Cal. "Start from the beginning and tell her everything you told me."

However breathless and jumbled his presentation may have been during his first clandestine meeting with Massey, he wasn't about to make the same mistake with Detective Stacy Porter. She would not be as patient or forgiving, so he had spent the day rehearsing it in his head, smoothing out any disjointed bits. He began with his interview with Daisy in North Carolina, describing her account of the attack. Porter looked bored, possibly because by now Massey had already told her that part. In the Spartan interview room with the harsh fluorescent lighting, the next part seemed far-fetched even to his own ears, but he kept his tone measured and laid out his research in order—the London Monster, Spring-Heeled Jack, and Jack the Ripper roughly corresponding to Daisy Wilcox, Wylie Gilbert, and Hayley Driscoll with their respective and fantastical modus operandi. Porter rolled her eyes at Massey occasionally, or huffed or mumbled "Come on . . . ," but Cal continued undeterred, encouraged by Massey, and the more connections he drew, the less agitated Porter became. He noticed her fidget less and concentrate more. Once or twice he even noticed her nod slightly. When he finished there was silence.

She rested her elbows on the table and leaned forward. "How did you find out about Daisy in the first place?"

"I'm Vice and Narcotics. She was in the life."

"CI?"

Cal shrugged.

"Come on," said Porter, smiling. "I'll show you mine if you show me yours . . ."

Cal grinned back but said nothing.

"Fine," she said.

"We brought Hayley's file," said Massey. Porter patted the top folder for emphasis and slid it over to him.

Cal realized this is what he had been waiting for. Helping. Working with the task force, working with Massey. In pursuit of a killer. But as he pulled the file toward him, he hesitated. He wasn't a profiler. He wasn't a medical examiner. Hell, he'd only been a detective for eight months now, and how much of that had he spent trying to get his sea legs? He didn't want to be a tourist in Hayley Driscoll's death. Her body was not a curiosity. And he knew that whatever hellish images he put in his head would stay there, according to Sydnor, and he was already fully stocked. Even if he couldn't remember them, even if they only allowed glimpses of themselves at night in his tattered sleep. But he told himself he wouldn't be here if Massey didn't think he could help. He looked up at the senior detective for reassurance.

Massey nodded. "Fresh eyes."

Cal opened the folder. He decided to work his way from a corner of the photo in, in an attempt to notice every detail, while slowly acclimating himself to the horrible scene. He braced himself for Hayley's lifeless body dumped onto the grassy ledge of Hooff's Run, throat cut, and hoping the rest of the damage—which Massey and Porter had successfully withheld from the press—wasn't too severe, too graphic. But the green of Hooff's Run and the brown of the brackish water over the streambed were gone. The photo was taken somewhere indoors, somewhere where the decor was primarily red. He looked closer and noticed that Hayley was sprawled on a bed, and from a small patch by her foot, the original color of the bedspread had not been red, but beige. His gaze moved up the photo and his eyes snagged on a large tattoo snaking around Hayley's waist. His eyes lost their discipline then and he looked into the victim's face. The mouth was stuffed with large feathers.

It was shocking enough that it took Cal a beat to realize the victim's hair wasn't blonde but dark, because the victim wasn't Hayley Driscoll at all, but Honey.

56

"WHAT?" SAID CAL.

"Shit," said Porter, reaching over to clap the file shut and slide it back. "Wrong file."

"You alright?" said Massey. "You look a little queasy."

"Hey, in for a penny . . . ," said Porter, shuffling through the files.

Cal's head swam.

Honey was dead. He'd seen her less than two weeks ago. He'd barged into her life, and now she was dead. Mutilated and murdered, according to the glimpse of the photo he had seen. It was too much of a coincidence, and Cal felt like throwing up. He felt a sharp tugging at the corners of his vision.

The words of the letter played across his mind:

Two more playthings,
Cheap lipstick and leather.
Carved like turkeys
Birds of a feather.

Though Cal was reeling, his mind raced ahead. There were two victims, one of them Honey. Did they both have feathers in their mouths? *Cheap lipstick and leather.* Was this an allusion to sex workers? Was the other victim one too? He tried to focus on the present.

Massey was speaking now, but Cal only caught half of it. ". . . using the language of folklore, referencing historical killings. Inciting mass hysteria, which we've thankfully been able to keep a lid on. I think Farrell here is spot on. He wants attention."

"Who?" cracked Porter. "The killer or Farrell?"

Cal looked at Porter. "Excuse me?"

"Come on, you don't like the attention?"

It took him a moment to recover from the shock of seeing Honey, but when he did, everything was suddenly clear. An electric current ran up his spine, and when it passed, he found himself sitting ramrod straight. His nausea, his exhaustion, his anxiety . . . all set afire and burning off as if they were fumes.

"*No,*" he said.

"Walk us through it—" began Massey.

Cal pointed to the folder, now back in Porter's grasp. "When did this happen?"

"Let's put a pin in that," said Porter, a rueful smile on her face.

"Cal, walk us through it again," said Massey, still kind and with his easygoing manner. Still eager to understand, to seek a connection. Cal noted that the detective had never actually used his first name before.

Jesus Christ, how could I have been so stupid?

"Try to see it from *our* perspective," continued Massey. "Help us understand. Of all the people in Alexandria, you just happen to be the one to stumble upon a dead body on the trail."

"Stumble is pretty generous," interrupted Porter, "seeing as how Tiny was damn near a hundred feet in the air." She opened another file. "Oh, and you knew him."

"I didn't know him."

"Report has it you arrested him."

"Detained. I let him go."

"After you two tussled," continued Porter. "Maybe that got under your skin. Asshole puts his hands on you, then you have to cut him loose? Still wearing your bracelets? That would have pissed me off . . ."

"Well, you seem a lot more vindictive than me."

Porter smiled. She was enjoying herself. It made him furious, but he knew he couldn't lose it. They *wanted* him to lose it. They had all along. He thought of the handcuffs. The bow. They were meant to get under his skin, to throw him. Cal looked at Massey. "There never was a note with the cuffs, was there?"

"How did you even see him?" replied Massey, ignoring the question. "I'm serious. I can't stand running. When I do it, I just sort of stare straight ahead."

"Or at my own feet," said Porter.

"Sounds to me like you both should run more," said Cal. "And maybe work on your situational awareness."

"Well, we know maintaining situational awareness is very important to you," said Porter. "Even when it's not warranted."

"We put surveillance at Hooff's Run after Hayley Driscoll."

Massey lobbed the fact at him, and Porter knew enough to let it land without chiming in.

Cal thought of his night in the ravine. From where they were sitting, it didn't look good. Hell, it didn't look good to him either. But his mind kept returning to Honey, the red sheets, the feathers, the bloody tangle of her midsection.

Massey continued. "Patrol was pretty surprised to see a man splashing around in the dark out there. They were even more surprised when they ran your plates, Cal."

Every time Massey used his first name, Cal's jaw flared.

"Though not as surprised as I was to put you and Hayley at the same time and place."

"What?"

"I have to say, I wasn't surprised one fucking bit," said Porter. She slid another sheet of paper across the table, face down. Cal hesitated, worried it might be another trick. Some new horror. Porter nodded at it. "Volunteers of Alexandria fundraiser last fall."

He remembered now. It was the nonprofit's annual gala, held in one of the large hotels along King Street. For a brief stretch in the months after the Very Hot Day, he attended several of these balls. They were an excuse for Alexandria's luminaries to dress up, get drunk, and have their photo taken being generous.

It was also an opportunity for them to corner Cal and pepper him with pointed questions about the worst day of his life. He felt like a morbid door prize. The fundraisers began with the Alexandria Police Foundation trying to raise money for much-needed APD resources. That year broke fundraising records, so the brass decided to deploy their "hero cop" to other Alexandria balls—libraries, parks, after-school programs—until it finally occurred to him he could say no. The parties all blurred together, but the Volunteers of Alexandria party must have been during that circuit.

Cal pulled the paper toward him and flipped it over. Sure enough, there he was. It was a group photo of the Volunteers of Alexandria staff, pulled from the internet. The staff were all dressed up and hoisting drinks, celebrating a successful event. At one end stood a wan Cal Farrell, clutching a beer like a life preserver and offering a distracted smile. At the other was a beaming Hayley Driscoll in a cocktail dress. He didn't remember seeing her. Then again, his memory wasn't optimal these days.

"Did you two chat that night?" asked Porter. "Let me guess: You made a pass and she shot you down?"

Cal ignored her and directed his answer to Massey. "The department sent me to half a dozen of those things. They did everything but raffle me off."

"Back to the ravine then," continued Porter. "So, did you jerk off down there or did you wait until you got back in your car?"

"Porter," said Massey.

"Go to hell," said Cal.

"After you, *Killer Callum*. Because you're wrong, Farrell. I don't know if you were *ever* right before Milton, but you're definitely fucking wrong now. Everyone in the department thinks you're wrong, and they don't even know about your creepy extracurricular activities. *Yet*."

"Porter, take a walk," said Massey.

"Yeah, Porter, take a walk around the corner into the two-way," said Cal, "and I'll pretend you're not there. Just like I'm doing now."

Porter leaned forward, the disdain coming off of her in waves. It reminded Cal of the warped, heated air above a grill in the summertime.

"Every night, I wish to God it had been you instead," she hissed.

"Porter . . . ," said Massey.

But Porter's voice rose, gathering strength and getting louder with each word. "But no. That *Killer Callum*—sick, broken fuck that he is—still gets to roam the earth is a fucking travesty!"

The sudden venom, the sheer, unmasked hatred, startled Cal. This went way beyond good cop, bad cop. Before he knew what was happening, she was climbing over the table. Massey grabbed her before she reached him. He wrapped both arms around her and hauled her away, toward the door. Cal peered over the table and was astounded to see both of her feet off the floor and kicking as her partner bore her backward. Her eyes were red and brimming and she continued to scream.

"You're lucky Virginia outlawed the death penalty. I'd throw the fucking switch myself!"

Massey shoved her through the door. He looked nearly as rattled as Cal, but once the door was closed, the detective leaned his back against it and exhaled. He let the silence hang for a moment, then grabbed Porter's overturned chair and dragged it back to the table. He collapsed into it.

"I knew she wasn't up for it," muttered Massey.

The whole display was over the top. What at first unnerved Cal now infuriated him. He didn't deserve to be in this room, let alone endure that bullshit.

"And the Academy Award for Best Actress in a Drama goes to . . . ," he said, pantomiming opening an envelope, "Stacy Porter in *Good Cop, Bad Cop*." He jabbed his finger at Massey. "I want my rep. *Now*."

"That was no act."

"Then fuck you both."

Massey looked at him. "Porter and Vance were engaged."

57

I T HIT CAL like a punch in the gut.

"He was patrol, she was a detective," said Massey. "They kept it quiet, but yeah."

They sat in silence for a while.

"I think about what happened to Vance every day," said Cal.

"Well, you two have that in common then."

"It happened fast. Too fast. I was right on Vance's tail on Duke Street and paused only to open Tiny's door. Vance ran ahead. I was two seconds behind him."

"So it's Vance's fault?"

"That's not what I meant and you know it."

"Protocol is you run toward it. You don't wait."

"*I didn't wait*," said Cal, leaning forward, his jaw clenched. "And how many active shooter events have you responded to?"

"Touché."

"You want to continue this conversation without my rep present? Tell me about Honey."

"You knew her?"

"Suspect me all you want, but don't insult me. You know I knew her, that's why I'm in here. So let's skip the foreplay and get down to it, yeah?"

"Fair enough. Regina DeMarco aka 'Honey' was found early yesterday afternoon in a suite at the Sun Dial Motel in Belle Haven."

"Belle Haven? That's Fairfax County."

"Where did you see her last?" asked Massey.

"Still going to pretend like you don't know?"

"Hey, you stumbled into our surveillance. We don't have it on you 24/7. Yet."

"Days Inn off of Route 1, southern Alexandria."

"Were you a client?"

"*No.*"

"Just a matter of time before we get the warrant to access her account on BackPage to get a list . . ." Massey let the insinuation hang between them. Cal ignored it.

"What happened to her? And no, I don't need to see the photo again."

"Working theory is that someone masqueraded as a john, and he was invited in. The suspect cut her throat, and seeing as how he was indoors—unlike Hayley Driscoll—he proceeded to take his sweet time. I'll say this, our gentleman caller is not queasy. And the feathers are a new touch. From the wing of a Canada goose, by the way. Very common. Lorna Mayberry was a receptionist from Landmark-Van Dorn, but she was found in Dyke Marsh at sundown, in a similar state. Mallard feathers for her, though, blue patch in the wing."

Cal stared off to the side, avoiding Massey's gaze. He didn't care if it made him look guilty. He needed to process this.

Massey blew out a long breath. "I'm tired, Farrell. Porter's tired. We're all fucking tired . . ."

Cal burst out laughing. Once he started, he couldn't stop. It made him light-headed.

"What?"

"Do you think," said Cal, wiping tears from his eyes, "you're more tired than me?"

"No, Cal—I bet you can't remember the last time you had a good night's sleep, can you? At least that's what the report from Dr. Julia says. Blackouts? Lost time? Come on, man . . ."

Cal felt bile rising in his throat. Massey turning on him was one thing, but Julia? He had trusted her.

"Look at it from our point of view for just one second. Once upon a time, a good cop sees something utterly fucking terrible. A nightmare no one should ever have to endure, even a cop. It's bound to mess anyone up. Big time. Add the other coincidences? Discovering Tiny? Your handcuffs in his pocket? Being spotted at Hayley Driscoll's crime scene? Now we have you photographed *with* her."

"It was a gala. Half of Alexandria was there."

"*You* came to *me* with Daisy Wilcox. And she spoke with you at the request of an associate, Regina DeMarco aka Honey, now gutted. You're connected to all of them, Cal. It's just a matter of time before we link you to Lorna Mayberry too. It looks *bad*, man. Am I supposed to believe it's a killer arborist or some folklore legend come to life? Come on. You're a smart guy. If you were in my shoes, it would look bad to you too."

Massey paused to let it all sink in. He placed his palms on the table.

"Listen, I know it's not you, not really. You're in the back seat when this happens, or somewhere else entirely. You probably can't even remember it. I'm just trying to do my job here. I just don't want anyone else to get hurt, and I know you don't either. Not really. So I'm asking you to help me out . . ."

Massey leaned forward, almost across the table, his arm reaching for him. Cal met his eye. Massey's face showed exhaustion, his eyes were narrowed with concern. Cal could practically feel waves of empathy rolling off of him, the polar opposite of Porter's explosive hatred or even Sydnor's indifference. The ache of the detective, the sadness and worry in his eyes, the desperate need to understand, to connect. Saying without having to that Cal was not the acts he committed, that they were separate, and if they could just get them out into the open, they could begin the process of freeing him. Name them and tame them and put them behind him.

How many people, wondered Cal, had given it all up to ease the suffering in poor Massey's eyes? To restore the kind detective's breezy smile and bask once more in its pleasing sunshine?

How long had Cal himself been seeking his approval?

"Last chance, Cal. It's escalating. I'm telling you, Regina DeMarco and Lorna Mayberry were far more . . . extensive than Hayley Driscoll. It was like a botched surgery. It's getting so much worse . . ."

Cloying or not, bullshit or not, Massey wasn't lying about that. People were dying. And Cal knew enough about serial killers to know that they often inserted themselves into investigations, trying to be helpful, because they either wanted the attention, wanted to get caught, or both.

And here comes Cal, he thought.

Hounding Massey for meetings. Tipping him to Daisy and floating theories about murderous arborists and centuries-old urban legends and killers by gaslight. How could he have been so stupid? It was all so fucking embarrassing.

And he was so very tired. Bone tired . . .

Cal sighed. He was just about to speak when the door to the interview room flew open. A woman in a tailored business suit with her red and gray hair trimmed in a fashionable bob stood in the doorway. In a firm, crisp voice, she said, "This interview is over."

Behind her stood Lavaar Sydnor.

Nick of time, thought Cal.

58

"Is Mr. Farrell a suspect?" asked the sharply dressed woman. Massey, surprised, said, "Person of interest."

"So you're not charging him then?"

Massey hesitated and Porter stared daggers at Cal from over Sydnor's shoulder.

"That's what I thought. This ambush is over." The lawyer faced Cal. "Let's go."

"You heard her," grunted Sydnor. "On your feet, kid."

Cal stood, some of his energy returned to him. He looked from Massey to Porter and back.

"Both of you can go to hell."

Massey chased an irate Sydnor into the hall, trying to explain himself, and Cal found Porter struggling to resume what must have been a losing argument with the older woman. The lawyer ignored her, keeping her attention straight ahead, in the direction she was walking, utterly unfazed.

Porter broke off her attempts with the woman and called after Sydnor. "Something's fucking wrong with him and you know it, Syd!"

Whatever firepower Porter had brought was nothing compared to the molten fury of Lavaar Sydnor. He glared at her and she stopped in her tracks. Then he stared down his old partner.

"That's some dirty fucking pool." He shook his head. "Same old Adam."

"If you knew what we knew . . ."

"You should have told me."

With that, Sydnor turned and followed the woman out the door.

Cal's head spun. He looked back at the two cowed detectives for a moment—Massey's face contorted with nausea and Porter's looking furious—then followed his rescuers down the hall.

Once the pair was out of view, any bravado Cal felt evaporated. He felt deeply foolish.

"How'd you know?"

Sydnor didn't break stride and Cal couldn't see his face, only the back of his head, his thick neck, and his tense shoulders. "Your poker face is for shit."

"Thanks," he mumbled. "To the both of you. It's not—"

"Not here," hissed the lawyer.

They ascended to the main floor and headed for the doors, the only sound the echoing, staccato report of the lawyer's heels on the tile floor. Cal saw Julia crossing the lobby, bag slung over her shoulder and heading home for the night, and he peeled off.

"Julia!" he called after her.

One look at her face told him it was true.

He already knew Porter hated him, although he hadn't known why or the depths of it until tonight, and it stung like hell to know that Massey had been playing him, but Julia's betrayal cut the deepest.

"Cal, I—"

"I never thought you of all people would sell me out. Maybe I'm naïve, but at a minimum, I thought at least some doctor–patient confidentiality would kick in."

"They asked me pointed questions. I had to answer. I'm sorry."

"You had no right . . ."

"I had no choice."

"Bullshit."

"Cal, I work for the *department*. It's my job to assess officer suitability."

"Jesus Christ, Julia, do you honestly believe I could do something like this? That I'm even capable of doing those things to those women? To Tiny?"

She was usually the one to make him squirm. He'd never seen her in turmoil before. She looked at her shoes, then finally looked him in the eye.

"I think you're very charming and very clever."

"You were right," said Cal. "I do have enemies here. I just didn't think you'd serve me up on a platter to them. Of all the things to feel stupid about tonight," he said, "I actually thought we were friends."

Tears brimmed in her eyes, but he'd been manipulated enough for one night.

He stormed out of the lobby and found Sydnor outside, standing beneath the large replica Alexandria Police Department badge on the building's façade. The older detective shot him a look as if he wanted to slug him. Cal ignored him and instead focused on the lawyer, who looked irritated as well.

"Thanks, Mom," he said.

59

HE BEGAN TO explain, but Meredith Farrell cut him off. Meredith Farrell, senior partner in Littlefield, Billings, and Hobbs, one of the most prestigious law firms in Washington, DC. Meredith Farrell, president of the Eco-Action Board of Arlington. Meredith Farrell, peak performer in anything she set her mind to and the scourge of anyone who dared stand in her way. There were mama bears and tiger moms, but Meredith Farrell was a great white with a juris doctor degree.

"Not here," she snapped.

"Did I just get a 'We'll talk about this at home, young man'?"

"Did I just leave a keynote speech because my son is suspected of being a serial killer?"

"If I had a nickel for every time I heard that . . ."

"You think this is fucking funny?" said Sydnor. "What the hell were you thinking?"

"I was trying to help," he said.

"What did I tell you?" he railed. He spun toward Meredith. "I told him to keep out of it."

"How are you even here, Mom?" asked Cal.

"Lavaar and I have known each other a long time."

"Please don't tell me you're dating, because I really can't handle any more craziness tonight."

"Lavaar worked with your father."

"What?" Every time Cal's head stopped reeling and the dizziness passed, something sent it spinning again. Out of the thousands of silent hours in the car together, or at their adjoining desks, or face to face across a table at lunch, Sydnor had never mentioned it. All Cal could do was laugh.

"Unbelievable."

"He was real good to me coming up in Patrol Division," said Sydnor. "Not everyone was."

It began to make sense. Why Sydnor had volunteered to take him on as partner, though nothing in his demeanor before or since had shown any enthusiasm for the role. The cover story had the ring of truth—there was logic in teaming him with a veteran detective, but Lavaar Sydnor surely had enough juice to say no had he wanted to. And who could blame him? A rookie partner with Cal's baggage? Baggage that was now open and spilled out all over the place.

"And you never once thought to mention that tidbit?"

"You deserved to make your own way. Didn't want you to think I was babysitting."

"But you were, though, weren't you?" He wheeled to his mother. "Jesus Christ, did you ask him to take me on as his partner?"

Meredith waved off the question. "That hardly matters right now. What matters is that you're in trouble, and thank God Lavaar called me as soon as he heard."

Cal turned to his partner. "And how did you hear?"

"Believe it or not, I still have people around here who prefer me to Massey. People know where they stand with me."

"Debatable," said Cal.

"You should be grateful," said Meredith. "Who knows how long you'd have been in there or what they would have gotten you to say."

Cal winced. He knew it to be true.

"Massey's clever," said Sydnor. "Sometimes too clever, but make no mistake, he's the real deal, and Porter wants your head on a pike. I told you to stay away. I God damn *told you* . . ."

"Enough!" bellowed Cal. His mother flinched. Sydnor's eyes widened, then narrowed, keen on Cal. Cal took a couple of deep breaths, then spoke in as controlled a manner as he could manage. He pointed at Sydnor. "This case may just be another shark or waterfall or whatever the fuck to you, but it's important to me."

"Why?" asked Sydnor.

"I don't need to explain myself to you. You damn sure don't explain yourself to me."

"You're being ungrateful, Callum," said his mother.

He looked at her, then back at Sydnor. "People cheating, crimes of passion, even murder . . . that's dawn of time shit. But this guy? He's an aberration. And I've seen enough of those. He needs to be stopped."

"Why does it have to be you?" yelled his mother.

Because a tax was incurred.

But Cal's anger burned out quickly, and with it, the fumes of his remaining energy. For months, Cal had been fighting currents he didn't even know existed. Now the enormity of what had transpired the past couple of hours hit him full force, and his exhaustion found another reservoir.

"Whatever. I'm going home now. Thanks for bailing me out."

"There is zero physical evidence," said Meredith. "That much was obvious from Porter. The whole thing is a fishing expedition, and no judge will entertain it. Even so, I will engage Detectives Massey and Porter in the morning to find out how metaphorical 'bailing you out' really is."

"Take sick leave tomorrow, kid," said Sydnor. "I'll talk to Massey and see if they were just trying to put the fear of God into you."

But Cal was already walking away.

Sydnor called after him, "And no more sneaking the fuck around!"

"You first," said Cal over his shoulder.

Cal found his car and closed his eyes once safely inside. He was furious, humiliated, hurt, reeling from too many revelations in too short a time, but mostly, he was scared. He found some loud music on his phone. The pounding drums and slicing guitars of the Pixies' "Bone Machine" synced to his car and blared through the speakers on his short drive home to Del Ray.

He felt like he was whitewater rafting on a river of adrenaline. He parked in front of his bungalow and slammed the car door. He wanted to put his fist through something. He wanted to howl at the moon. He didn't get the chance.

"Took you long enough."

Cal stared into the shadows of his small front yard.

"Heather?"

60

HEATHER WAS AT the side of the walkway leading to Cal's front door, sitting in the deep shadow of a tree. She rolled forward into the light cast by his small porch. Backlit, her red hair was vivid in the night. He took two quick steps toward her.

"Are you okay?" he asked.

She didn't appear to be in any distress. She even wore her trademark smirk she used when she teased him. He broke his gaze, looked up and down the street, then stared at her again. To make sure she wasn't a hallucination.

She laughed at him. "It looks like I should be asking you that question."

"Work stuff," he said, waving it off. For detectives, it was a phrase that shut down unwanted inquiries from prying civilians. It intimated any number of uncomfortable or gruesome topics and served as the conversational equivalent of "Employees Only Beyond This Point" signage. Maybe that's why they called it a cop-out, he thought.

"Sounds like you need a drink," she said.

He rubbed his neck. "Probably."

"You know, you've never invited me over. And now I know why."

"Why?"

"You don't have a fucking ramp."

"Shit . . . I'm sorry."

"I'm fucking with you, Cal."

"Right. Ha."

"Am I invited now? It's cold out here."

"Of course."

She lifted her arms then. It wasn't like that day in January at Jason's house, surrounded by laughing friends, when she flung her arms wide, threw her hair back, and closed her eyes. This time, she cocked her head, raised an eyebrow, and twirled her hands at her wrists as if to say "ta-da."

He took her meaning and scooped her from her chair. He climbed the three steps to his front porch with her in his arms. It was a far better exertion than putting his fist through something. He suddenly had a hard time remembering why he had been so worked up moments before. One hour ago may as well have been one year ago. The only thing he was conscious of was her warmth and her comfortable weight in his arms. He remembered the sensation well. He had practically memorized it. And every moment between holding her in January and again now pulsed with a phantom ache he was only now aware of.

He squared up to his front door and muttered, "Damn it."

"Door locked?"

"Yeah, sorry. Just a second . . ." He turned to take her back down the steps to her chair so he could have his hands free. She stopped him with a hand on his chest.

"Which pocket?"

"Um . . . right."

He stood frozen as she slid her outside arm down the front of his pants, searching for his pocket. She found it and slipped her hand inside. He stood frozen. She smoothed her hand down his thigh until she grasped the keys and drew her hand out slowly.

"And . . . ," she said, dangling the keys in front of him. "Voilà."

She fit the key into the lock, then pushed the door open. Cal crossed the threshold into his darkened bungalow. Without sight, his other senses affirmed her presence. He felt her warm breath tickling his neck. This close, he could smell her hair: honeysuckle. They had never been this close for this long, he thought.

He cleared his throat. "Light switch is on the wall there."

Her hand found it and the room flooded with light. She looked into his eyes. He surveyed the room, looking anywhere but at her, but she kept her calm gaze on him. Finally, he turned his face toward hers. She waited for his eyes to settle on hers, then turned off the light again.

He felt her lips against his. Incredibly soft, almost impercep-tible at first. He tasted her lip gloss, something between vanilla and cinnamon.

One moment he was in the doorway, his brain numb and his pants unbearably tight, and the next they were on the couch, her arms around him, tugging at his shirt, and her mouth now wet and luscious and hungry. His day had been a roller-coaster and now it felt as if the car was shaking loose, rocketing toward the next peak, and about to fly off into space. His breath grew ragged. He was light-headed, his hands fevered. His heart pounded like it was going to explode from his chest. He had dreamed of this moment for more months than he cared to admit, and it felt so right, so perfect . . .

But there was something wrong too. A few somethings.

"Whoa," he said, and rolled to the side. "Whoa."

"What?" she said. "What is it?"

"Just," said Cal, breathless. "Just a minute."

"Why?"

"Jason. For one."

She pulled him back down by his collar. "Don't worry about that."

"I have to. He's my friend. He's your boyfriend."

"Not really."

"Did you break up?"

"Are you writing a book? I don't care."

He pulled away and sat on the far end of the couch, elbows on his knees, and caught his breath.

"I don't deserve you."

"Oh, fuck you. That's even lower than 'It's not you, it's me.' If you don't fucking want me . . ." She sat up and scooted back to the other end of the couch, facing him, her legs separating them. "The last thing I need is for you to make excuses . . ."

He reached over and put his hand on her shin.

In a low, calm voice, he said, "I'm not making excuses. I want you, Heather. More than you know."

She glared at him. She leaned back against the arm of the couch and folded her arms.

He could barely face her, but he forced himself to.

"That day . . ."

"Cal, the last thing I want to talk about right now is *that day.*"

"I have to."

She looked away. "Out with it already then."

He gestured to his head. "I have holes. Blank spots. I mean, I know what happened, I have the facts, but I don't really remember. I remember that I saw you, you gave me your badge, and I entered the office. I remember squaring up against the conference room, wheeling in, and then . . . nothing. I came to in the back of an ambulance."

"That's okay . . ."

"It's *not.* When I was out of it, a narrative started to form. A bullshit 'hero cop' narrative. It had a head start. And it's what the city wanted, it's what Jason and your friends and family wanted, and if I'm being honest, it's what I wanted. But the truth is, it wasn't heroic. And my peers are pissed that I made detective ahead of them. Some cops just don't trust me. And some whisper 'Killer Callum' when I walk by."

"Hey," she said softly now. She leaned forward and squeezed his hand. "Me too."

"You? How could that possibly be?"

"My friends are cool, and most of my coworkers are too, but everyone else?" She shrugged. "No one looks me in the eye."

The thought of Heather experiencing similar indignities, or worse, made his fists hungry for a wall again. "Why?"

"Ever heard of a sin eater?"

Cal shook his head.

"Back in ye olden times, someone in a village, usually a poor person, would get paid to eat a meal over a dead body. It was a way of taking on the sins of the deceased. As you can imagine, the dude paid to chow down over a corpse to absorb its sins would not be super popular. And the more he did it, the more of an outcast he became." She pointed at her chest, then at him. "We got a full helping that day. And then some."

He always felt there was more to the department's resistance to him. The array of reasons didn't make sense. He had responded, however imperfectly, and his fellow officers should have cut him some slack. He could never quite put his finger on it, and Heather had just articulated their detachment in a way even Dr. Julia couldn't when she discussed concepts like displacement or phobias. They didn't resent him because of the promotion. Maybe some did, but that was just the excuse.

They resented him because he was a memento mori. A reminder of death.

"So I'm a walking funeral then."

"And I'm a rolling cautionary tale. What can I say? We sin eaters are a tough hang."

"Still," he said. He forced himself to meet her eye. "I'm no white knight, Heather."

She was silent for a moment, considering this, then burst out laughing. Her head fell back and she laughed into the air, her body convulsing with it, her arms thrown out to the sides.

"That's . . . not the reaction I was expecting," he said.

"Jesus Christ, Cal, do you think I give a shit?" She caught her breath and reached out and touched his face. "You beautiful, stupid man. Is that why you think I'm here? Because I think you're my knight in shining armor?"

"I'm learning tonight I'm clearly mistaken about a number of things . . ."

"Look, we both did the best we could that day. I've had to wrestle with a lot of anger, a lot of *why me*, a lot of 'If I only did this instead of that' . . . but the truth is it was all on that asshole.

Him and no one else. But at the end of the day, the scoreboard has
him dead and us alive. And last I checked, when I met you, you
were running *toward* him. So as far as I'm concerned, no one was
there except me and you, so no one else has the right to have an
opinion on the matter. And beating ourselves up is a colossal waste
of whatever time we have left."

She touched his forehead with her fingers, swirled them as she
had that day in the hospital.

"He's living in there rent-free. Evict him already. I have."

He blew out a deep breath. He didn't realize how much he
needed to hear that until she said it.

"Been carrying that around a while?" she asked.

"Yeah."

"Well, you're dumb. I'm not here because you're my hero, Cal.
I'm here because I know you want to fuck me, and I want you to."

His erection roared back.

"That obvious?" he asked, laughing.

Her insouciant, lopsided grin returned. "I knew I wasn't
wrong."

"No, you most definitely are not wrong. I've wanted you since
earlier than I care to admit."

She leaned back again, hands folded behind her head, taunting
him now. "We have to work on that guilty conscience of yours."

"About that. So you and I are sorted, but what about Jason?"

"Look, Jason is used to getting what he wants, and when we
were friends, he always chased me. And then that day happened
and suddenly," she said, gesturing at her legs, "I was pretty easy to
catch. He swore up and down he still wanted me, and it sounded
like a good deal. He stuck by me, and who else would want me,
right?

"*Wrong.* I realized how fucking stupid that was. I was scared
and feeling sorry for myself and couldn't imagine bouncing back
and all of the stuff you would expect. But I'm still ten million
kinds of fucking awesome. I'm still *me*, so why settle?

"Plus, it's horribly unfair to him. He's the most caring,
loyal, wonderful guy, and he deserves someone who wants him

unconditionally. We fell into a relationship, and yes, technically, we're still in it, but we don't touch. Not like that. There's no passion. It's like a game of chicken and neither one of us has the guts to jerk the wheel, you know? But I don't need any more friends, Cal. If I want companionship, I'll buy a dog. What I need is to live again. I want to be with someone who looks at me the way you do. Who can't even fucking hide it. Now, do you have any more questions, or am I free to go, Officer?"

"You're not going anywhere."

He leaned over and kissed her. Slowly this time. His head swam with it, as if he'd had too much wine.

"One last thing, though," she said.

"Yeah?" he said, kissing her neck.

"Next time you need absolution, see a priest, not the raging hottie waiting for you. Now go get my chair. Then take me to your bedroom and take your pants off already, you big dork."

61

CAL CALLED IN sick the next morning. Sydnor texted him, telling Cal to lay low until he could suss things out. Cal didn't care. He wasn't asking permission. Messages from his mother filled his voice mail as well, but he ignored them as much as Sydnor's texts.

He had company.

Heather called in sick too. They spent a long lazy morning in bed together until Cal cooked them breakfast. Then it was back to bed. Despite being a person of interest in multiple homicides, he had never been happier. He told her so, leaving out the events of the interview room. She told him they deserved it and he allowed himself to believe her. Weren't they owed some hard-won happiness? And even if it was a cold, uncaring universe—and there was plenty of evidence to support that—didn't that prove her point all the more? Weren't they duty bound to seize whatever joy they could?

Try as they might to shut out the world, it still managed to penetrate their bubble. He came out of the shower in the afternoon and Heather was lounging in bed on her phone.

"Christ," she said, shaking her head.

"What's wrong?"

She held up her phone and sighed. "Article in the *Post* about the murders. This fucking city . . ." She slammed her phone down suddenly. "I crave more sustenance! Fetch me snacks, cabin boy!"

"Aye aye," he said, smiling at her. He cinched the towel around his waist and palmed his own phone on his way out of the room. Alone, in the kitchen, he pulled up the *Post* and scrolled until he found the article. The department admitted there was a link between Hayley Driscoll and the double event of Regina DeMarco and Lorna Mayberry. The goriest elements were left out, but it was clear from the article that the new victims' throats had been cut, and Beth Naff alluded to the fact that the subsequent mutilation had been "'considerably more extensive,' according to lead detective Adam Massey, and that the task force was 'pursuing a very strong lead.'" The article was the first place to mention "Old Town Jack."

The article then pivoted to the public's mounting frustration over the perceived lack of progress in the investigation, and the debate over a curfew. Panic was setting in. Now *#OldTownJack* was trending on Twitter, becoming a story in itself. The echo chamber was in full swing, a closed circuit.

"*Snacks!*" cried Heather from the bedroom, dramatically. He could picture her naked form, her forearm flung across her brow in swoon. He smiled and left the phone in the kitchen.

Cal banished thoughts of anything related to Old Town Jack from his head. His Del Ray bungalow was the whole world. They were giddy and bingeing on each other—laughing at each other's jokes, listening rapt to each other's stories, making out constantly—when Cal reached under the bed to retrieve an old photo album. Something pricked his finger as he stretched for it. It didn't stop him from pulling out the album and sharing a lovely afternoon with Heather.

They lounged in bed, her laughing at pictures of a young, sullen Cal looking suspiciously at the camera.

"You were cute."

"*Were?*"

"Are you okay?" she asked.

"Never been better. Why?"

"Your eye," she said, pointing to her own. "It's twitching."

"Happens sometimes," he said. "Particularly when I'm happy."

She leaned over and kissed the twitching skin by his eye. "Still cute."

At four o'clock, she prepared to leave. She hugged him and made that little noise he loved so much.

"Call in sick again tomorrow," he said. "Stay here."

"I *have* to go in," she said. "There's only so long one can suffer from 'food poisoning.'"

"Tell them you were sure the clams were good this time."

Heather laughed, but there was a sudden shift in her mood. She looked as if she might cry for a moment and he couldn't bear it.

"I wish we could do this forever," she said.

"What do you mean?"

"Hide."

"I don't want to hide anymore, Heather."

She looked up at him, her lips tilting into that cocky, lopsided grin that drove him mad.

"Good."

They smiled at one another for a moment.

"I'll tell him for you," said Cal.

"I can't ask you to do that."

"You didn't ask. I volunteered."

"I don't know, Cal—"

"I do." He knelt down beside her. "I want to make you dinner. I want you to spend the night again. I want to wake up with you. I don't want to waste another second."

"It wouldn't be fair."

"When has the world ever been fair to us?"

"Listen to you, playing that card. Shameless, Farrell."

"Shameless and selfish," he said, grinning. "I'm tired of playing fair. You're all I want and the clock is ticking."

She closed her eyes, drew a deep breath, and blew it out.

"We're both really fucked up, Cal."

"But in really complementary ways," he said, and she laughed.

He kept a weather eye out as Heather's custom van lifted her chair. It was far darker than it should be for the time of day. Black anvils of cumulonimbus clouds piled overhead, getting ready to pound Old Town with rain. Heather noticed the rolling thunderheads too and made a face.

"Hope I make it home before it opens up."

When her seatbelt was buckled, she kissed him. He kissed her back and they stood that way, on the street in front of his house, kissing with abandon, as if it was the last time they'd see each other.

"Be gentle," she told him.

He nodded. She rolled up her window, put the van in gear, and pulled out onto the street. He watched until the van turned onto Mount Vernon Avenue and was gone. His waving arm fell and he glared at his empty house.

He walked inside. He smelled the pesto they ate on the couch. He smelled their endless sex in his bedroom. He smelled her perfume high above it all like a thin shroud. He got on his hands and knees beside the bed, then flattened himself. He reached until his finger brushed against a sharp edge. He grasped it carefully and brought it out to the light.

He turned it over in his hand and studied it.

Crampons.

CHAPTER

62

CAL READ A lot of books in the Navy.

Cell phones didn't really work at sea and they weren't allowed for operational security, so analog entertainment was the best way to pass the downtime. There were card games and movie nights on the mess deck, but as much as Cal enjoyed the camaraderie, he preferred tucking himself into a corner of the ship, in the lee of the wind, and getting lost in a book. Reading above decks cleared his nose of the stale, rank air of his cramped berthing area and filled it with clean, salty sky. He'd burn through whatever books he packed for a long deployment, then have to go in search of others to trade with. Once, he'd swapped books with a senior chief who passed him a short story collection that included Stephen Crane's "The Open Boat."

Stories of disasters at sea were always a dicey proposition as it seemed to tempt fate—sailors are a superstitious lot—but Cal was sucked in immediately. The story shared the predicament of four men in a small boat on the open sea after their ship sinks. They attempt to ride the perilous surf to shore, but they are weak after their suffering and the water is icy and rough. The exasperated narrator laments: ". . . if I am going to be drowned, why, in the name of the seven mad gods who rule the sea, was I allowed to come thus far and contemplate sand and trees? Was I brought here merely to have my nose dragged away as I was about to nibble the sacred cheese of life? It is preposterous."

It *was* preposterous, thought Cal at the time. Such a powerful story, so much emotion, so much hope and dread only to use a phrase like *the sacred cheese of life*. Crane must have really liked cheese, he thought. It tickled Cal so that he committed it to memory.

It wasn't so funny now. Sand, trees, cheese. Life.

Happiness.

He was so close to shore . . .

He turned the crampons over in his hand. The weak light in his bedroom caught the length of the spikes, but not the tips, which were gummed with dried sap. He sat on the bedroom floor for a long time and worked on his breathing until his eyelid stopped fluttering, his heartbeat slowed, and his panic subsided, even as dark clouds crackled outside and the storm finally opened up.

So close.

He thought of the Very Hot Day. Nothing about that morning stood out, except the heat, and even that wasn't remarkable for a sweltering Alexandria summer. Then he had a single cuff on Tiny and the world spun off its axis. Nothing had been normal since. The time between his scuffle with Tiny and pressing his back against the wall beside the door to the conference room with pistol drawn could not have been more than five minutes. And the next thing he knew he was dazed and covered in blood in the back of an ambulance. Life as he knew it was over. Since then the only emotions he'd felt were fear, guilt, regret, foolishness, exhaustion, and most of all dread, heavy and thick around his heart like a weighted vest.

He'd been adrift in a black sea since that day, alone and just trying to keep his head above water. And this week, he'd glimpsed the shore. Hope.

He would be damned if he was going to give it up.

He threw the spikes aside, snatched his keys, and went out into the driving rain.

CHAPTER

63

CAL GOT DOUSED in the few bounds it took between his front
door and his parked car, and after a short, five-minute ride,
he got drenched again bolting from his car to the Alexandria History Museum at the Lyceum on South Washington Street. He
shook himself as dry as he could in the shelter of one of the Greek
Revival building's massive columns. There was a crack of light-
ning, so close—loud and overpowering—that it made him jump.
His heart raced and his vision began to telescope, but he clamped
his eyes shut and pressed the heels of his palms to his temples as if
trying to restrain his vision.

Ebb and flow . . . come and go . . .

He opened his eyes again and his vision cooperated, for now.
He looked at his watch—it was almost five o'clock—and he pushed
in the massive, wooden door, spilling into the tranquil lobby.

The heavy door closed behind him, and it was like entering
a vault. He could barely hear the rain beyond the thick walls of
the museum. He hadn't just sheltered from the storm, it was like
tumbling down the centuries. At the other end of the lobby, a sign
read "Building a Community, Alexandria Past to Present." Off to
the side stood a bronze bust of a colonial man Cal didn't know.
To his left sat twin lighthouse lanterns, glowing Fresnel lenses as
large as a man's torso. Directly across from the twin lenses was an

information desk, and two museum employees stood speechless and blinking at the soaked, panting man who had barged in at closing time.

"Sir," said an old lady behind the desk in an authoritative voice, "we're closing."

"It's okay, Eunice," said Jason Blye, a curious look on his face. "He's my friend."

"Still," she said, glaring at Cal.

Jason approached Cal, who stood there, disoriented.

"Hey, man," said Jason in a voice low enough so that his coworker couldn't hear. "Are you okay?"

"We have to talk."

"Can you give me a half hour? I'll meet you down the street at Southside? You look like you could use a drink—"

Cal shook his head. "Now."

Jason hesitated, but said, "Okay, let me take care of her. Wait in there." He nodded toward an exhibition room, then turned back for the old lady. "Eunice! It's all wet and slippery outside, why don't you let me walk you to your car . . ."

"He can't be in here after we close, Jason."

"It's okay, Eunice, he's a detective."

Eunice made a face, clearly finding the profession distasteful.

Jason helped the old woman from behind the desk and escorted her out of the lobby and down a corridor. Cal drifted through the nearest open doorway, slipping into the large exhibit room off of the lobby. Behind him, he heard Eunice's complaints getting louder, clearly meant for him.

"You better mop up after him. He looks like a drowned rat. He's going to destroy the parquet . . ."

"Yes, Eunice . . ."

Their voices faded as Jason shooed his coworker off.

Then the silence of the exhibition room was total, so much so Cal could hear his heart pounding in his ears. He closed his eyes and continued to work on his breathing. He needed to be clear-headed for this conversation. He'd had plenty of difficult conversations, like notifying the families of deceased Alexandrians. They were the worst part of the job, but there wasn't an element of personal betrayal. This was a new flavor to his usual dread. Jason had been his best friend these past months. Supportive, always willing to talk, always going out of his way to include him, but one thing had lasted longer and ran deeper than his loyalty to Jason: he had loved Heather since the moment she woke up and touched two fingers to his brow. Cal liked Jason, but on a subconscious level, he kept him at arm's length for that very reason. Now something had to give and it wasn't going to be Heather.

He took several deep breaths and tried to take in his surroundings. The exhibition room was dedicated to Alexandria's history as a seaport. A silkscreen of historic Old Town as it looked in the 1800s covered the entirety of one wall. Mannequins sporting colonial garb and sailors' uniforms stood at attention in glass display cases. Overhead hung a refurbished small boat.

An open boat.

Cal's vision was clear now, no eye twitching, and his heart had settled down, beating normally again. He smiled and thought of the sacred cheese of life. He thought of Heather. It was a sign.

Most people never look up. Heads buried in their phones, their navels. Anywhere but up. But Cal did, which is how he noticed the nautical tableau overhead in the first place. The fishing net, the brightly plumed waterfowl on invisible wires, and the open boat suspended by knotted ropes and pulleys.

His heartbeat spiked again.

He reached for the gun at his hip, but he wasn't wearing it. Then there was a sharp pain at his throat, high and clear like a falsetto. The pain jolted him like an electric current, and it drew his eyes down, away from the boat. He clapped his hand over his throat, but blood already cascaded over his fingers.

CHAPTER

64

*I*F NOT FOR *the blood, he might not have remembered.*
    Cal took a deep, silent breath, blew it out halfway, and wheeled into the threshold. He took two steps into the room, his pistol raised, and it was like passing into another dimension.

    Cal had seen gruesome things before, but those horrors were a direct result of their settings. Accidents, beatings, overdoses. In those instances, he had context. A warning or a few seconds to prepare. But there was no context for this—the juxtaposition of what he was seeing with where he was seeing it. Had he been on a battlefield, it would have been reasonable to expect the gory results of a battle. But a battlefield in a conference room shattered reason.

    Time slowed.

    The conference room had been the site of the most mundane thing in the world—a meeting. Two people were still seated. A woman's head and shoulders were slumped over the table, her arm unfurled, her head in the crook of her elbow. Blood and gray matter flowed over her arm, as if she had fallen asleep and pitched forward into a bowl of soup. A man sat across from her, still upright, his mouth hanging open, as if he'd been in the middle of a sneeze, but there was a crater in the back of his head and his lower jaw was in pieces on the table in front of him. Chairs were thrown back and to the side, their perforated owners entangled on the floor, as if frozen in some crimson bacchanal. If not for all the blood, in such volume and in such vivid hue, the conference room would have been as drab and indistinguishable as any other, in varying shades of beige, illuminated by fluorescent bulbs. Instead, the blood assaulted his senses. It pulsed in his eyes. It invaded his nostrils with its charnel smell and the sharp tang of gunpowder. In an instant, every one of his senses was filled to capacity, more than he could process.

He took it all in in the space of microseconds, finding the one person still on his feet—James Allan Milton—though he did not yet know the man's name. At this moment, he was just the minotaur in the center of the maze, the butcher in the slaughterhouse, dressed all in black, a rifle swinging from a harness, a pistol in a holster. Milton stood in the midst of the carnage, at the other end of the table, as if presiding over a nightmarish staff meeting. Cal understood then why Milton had returned here, to this dead end. It wasn't just the scene of the crime, it was the seat of his power. A bloody throne room. The climax of his dark victory.

Before Cal finished his two steps into the room and before he could mouth the words "Drop your weapon," Milton began to swing his rifle up and toward the doorway.

Cal fired twice.

Milton bucked backward, arms flailing. He slammed into the far wall. Cal's rounds had struck the man at center mass. Too late, Cal noticed the black bulletproof vest worn over Milton's black tactical clothing. Milton's arm was up again. This time, the barrel of the pistol was under his own chin.

He smiled at Cal.

"Game over," said James Allan Milton.

Cal shouted, "Don't!" He rushed forward, pistol pushed in front, but he stumbled. His gaze jerked from Milton to the floor. The toe of his boot lodged between the head and shoulder of a woman shot through the eye. Her body rocked and sent a ripple of blood rolling across the floor that washed up onto the shore of a dead man's face. There was the roar of a gunshot. The corner of the conference table rushed up at him. A hard blow, then stunned silence.

Cal came to on his hands and knees.

He was in the blood.

His hands and knees were slathered in it. He couldn't remember how he got there. He didn't know where here was.

He only knew there was a bad man.

He got to one knee and looked toward the other end of the room. There was Milton, seated against the far wall. His legs were spread like he didn't have a care in the world. He wore a horrible grin like it was all a big joke. Cal did not understand. All he knew was that he had to stop him.

Go go go.

Cal's hands joined in front of him. His pistol dripped blood. The room whirled around his front sight, but he kept it thrust forward, fighting the spins. His first shot went wide. It blasted the drywall two feet to the side of Milton's head. There was blood on the wall behind Milton, a trail of it clear up to the ceiling. It didn't matter. Cal fired again. Closer, but still off. He had to stop the shooter before he snapped out of it and returned fire.

Cal got to his feet, but the dizziness was overpowering. There was a ringing in his head now too. It sounded muffled, far off, and when he got a bead on it, it darted away, coming from somewhere else. Taunting him. Then the rings multiplied, like a swarm of buzzing mosquitos, coming from everywhere at once, and he realized they were coming from phones. Phones in jacket pockets, phones on the table, phones on the floor, submerged in the blood. When he realized they were phones—ringing and buzzing and rattling—it dawned on him they were loved ones checking in. Husbands, wives, children, mothers, and fathers trying to alert them there was a gunman in Old Town.

Please be safe.

Call me when you can.

Just let me know you're okay.

I love you.

Why aren't you picking up?

As disoriented as he was, his own blood boiled. He stumbled toward James Allan Milton, enraged, steadying himself on the slippery edge of the table, sloshing through the blood. Firing as he went. James Allan Milton, jerking now, red blooms opening up on him, yet still smiling. Still a threat. He had to get to him no matter what. To stop him.

Go go go.

The room was in a full whirl and picking up speed, but Cal fought the vertigo as hard as he could, until he was hunched over James Allan Milton. He had to neutralize him, now, before he killed again. He planted his feet in the swirling blood and steadied his right hand with his left, and fired. Again and again, until the gunshots obliterated the ringing phones and that maddening grin and Cal's slide locked to the rear. The spent gunpowder roared in his nostrils and the creeping darkness at the edges of his vision overwhelmed him finally and he fell forward.

65

C AL AWOKE IN a hospital room at night, his throat bandaged and itching beyond belief. He was woozy, his tongue thick. It didn't take him long to realize he was medicated, though he did not understand why. He reached to touch his throat but found he couldn't move his arms. They were lashed to the sides of the bed. He tried to look, but his head was immobilized too. His eyes grew wide then, panicked, and one by one, people came into his field of his vision. A doctor, two nurses, his crying mother.

"I don't belong here," Cal tried to say, but the words came out wrong and the doctor cut him off.

"Mr. Farrell, please don't speak," said the doctor, a tall, fit man. Or perhaps he was just tall because he was looming over Cal. It was hard to tell. Cal pulled at his restraints.

"Sir, please relax," he continued, speaking calmly but firmly, as if to a child. "They're for your own safety."

"Can't you prop him up?" he heard his mother say.

"Here, on the side," said one of the nurses.

He heard a whirring, and the back of his bed raised slowly, his field of vision rotating from the ceiling to the rest of the room. The nurses backed up slowly. They looked professional, but not kindly. In the corner of the room stood his partner, Sydnor, looking grave. Beside him stood Dr. Julia, whose eyes were red and puffy. Even Jason, who looked drawn and distraught, his shirt splattered with blood. Outside his room, framed in the small window, Massey passed by, then Porter, circling like sharks. The adrenaline of being restrained managed to thin the fog of whatever was in his system, but dark tendrils were slowly creeping back toward him. He had awakened from one nightmare into another.

Cal clenched his fists and pulled hard, his biceps flaring, trying to get free or at least maintain his lucidity, but the doctor put his hand on Cal's shoulder.

"I need you to relax. Otherwise, we're going to have to sedate you again. Do you understand?"

Cal nodded what little he could in the restraints.

"My name is Dr. Delahaut. Without speaking, do you know why you're here, Mr. Farrell?"

He didn't quite know how to answer. Considering his options were limited to a tiny nod or a shake and whatever incredulous expression he could convey with his eyes, he decided not to answer at all. The doctor continued in calm tones.

"You hurt yourself. You arrived in Mr. Blye's—"

"Jason," said Jason absently, his arms wrapped around himself and staring at the tile floor.

". . . Jason's place of work in quite a state, apparently. Jason left you unattended and returned to find you writhing on the floor . . ." The doctor hesitated then. "A self-inflicted laceration to your throat."

"I was only gone for a minute," said Jason. Cal's mother rubbed his back. "Jesus Christ . . ."

"You were lucky, Mr. Farrell," continued Dr. Delahaut.

Cal heard he had barely missed the windpipe, but the doctor was droning on, losing him, so he tried to read what he could in everyone's faces. His mother looked like she was in more pain than Cal. They had not spent much time together these past couple of years, and seeing her made him feel powerfully guilty. Perhaps if he hadn't drifted so far away from her and his sister, he could somehow have avoided this situation. Fortunately, whatever drugs were in his system wouldn't allow those thoughts, or any, to take root. When he drifted back to the conversation, Dr. Julia was talking in a low, hushed voice.

". . . in such a dramatic fashion, in an exhibition space no less, the self-loathing must have been more profound than I realized." She looked at her feet, ashamed.

"Don't beat yourself up, Doc," said Sydnor. "He had us all fooled."

Cal looked at Sydnor. He thought he could not feel lower until he saw his partner's eyes. You always knew where you stood with Sydnor, and his quiet recrimination reverberated like a judge's gavel. Cal closed his eyes then, let his arms go limp. With that decision, the fog rolled back in, thick and dark.

"I knew he was hurting . . . ," said Jason, sounding far off. "The weight of the world on his shoulders. But we had no idea . . ."

We.

Heather, thought Cal.

With great effort, he pried his eyes open again. The doctor was ushering everyone out. First his mother floated by, and she bent over to kiss his cheek. He was too numb to feel it.

Everyone filed out of the room, but Jason lingered. His friend blew out a shaky breath, holding back tears. Then he bent close to Cal's ear, as if he too might kiss his cheek, and whispered, "Don't worry, I'll take care of Heather . . ."

66

CAL REVOLTED.
Thrashing, kicking, wrenching his head against the restraints as if having a seizure, until he felt the warmth of his own blood seeping from his throat to his chest. He didn't care. He would break free and strangle Jason before anyone could stop him.

Instead, the doctor quickly ushered Jason out of the room. A nurse approached with a needle, and darkness fell.

When he awoke later, sunlight streamed through his windows. Midafternoon, he guessed. He followed the shaft of light and the long shadows to his hands, which were lashed to the rails. He knew then he needed to be smarter. Every bad reaction only proved everyone's point that he was unhinged, and very likely a killer.

His eyes continued their sweep across the room to his mother. Meredith Farrell was indomitable, in both her family and her profession, but she looked small and frail in a recliner in the corner of his hospital room. Guilt washed over him. He had done this to her.

Not me, he reminded himself. Blye.

He forced himself to breathe, to really breathe, using the exercises Julia had taught him.

Before she had turned on him.

Don't think about that. Forget guilt, forget anger. Forget every-thing but deep, cleansing breaths, in for six, out for eight. That's better.

The more he breathed, the calmer he grew, realizing it wasn't really Julia's fault at all. Or Massey's. Or even Porter's. They'd been manipulated, just as Cal had been. If he hadn't noticed it, how could they?

Jason wasn't just killing people. He wanted Cal to take the fall.

But why?

There was no way to know, lashed to a hospital bed in Inova Alexandria Hospital. It was the most maddening, helpless feeling in the world, and his muscles began to tense and his breathing grew shallower and quicker and—

Breathe, Cal. Think of something that brings you peace.

He thought of Heather. Their stolen time in his bungalow, lounging in bed, laughing and learning about each other and fall-ing in love.

Jason had Heather. He could be toying with her right now. She could be tied up like him. Or she could already be dead. Hanging from a tree or gutted like a fish somewhere, or the victim of some new horror, waiting to be discovered at any moment.

Ebb and flow . . . come and go . . .

Difficult as it was, he knew maintaining his composure was the only way he was going to get out of here. He began by lis-tening. Dr. Delahaut returned shortly after he awoke, with Dr. Julia in tow. His mother roused herself from her corner chair and smoothed her dress pants, going from sleep to lawyer mode in seconds. Dr. Delahaut explained they were waiting for the deep laceration at his throat to heal before transferring him to an inpa-tient behavioral health center in Mount Vernon for a seventy-two-hour hold. He apologized for the restraints, but explained it was either physical or chemical restraints if there was an acute danger to a patient or others.

Meredith began to protest, but Cal waved a lashed hand to draw their attention.

The doctor turned to him.

"We must be cognizant of your safety and ours, you understand . . ."

Cal was furious, but if he was going to get out of here, either legitimately or through escape, he needed to commence Operation Model Patient now. He nodded as much as the bandages would allow. He radiated kindness and innocence and compliance through his eyes. *I understand. No hard feelings. A fucking songbird will land on my finger if I extend it.*

He pinched his thumb and forefinger and pantomimed writing.

Dr. Delahaut smiled in return. "I'm sure this is a lot to process, Mr. Farrell, but I assure you, this is for the best. There will be plenty of time to discuss specifics and answer questions, but right now the most important thing for you to do is rest."

Cal smiled beatifically.

Of course, Doctor. My bad, you smug motherfucker.

Seventy-two hours was an eternity if Jason had Heather, but he guessed Massey and Porter were hounding a judge to get a search warrant for his bungalow in Del Ray—if they hadn't already, to make sure Cal went from the hospital straight to a jail cell. Any evidence they had was circumstantial, but slashing your own throat in a museum sure made it look like he was buckling under the strain of *something*. Massey was a local hero and could sweet-talk suspects into confessing anything, so how long would it take before a judge succumbed? Cal could only hope the Fourth Amendment could withstand the barrage until he figured a way out of here.

Dr. Delahaut examined Cal, then left him alone with his mother and Dr. Julia. Julia noted that his mother had been there all night.

"Go home," said Julia. "Get a shower. You heard the doctor. Nothing is going to happen for a while. I can stay."

Meredith gave Cal an uncertain look. Cal met her gaze and offered her a sympathetic smile.

Go on, Mom. It's okay. I promise not to slit my throat while you're gone.

"Just a fresh change of clothes." She squeezed Julia's hands. "Thank you, Dr. Mohr. I won't be long."

Julia watched her leave, her back to Cal. When she turned back to Cal, her face was a storm of emotions. During their sessions, she remained relatively breezy—her expressions ranged from furrowed eyebrows to bright smiles. He had never given her cause to look grief-stricken. Or angry.

"I'd like to think I'm a damn good judge of character, Cal. I've been burned before, sure, but if I'm wrong about you then I have no business doing this job. Please, please, please tell me you're not a fucking serial killer."

He gave her an impatient look. He held up his hands, cinched at the wrists. He pinched his thumb and forefinger and pantomimed writing.

She looked nervously around the room.

"I'm going to loosen one of your wrists. A little. Just so we can communicate. Don't make me regret it."

He cut his eyes toward the uniformed officer stationed outside the door and made an expression that roughly translated to *What do you think I'm going to do?*

She must have agreed their surroundings were sufficiently insurmountable and retrieved an iPad from her bag. She laid it in his lap, a Notes app already open.

He tapped furiously. *Not only did I not do this, I know who did.*

She shook her head. "Convince me, because right now you sound paranoid and grandiose."

This was taking forever, but he willed himself to go slow. To be understood.

I know I sound crazy. For a while I thought I might be but turns out just a patsy.

"How so?" she asked, curious now.

He gestured for the iPad and she handed it back.

I'm seeing a woman, the survivor from that day. I've been in love with her for months. Jason Blye's girlfriend.

"Your friend who was here last night?"

Cal began to nod, but it hurt, and the bandages around his neck made it difficult. He breathed through his nose like an irritated bull and typed furiously, ignoring syntax and the autocorrect that nipped at his words.

Yes! I'm guilty of being a shorty friend and terrible detective but that's it. Heather and I want to be together. Happy for the first time. Tired of being miserable. Went to museum to tell him man to man. HE cut my throat, not me. I hate myself, but not THAT much.

"You're saying *Jason*—"

The door to the hallway swung open, revealing a grinning Jason holding a bouquet of flowers.

"Speak his name and the devil appears," he said, strolling toward them.

67

"SERIOUSLY THOUGH, JASON *what?*" he asked.

Julia recovered without missing a beat.

"I was trying to get through to him that he has more reasons to live than not, including his friends." She put her hand on Jason's shoulder and gave it a squeeze, smiling brightly at Cal. She spoke louder, as if Cal was hard of hearing. "Especially this friend here, who saved your life."

"Well, he's my best friend," said Jason.

He blushed and looked at his shoes. As he did so, Cal hit the trashcan icon at the bottom corner of the iPad's screen. The note whooshed away silently.

Jason continued, looking at Cal now, "Heather and I both love him very much. She's in *knots* about this. I'd bring her by, but how much more trauma can one girl take, you know?"

Cal kept his eyes locked on Jason's and pursed his lips. Cal dared not look at Julia at that moment, and hoped she was studying Jason's face as much as his own.

She chimed in without hesitation.

"You see, Cal? You're not alone. I know things seem awful now, but this is where we rebuild. We're going to take it one day at a time . . ."

"Is he really necessary?" said Jason, jerking his thumb toward the door and the uniformed officer beyond.

Julia clasped her hands together, cutting Jason off. It made a sharp, clapping sound in the confines of the room. The officer's face appeared in the window briefly, and, satisfied it was nothing, turned his back to the door again. "We're not going to focus on anything *beyond this room* right now," she said, fixing Jason with a brief but intense glare, as if she were a mother steering a father around a touchy subject in front of their child. He wouldn't be surprised if she resorted to spelling out words in front of him. *We'll worry about the I-N-V-E-S-T-I-G-A-T-I-O-N later, dear . . .*

She's really selling it, thought Cal. She brought Jason into a little conspiracy of two to keep him unaware of what was really going on.

Whether Jason fell for it or not, he played along.

"Ah," he said, his eyebrows lifting. "Of course. I really should go anyway. I just wanted to see where things stood. Don't want to get in the way."

"Thank you," said Julia, offering her warmest smile.

"Doctor, may I give you my number? If there's anything you need, please don't hesitate to reach out."

"Of course."

Cal watched intently as they huddled close to one another, exchanging numbers and programming them into their phones. He felt a chill run the length of his body and fought the urge to rebel against the restraints again.

They parted finally and Jason moved to the door. Before leaving, he turned around and looked at Cal.

"I'm behind you every step of the way." Jason gave him a thumbs up. His face drained of warmth, and his eyes cut to Julia, who was facing Cal at that moment. The implication was clear.

Play along or she's next.

Cal stared at him, but with his loose hand, returned the gesture.

"It's always been me and you, pal," said Jason. "I'm with you to the bitter end."

Then he was gone.

Julia stared at Cal, her wide smile fixed in place until the door closed behind her. She walked over to the door, glanced through the window, then turned back toward Cal. Her smile vanished.

"Fucking hell," she said. She began pacing in the middle of the room, muttering more obscenities. Cal tried to wave his hands to get her attention, but strapped as they were to the bed, it was futile. She was shaking her hands in front of her as if air-drying them. Suddenly, she stopped in her tracks and fixed her gaze upon him. It was so intense he thought he could feel twin holes boring into his chest.

"It's really him, isn't it? He's a fucking psychopath."

Cal had already typed a message.

I remember the very hot day now. All of it. You know me better than anyone. I may be refreshingly fucked up, but I'm no killer.

She looked at him. A mixture of hope and sadness.

All that matters now is Heather. Call her. Send Sydnor to pick her up. Don't care if I rot in here, but she's in danger. PLEASE.

He tapped out Heather's number.

Julia kept the phone to her ear and Cal heard the muffled rings, heard her voice mail. His stomach fell. Julia stared at him, fear creeping into her eyes.

"What are we going to do?"

Cal was already typing.

CHAPTER

68

THEY SETTLED ON a plan. After sunset, a klaxon blared. Blue lights strobed in the overhead.

Cal held Julia close, by the elbow, mostly to keep himself steady. They were down to the first floor now. He kept his head down with his hand up by his bandaged throat as nurses bustled past.

Earlier, Julia had gone to the nearest department store and returned with fresh clothes, a hoodie, and a cheap pair of running shoes. Then she released Cal from the restraints holding him to the bed, and excused herself.

Cal was considering how he was going to get past the guard stationed at his door when all hell broke loose. Julia had pulled a fire alarm. After a minute, she burst back into this room and said, "What the hell are you waiting for?"

They darted to the nearest stairwell unseen among doctors and nurses wheeling patients out of their rooms. Now they were on the first floor, steps from freedom, when they froze in their tracks.

"Farrell!"

Cal whirled to find Detective Stacy Porter, weapon drawn. He kept his hold on Julia, pretending to point an invisible gun at her back.

"Don't!" cried Julia. "Please don't let him hurt me . . ."

Cal was amazed at her improvisation skills.

"Hands up," said Porter. "And step away from the doctor." It was a command, but Cal also detected a note of rueful glee. Stacy Porter didn't need any more excuses to shoot him dead. She had never liked him. As a suspected murderer, she liked him even less. And now he was trying to escape with a hostage.

APD would pin a medal on her. Like they had pinned one on him once upon a time.

She took a step closer.

Cal took a step closer as she did, which Porter didn't expect. Suddenly, the distance between them was halved. She blinked. He shoved Julia into the detective hard, something else Porter didn't expect.

Porter moved her gun to the side as Julia collided with her. Cal followed close behind, practically riding on top of Julia. As the psychologist fell to the floor, Cal caught Porter's gun hand as it whirled back to the front. There was no time for regrets. It was him or her. And if it was her, Heather died. He jerked Porter close, pulling her off balance. He bent his other arm and drove two savage strikes of his elbow to the side of her head. Her knees buckled. Her gun fell to the floor and clattered away.

He caught her as she went down and laid her gently on the floor.

Then he held his hand out to help Julia up.

She scuttled away from him slowly, a look of shock on her face. Maybe horror. Certainly reevaluating her decision. She picked up the gun from the floor. She didn't point it at Cal, but she didn't hand it over either. A bridge too far.

"Sorry," he mouthed and ran into the night.

CHAPTER

69

THEY WOULD BE looking for him on the surface streets and Metro stops. But Cal sprinted for Fort Ward Park. The park covered over forty acres and featured a restored Civil War building turned museum, earthworks, and sprawling grounds used for reenactments, picnics, and play.

And enough woods to lose himself in.

The park was closed and deserted. He skirted the bowl of open green space, charged up its grass hill perimeter, and headed for the tree line. Once in its shadow, he caught his breath and his bearings. The park began a mile north of the hospital and stretched nearly all the way to his destination, Fairlington, the neighborhood at the northern end of Alexandria.

He heard faraway sirens. He picked up the pace again.

He touched his bandage. His pain medication had worn off and his throat throbbed. It was superficial enough that Jason had missed the windpipe but deep enough that the doctor told him not to speak. The increasing itching of his stitches was driving him mad. He concentrated instead on his forward progress. The grass was wet and the fallen leaves were slick. The trees thrashed in the blustery night air. Clouds raced overhead, allowing temporary glimpses of a quarter moon. He was only a couple of miles from his destination, but sticking to the woods and the shadows added distance to his route.

He couldn't get there fast enough, but he rejoiced at the sensation of his body free and at speed. He had been lashed to a bed for . . . he didn't quite know how long. Nor did he know how long Heather had been at Jason's mercy, but at least he was unshackled again.

In more ways than one.

The run helped him burn off the remaining drugs in his system and sort his jumbled thoughts. He was free to think. And remember in full.

Since waking up in that ambulance, the Very Hot Day was a story someone else had told him, not something he had experienced firsthand. A memory, once removed. Now he could play it back in his head in vivid, garish detail, like a lost episode of television, restored and recolored.

Wheeling into the ATMA conference room. The ripple of blood set in motion by his boot. Milton giggling. Cal going down and coming back up to discover Milton with half his head missing. Not believing it. Yet still hearing that maddening giggle. Desperate to silence it, to stop him . . .

How much was disorientation? How much was rage? Terror?

Even knowing what happened, even feeling it, Cal supposed he would never really know the answer to those questions. All he knew for certain was that he had emptied his pistol into an already dead man. Everything else was beside the point.

The city was in shock. It was awful and it was only going to get worse once the full extent of Milton's rampage was known. Thoughts and prayers weren't going to cut it. There was no upside. Just inexplicable loss and bottomless grief. No silver linings. So the City of Alexandria created one by responding with as much of the truth as it dared.

An officer of the Alexandria Police Department neutralized the shooter. An officer engaged James Allan Milton and shot him.

Technically, it was all true. Did the media, and the public, really need to know the single tiny, semantic detail that Cal's rounds were postmortem?

Did the department need a hit to its own credibility on top of this tragedy? Did the city really need to shake the gossamer faith its people still had in its institutions?

Not willing to risk it, they made an unwitting hero out of Cal while he was unconscious in the back of the ambulance. In the aftermath, they made him a detective, then quickly hustled him offstage to Vice and Narcotics, with Sydnor as babysitter. Though Vice and Narcotics still displayed a powerful array of the damage people can do to themselves and others, it was more subtle than Violent Crimes, considering. And they ordered him to meet with Dr. Julia, who would let the department know if the wheels started to come off.

The department and the city moved on.

Except word had clearly gotten around. Half the force resented his quick promotion, believing it undeserved. Others were spooked by him. And a handful—Porter, Adelphia—flat-out hated him.

Killer Callum.

Now, the debate would rage whether it was that terrible day that did it, or had it always been there inside him, waiting to come out?

Bent and broken from the trauma of that Very Hot Day, hero cop Cal Farrell snapped.

It was an irresistible story, even if it was bullshit.

Cal heard a thrumming nearby. He dove off the trail and crouched behind a tree.

A Parks and Recreation vehicle roved the grounds. It sounded like an all-terrain vehicle. The park wasn't as anonymous as he thought. The RCPA didn't normally patrol at this hour. They were looking for him.

The ATV idled for a moment, then a spotlight punched a hole in the night. The light swept up the grass hill and the tree line. It passed back and forth, lighting up his tree. Cal pulled his limbs in tight and held his breath.

Finally, the four-wheeler lumbered on.

Cal stayed low until its rumbling faded, then he resumed his jog north.

Cal realized the chances of his surviving the night were slim. He was a murder suspect, he had just viciously assaulted a detective, and was now the subject of a massive manhunt by his own department. Those who didn't trust him would have no problem believing his trauma had turned him into a bloodthirsty killer. It didn't matter that wasn't how trauma worked—it was a tidy story, all wrapped up with a bow. There weren't enough Dr. Julias in the world to convince the cops hunting him otherwise.

His career was over, his life likely soon to follow.

Yet he felt liberated.

For the first time since last summer, he had his memories back. He saw the facts with clear eyes. He felt whole. But there was something more.

He had figured it out.

In the Lyceum, before the blade came, he had looked up. He saw the knots and the pulleys, and he knew. It was like the warm, tickling sensation he felt after swimming as a child, when the water clogging his ear canal suddenly drained. Or the satisfying vibration of a lock's tumblers fitting perfectly against a key before turning.

He had reached for his Glock.

And in that moment, Blye—brilliant, evil Blye—knew it too. And cut his throat for it.

That was the irony. The first time Cal truly felt like a detective it nearly killed him. And now he was on the run.

But none of that mattered.

Only Heather mattered. And stopping Blye before his eager coworkers shot him or Blye finished the job himself.

Cal ran faster.

He told himself Heather was still alive. She had to be. The running helped to keep his mounting hysteria in check, helped to organize his thoughts. Blye was smart. Smarter than anyone, especially Cal, had given him credit for. Blye had been at work when Cal went to confront him, to tell him about Heather. And Cal had been with Heather all day before Blye cut his throat.

Which meant Blye would have had to kill her afterward, which he wouldn't have done. Not yet anyway. Not with Cal, the perfect patsy, strapped to a hospital bed. Any murders committed while he was secured in the hospital would go toward clearing Cal and implicating Blye.

Then again, now that Cal was free, all bets were off.

He ran flat out.

CHAPTER

70

CAL EMERGED FROM the woods on the Alexandria side of Fairlington into a quiet, tree-lined neighborhood of condos and townhouses. As he crossed an overpass that bisected I-395, leaving Alexandria for Arlington, he wondered if the Alexandria PD were still figuring out how to message that last year's hero was this year's psycho killer, or had they already blasted his face all over television and social media? He hoped for the former. Maybe APD wouldn't throw their hero under the bus as quickly as they had manufactured him.

Halfway across the overpass, an endless stream of white headlights and red taillights whooshed below him. He felt vulnerable, too out in the open. He may as well have been on a high wire.

He picked up the pace, keeping his head down and concealing his bandage from the headlights of passing motorists or the prying eyes of late-night dog walkers.

He finally arrived at Blye's neighborhood. His street consisted of three-story buildings, broken down into condo units. Each first-floor unit had its own small, fenced-in yard that backed up onto a larger, common green.

Cal bolted toward the deep shadows of a copse of trees. From here, he could see Blye's fence. Just over the fence, he could see Blye's small deck and the windows of his den. No lights were on.

Cal didn't know the exact time. It was late, but not that late. Blye had always been a night owl. The reasons for which now gave Cal a chill.

Cal swept along the lawn, keeping low until he was at Blye's fence. He tested its gate quietly. Locked. He looked around again, then backed a few steps. With a running start, he leaped, grabbed the top of the six-foot-tall wooden fence, and pulled his chest and one leg over. He pulled his other leg over and dropped into the yard in a crouch. He moved quickly and ducked behind the cover of a wrought-iron table and waited.

How many times had Cal had drinks at that very table? Beers after work with Heather and Blye? Saturday night parties? Sunday afternoon games?

He shook his head hard to clear those memories and instantly regretted it. Pain flared at his throat and he cupped his bandage there. Still dry.

No lights came on in Blye's or any other unit. Satisfied that the commotion getting into the yard had been minimal, he advanced to the back deck. He expected the door to be locked but tested the knob just the same. To his amazement, it wasn't.

Maybe Blye wasn't as smart as he thought.

No, thought Cal, he is. *Deadly smart.*

But even deadly smart people can get overconfident. And with luck, Blye still thought Cal Farrell was lashed to a bed at Inova Alexandria Hospital, slowly losing his mind. He gripped the knob, then pushed the door open quickly. Less chance of creaking hinges. With one fluid motion, he was inside Blye's home. He knew the layout well and didn't need lights.

Cal realized then that he was unarmed. If Blye was asleep, he would wake him with a hail of punches to the face. Jason, his best friend, always there for him, always willing to talk, always pulling him out of his shell when he didn't even know he needed it. And all of it a lie. He passed the kitchen and the island. The last time he was standing here was with Heather and Carly. Carly was gorgeous and charming, but he mostly remembered Heather's shark dress from that night and holding her in his arms.

By that time, Cal calculated, Blye had already slashed Daisy Wilcox and hoisted Tiny seventy feet in the air.

Cal pulled a knife from the butcher's block.

He held his breath outside Blye's bedroom door. It was slightly ajar. He pressed the blade against his thigh. He peered in quickly, then jerked his head back. The room was empty, the bed made.

Before making his escape at the hospital, Cal reached inside his pocket for the personal effects Julia had snagged from his clothes. He pulled a small penlight from his pants pocket and shone it around the room. He wasn't sure what he was hoping to find, but he moved toward the dresser. He opened each drawer and carefully moved his hand among the contents. Sweaters, gym gear, T-shirts, underwear. The top drawer held more miscellany. There was a tin and he opened the top. There were penknives, coins from around the world, contact lens cases, and other random trinkets. He closed the lid and was about to shut the drawer when he thought twice.

He opened the tin again and removed one of the lens cases.

He unscrewed one side and shone his light inside. Floating in a small pool of saline solution was a glowing orange lens. He shone his light away and the glowing ceased. When he swept his thin beam over it again, it glowed again as if lit from within.

Retro-reflective lenses.

Daisy.

Cal was weighing what to do next when the room flooded with light. He whirled around to see the barrel of a gun pointed at his face.

71

"LET ME GUESS, it's not what it looks like?"

Detective Adam Massey stood in the doorway, his pistol pointed at Cal's center mass. He still spoke in the same charming manner, but there was a hardness in his eyes and his smile was devoid of mirth.

"Because it sure looks to me like you're skulking around your best friend's condo in the dark with a big-ass knife. Hours after you knocked out my partner. She says fuck you, by the way. Now toss the knife—gently—on the bed."

Cal dropped the knife and held up his hands. Massey walked backward and motioned Cal to follow, out of the bedroom and into the living room. Cal tried to talk, to explain himself, but it hurt and it came out as a warble.

"Don't bother," said Massey and laughed. "You fucking psycho."

He motioned Cal toward the kitchen side of the island, with no escape. Massey stationed himself on the living room side, keeping the big island between them.

Cal looked around.

"Don't even think about it, kid. There's no way out."

Cal shook his head, his jaw clenched. He brought his hands together slowly.

"Ah, ah," warned Massey. "A lot of people would prefer I shoot you dead—Porter being at the top of that list—but where's the fun in that? Still, if you make me, I'll do it. Without a scintilla of hesitation or a nanosecond of lost sleep."

Cal mimed writing with a pen on paper.

Massey's eyes narrowed.

Come on, said Cal's expression.

Massey glanced around and saw a desk behind him. He tossed Cal a pen and a sheet of paper. Cal scribbled feverishly.

"This just keeps getting better and better . . ."

Cal glanced up from his paper, annoyed but curious.

"I mean, Sydnor and I making our big collar? That put me on the map, but *this?*" Massey whistled. "Nabbing Alexandria's very own serial killer, who just happens to be Alexandria's white knight? Are you fucking kidding me? I'll be able to write my own ticket. And by ticket, I mean memoir. We're talking book tour, speaking circuit, consultant, cable news talking head. Holy shit, man, I should almost thank you . . ."

Cal finished and spun the sheet around.

Blye is the killer. Remember Daisy? The glowing eyes? I just found the contact lenses in Blye's dresser.

"That I'm sure you planted. Nice try."

Cal scribbled again.

PLEASE SEND A UNIT TO HEATHER HAYES' APART-MENT. She is in DANGER. She's the survivor from Milton and she's Blye's girlfriend. We're having an affair. I went to the Lyceum to come clean. There's a boat there hanging from the ceiling with the same knots used on Tiny. I saw it and Blye cut my throat. LOCK ME UP FINE JUST GET HEATHER! PLEASE!!!

Massey read the note, then scrutinized him.

"By the way, screwing your best friend's girl? Surveillance picked up on that. You really are a creep."

Best friend is serial killer, so guilt = 0. You're supposed to be some great detective, so THINK. Why would I go to a public place to slice my own throat? Even if it was a cry for help, as soon as I get that help, I escape? Use your head and GET HEATHER.

Massey stared at him, his lips pursed, deep in thought. It would have been so much easier if Cal could actually talk his way out of it, but he had laid out the best case for his innocence. There was still one more thing to try. He grabbed the paper again and scribbled one more line.

You'll still be the fucking hero. Even bigger than before. But not if she dies. Then you're nothing.

Cal slid the paper around for Massey to read, but each time he didn't slide it quite as far. Massey leaned over the island to read it. Cal gripped the pen in his hand.

A phone rang.

Cal and Massey looked at each other. Cal eased his grip on the pen slightly.

Massey motioned to Cal to back up. The detective moved toward the kitchen counter. He reached into the shadows beside the coffee maker and retrieved a cheap, plastic phone. He set it on the island. They stared at it for a moment.

Cal pointed at the burner. He raised his eyebrows as if to say *Can I?*

Massey nodded, apparently willing to let it play out a little longer while he made up his mind.

Cal put his finger to his lips, motioning Massey to be silent, then put the call on speakerphone. He set the phone on the island and watched it, not sure what he wanted to happen. He cut a quick glance at Massey, who was staring at the phone, leaning over the island just slightly.

He kept his hand down by his thigh, wrapped around the pen. There may not be a better chance, he thought.

"Cat got your tongue?" asked Blye.

Massey looked at Cal then, and the detective looked considerably less confident.

"So, since you're answering my phone, it's safe to say you're snooping around my place. Maybe I should call the cops?"

Blye laughed then. He sounded almost manic, like when he hosted his parties and wanted everyone to have a good time.

Just as quickly, the laughter stopped.

"Heather, say hi . . ."

There was silence.

"Oh, looks like the cat got her tongue too."

72

MASSEY WENT WIDE-EYED. Cal gripped the edge of the island and clenched his teeth to stifle a scream that had been building for days.

Blye cracked up again.

"I'm just fucking with you, Cal. She's fine. For now."

Cal's head swam with relief. He thought his knees might give. He swallowed hard. It hurt and it brought him back around. Massey was staring at him with something like contrition in his eyes. It only made Cal angrier, so he stared at the phone.

"I think it's time the three of us had a chat. I'm going to text you an address. I really can't emphasize enough when I say just the three of us. I can't imagine you have any friends left at this point, but if I get the sense you're not alone—if so much as a cloud passes over the moon and casts a shadow—all of the suffering our poor girl has endured will be but an *aperitif.*"

Massey remained silent.

"Jesus," said Blye, starting to chuckle. "Clap or something so I know you understand . . ."

Cal brought his hands together. In the stillness of the kitchen, the report sounded like a gunshot.

"You have one hour. If you're a minute late, I start cutting."

The line went dead. Once he was sure they were disconnected, Massey muttered, "Shit, Farrell . . ." He holstered his gun. "It would've been so much fucking easier if it was you."

Massey only looked sheepish for a second. He looked at his watch and his expression became determined.

"Alright, we have one advantage. He thinks you're alone, so he won't see us coming."

Cal wrote in all caps.

JUST ME AND YOU. NO OTHERS.

"Couldn't agree more, Farrell. The cavalry would just spook him and get your girl killed." Massey broke into a wicked grin. "Besides, this is my fucking collar. Let's roll."

Cal followed Massey out the back door. They exited Blye's yard and crossed the shaded common green.

"Get the address yet?" asked Massey.

Cal looked at the phone. He was gripping the burner so tightly he forced himself to relax his hand for fear of crushing it.

Nothing yet.

When he looked up, a tree in the corner of the yard seemed to unfurl another branch. By instinct, Cal tried to draw a weapon but he still didn't have one. There were two snaps of suppressed fire.

Massey's head snapped back. He crumpled to the ground.

Cal bounded for him, but Blye stepped from behind the tree, his arm now raised at Cal.

"Be smarter than Detective Massey."

Blye leveled a Glock at Cal's face next, its silencer extending the profile of the weapon. The barrel looked endless. Cal stopped, his chest heaving. He looked at the fallen detective from the corner of his eye. The contours of Massey's face were all wrong. The back of his head was missing. At night, in the shadow of the tree, it was hard to see more detail than that. Cal supposed that was what passed for luck.

With Massey dead, there was no backup. No cavalry. No plan. Heather's best chance of survival was snuffed out before Massey could even get his car keys out of his pocket.

Cal glared at Blye, fighting to control his breathing. He balled his fists at his sides, waiting for an opening.

"I get it, Cal, you're angry," said Blye. "I'll explain everything, but right at the top? If you try to take me out, Heather dies. Alone in the dark. I don't know what'll run out first—food, air, or sanity—but she'll die screaming herself hoarse. And really, hasn't she been through enough?"

73

"KEEP IN MIND," said Blye, "even if you were faster than a speeding bullet and managed to overpower me, who are your 'friends' in the Alexandria PD going believe? Me? Or the psycho in police-mandated therapy? The weirdo who inserted himself into grisly homicide investigations? The creep who visited a hooker in the middle of the night when absolutely no one asked him to . . ."

Jesus, thought Cal. How long had Blye been following him? Hell, he didn't even need to follow Cal. How much had he spilled voluntarily to Blye over beers for months?

"Best part? You escaped from the hospital and came straight here. To the boyfriend of the girl you're fucking. Your prints are now all over my place. For fuck's sake, I watched you grab a *butcher knife* through the window." Blye chuckled. "I was laughing so hard I almost fell out of the tree . . ."

Blye tossed his car keys at Cal.

"You're driving. No wrong turns, no waving down other drivers, no driving us to a police station or into a telephone pole. Don't even change lanes without signaling. I know it's counterintuitive, but any knight in shining armor bullshit will absolutely result in game over for your little crush. Nod if you understand."

Cal studied him. After a moment, he nodded.

He passed Blye on his right, moving deeper into shadow and keeping his right side obscured. As he did, Cal slipped the phone into his pocket.

"Oh, and I'll take that phone," said Blye.

Cal fished the burner out of his pocket and tossed it at Blye's chest.

Blye caught it, grinning in the moonlight. "Nice try. Now it's time for a road trip. Don't want to keep our girl waiting."

Cal looked once more at Massey's body, its growing dark halo mixing with the shadows. Blye stepped forward and pointed the gun at Cal's face.

"Let's go," said Blye. "We're out in the open."

They left the common green and found Blye's SUV on the street. Blye climbed into the passenger side. Cal climbed into the driver's side and found Blye already buckled and pointing the weapon low at him. He looked at the pistol, then glanced over his shoulder into the back seat. The seats were folded down, connecting the back seat area to the load space of the trunk. There was a blue tarp spread out in back.

"I really learned my lesson after that homeless guy. He smelled like piss and vinegar, let me tell you. Could've knocked a buzzard off a shit wagon. You have no idea how many times I had to clean it."

Blye led them out of Fairlington and onto I-395 north, toward DC. Just when Cal thought they were heading into the District, Blye instructed him to take the last exit before the Fourteenth Street Bridge. The ramp peeled away and deposited them onto the George Washington Parkway, heading south toward Alexandria.

"I can't believe we're finally here," said Jason.

The killer was practically vibrating in his seat.

"I've been so far ahead of you, it's hilarious. Like that night you were in the tunnel. I was literally watching the cops watch you. But I'll give you *some* credit. You figured it out, didn't you?"

Cal looked over at Blye, unable to hide his contempt.

Blye nudged Cal like they were still pals. "Yeah, you did. I saw you reach for your gun. You decided to become a detective at, like, the last possible second." He drew a finger across his throat and made a whistling sound.

An airliner was coming in for a landing to their left at Washington National Airport, the Potomac River a dark sliver beyond it. To the right, the buildings of Arlington's Crystal City neighborhood stood in the distance above the tree line. Everyone and everything felt remote, out of reach. The two of them and the wide, tarp-covered berth behind them was the whole world.

"You know," continued Blye, "I could have led you to another exhibition room, but I led you to *that* one. I honestly don't know why. Maybe I did it on purpose, but it's been like walking around with a constant hard-on, you know? Lucky for Carly, I guess. Had her all lined up next to gild your guilty lily, but honestly, it's a relief to finally get to this stage."

Blye went silent for a moment, lost in thought, then burst out laughing. "God damn but you were flopping around! Like I'd just landed a grouper or something. Wildest part? Your eyes were open, but you didn't even see me." Blye waved a hand past his own face. "You were *gone*. I literally had to pry your hand off your throat to get your prints on the knife." He added air quotes. "'As I valiantly pried the knife away from you,' I mean. At great personal risk to myself, I might add."

The dark highway led into the northern reaches of Alexandria. Blye instructed Cal to get off the parkway. Cal turned left, heading toward the river in Old Town North. Cal realized that, after everything he had been through today, and how far he had come, he was only a mile from his home. He passed this street along his running route every morning.

He never felt farther away from his life and everything in it than that moment.

"Pull over," said Blye. "The rest of the way is on foot."

74

THEY WALKED NORTH along the trail, Cal in front, Blye a few steps behind with the gun trained on him. Blye need not have bothered. Cal wasn't going to run. And in the dead of night, with a thick band of wilderness to their left and a bluff that dropped to the dark Potomac below to their right, there was no one to signal. Even if he could, he wouldn't because it would doom Heather.

Cal's throat itched. His whole body itched. He felt like he could burst out of his skin. It was even worse than being bound and helpless in a hospital bed. Worse than sliding around a blood-soaked floor at the museum, a fishing boat suspended above him by familiar knots. Worse even than his Very Hot Day, now Very Clear. Nothing was worse than this. Heather alone, somewhere ahead of him, terrified. Maybe in pain.

He realized he was taking the word of a psychopath that she wasn't already dead.

"Stop," said Blye suddenly. He had gone quiet on the trail, but now he ordered Cal to turn around. He pointed at a tree with his gun.

Cal didn't recognize it until he saw Blye's smile in the moonlight. He had approached the tree in January from the north.

He jerked his head upward, feeling his stitches pop. He craned his neck to peer wildly into the canopy, but it was too dark to see.

"She's not up there," laughed Blye. "Give me some credit . . ."

Cal lunged. It was the thought of Heather in the tree, the laughter, the maddening itching, the pain at this throat. It was all too much. Before he could stop himself, Cal landed a savage blow to Blye's face. The killer sprawled in the grass beneath the tree.

Cal advanced on him, but Blye recovered quickly, coming up with the gun. He pointed it at Cal's chest.

Blye spit. "You get *one*," he said.

Cal didn't care about the gun, but he stopped anyway. Unleashing on Blye felt good, but it was counterproductive. Losing his temper was stupid and selfish. It would not help Heather.

Ebb and flow . . . come and go . . .

"Just taking a stroll down memory lane," said Blye.

He lowered the gun and walked past Cal. He leaned against the tree as nonchalantly as if he were a jogger taking a breather on the trail. He rapped on the trunk with his knuckles. "I don't think you appreciate yet just how much work I've put into all this. First, there was finding the guy. It's not like he kept a schedule. Then there was getting him into the car. That part wasn't so tough really, but getting him out after I dosed him? Then scaling that tree? Hell, I'm not even wild about heights. I had to buy all the gear, take test climbs, all for the chance of you running past. I mean, the fucking logistics involved . . ."

Blye massaged his jaw where Cal had punched him. When he spoke again, his voice was hard and cold. "By the way, those crampons are under your bed right now."

Blye rubbed his thumb and forefinger together and bobbed his hand as if dropping invisible seeds.

"There's a cute little bangle bracelet Hayley was wearing, too. A ring from Honey, a necklace from Lorna. Cheap things, but that's not the point, is it? All sprinkled about . . ."

He pushed himself off the tree trunk and approached Cal, looking up into his eyes. "I'm so far ahead of you it's not even funny. Every time I've ever seen you, I lapped you and you had no fucking clue."

Cal balled his fists. Blye was showing off. Everything out of the man's mouth was about proving how much smarter he was than Cal. He wasn't going to kill him or Heather . . . yet. Cal wagered Blye wouldn't hurt them, really hurt them, until he had the opportunity to gloat first. To peacock in front of both of them. He relaxed his hands.

Blye pointed at the bandage at Cal's neck.

"Careful. You're bleeding."

He turned his back on Cal and walked farther down the trial.

"Onward . . ."

75

THE MASSIVE SILHOUETTE of the dark, five-stacked structure loomed in the distance. Cal had run past the old coal-fired power plant along the river hundreds of times. Now he shuddered when he saw it.

Last December, Blye, in an effort to cheer up Heather, had taken them all on a Potomac River boat cruise. The cruise picked up in Old Town and dropped off in Georgetown, where they ate a large seafood lunch. Cal felt out of place, but Jason had convinced him to come. When Cal wavered, Jason laid a small guilt trip on him. "Come on. It's her first outing. She loves the water and I think it might help. And I'm going to need another strong back getting the chair on and off the boat."

Cal had never been able to say no whenever Heather was concerned, and Blye knew it.

He'd been manipulating Cal that long.

From the land, the shuttered power plant stood like a battlement over the treetops, and from the river, it was a stark landmark in Old Town North.

"Jesus," said Jason, shivering beside him on the deck of the boat. "Creepy much?"

"Yeah," said Cal, but he was stealing a glance at Heather, surrounded by her girlfriends. It was a mild day for December, but on the water, at speed, the wind was cutting. Heather didn't care. She insisted on staying on deck, so everyone else did as well. The wind was in her hair and she wore a bright smile, looking like what Cal imagined was her old self.

"Looks like a fucking super-villain's lair," laughed Jason. "Come on, let's have a drink . . ."

Now, as Cal tried to orient himself, he remembered what he knew about the plant. It provided power for generations, but it had been the number one polluter in the area, covering nearby homes and businesses in black coal dust. The local government's crusade to get the plant shut down was finally successful in 2012, but the company had a prepaid lease on the property. There had been many plans for what to do with the land that went nowhere. The last he read, it was going to be subdivided, turned into a mixed-use development with retail shops and green space. Just as soon as the parties involved could all agree to dismantle the monstrous facility and decontaminate the land and groundwater.

For now, it remained a neglected husk, blotting out the night sky as they approached.

Blye passed several DANGER and KEEP OUT signs along the chain-link fence until he found the spot he was looking for. He grabbed a section and it unfurled without protest. He gestured at the fresh gap. "After you."

Cal ducked inside.

Blye followed, then pulled the fence taut again and hung it back in place. "This is a private party." Then he took up the lead again. He walked straight toward the ramshackle structure until they were completely eclipsed by it, lost in its shadow, the moon hidden.

They walked along the structure's façade until they came to a heavy door. Blye bent to a combination lock and flicked his wrist back and forth with quick, practiced ease.

How many times had he been here? How many times had he used it?

There was a click, then Blye jerked the lock down and swung the door open on oiled hinges. By the condition of the rest of the building, the door should have sounded like hundreds of nails on a chalkboard at once, but it was silent. Of course, Blye had prepared for that too.

The black maw of the door seemed like a portal to another world altogether. Blye stepped inside and was swallowed whole.

Cal's pulse quickened and his vision tilted for a moment.

It was most certainly a trap. Blye could have shot him at any time since his condo, but he chose not to. Maybe he was just waiting for a dark, out of the way spot to do it, like this. A place to really take his time, like with Honey. Maybe he had learned his lesson with Tiny and just didn't want to haul a body around, increasing his chances of exposure.

Or maybe it was just fun and games to Blye, making Cal follow him into the dark. Like his partner said upon seeing the body of Tiny hanging so high in the tree.

One hell of a flex.

These thoughts were quiet, calling from the back of his mind. Cal's heart pounded in his chest and he struggled to keep his breathing even. It was impossible to tell, staring at the impenetrable black of the open doorway, if his vision was telescoping or not. He was back at the threshold of the conference room on that Very Hot Day, the sweat cooling on his neck in the air conditioning, his vest cinched too tight and constricting his chest. For so long, everything beyond the threshold had been black and unfathomable. He knew now, in excruciating detail, what lay beyond dark doors. And its cost.

None of that mattered. Heather was in there somewhere. Cal quietly palmed the combination lock and tossed it into the weeds. Then he stepped inside.

He looked around, straining his eyes in the gloom, careful this time to turn his shoulders instead of his head. It was oppressively hot in the space. The building seemed to collect and compress the humid air. His stitches ached and itched like mad and blood still seeped through. He ignored it, trying to suss out the contours of the room.

There was an oiled whir behind him. Cal whirled, but it was just the sound of the door swinging home. The chatty Blye said nothing now. The dark settled about them for several moments.

His eyes had already adjusted to the low light of the trail and he felt them reaching out further now—his irises widening, his pupils dilating, drinking in as much light as he could. Just like his days aboard ship with its quiet night watches. Fumbling about in the dark for several minutes before his eyes adjusted. Cal had always liked standing lookout on the night watch. Scanning the darkness ahead of him as the ship sliced through the night sea, hundreds of men and women sleeping soundly belowdecks as he stood watch over them. They trusted the watch with their lives, counting on it to guide them safely through the night and closer to shore. It was a sacred charge. An honor. It was how he had felt about being a police officer, before the Very Hot Day had turned everything on its head.

His eyes were adjusted now. He saw clearly for the first time in a long time.

Cal took the opportunity to slide his hand into his front pocket and found what he was looking for. Palmed it. Put it to his mouth as if kissing a rosary.

"Let there be light," said Blye. There was a click, then a bright beam in Cal's eyes. It was searing. Without thinking, he jerked his head and felt another stitch pop. More blood.

He was fully blind now.

Blye rushed at him.

CHAPTER

76

BLYE GRABBED CAL by the shirtfront and jerked him forward. He pushed him through a labyrinth of corridors, corners, and stairwells. Still seeing spots, Cal tried to count the steps, but he was completely disoriented. Every time he thought he had a handle on his position or a direction, a rattling slap would lash out from the darkness.

Cal gritted his teeth. He allowed himself to be borne along. He memorized every blow, adding each one to Blye's tab.

I'll kill you, Jason. I'll kill you, Blye.

Cal collided with a door and whirled around. He squeezed his eyes shut again and again, hoping to blink away the floating pink dots obliterating his vision.

"Settle down," said Blye. "We're here."

Cal heard the oiled whir of another door swinging wide. He felt a breeze from the change in pressure. He sensed that he was standing on the precipice of a cavernous space. He heard Blye's footsteps advancing into it, and over them, a blessed sound.

Heather, cursing.

"You piece of shit, let me out of here! You fucking filth!"

Cal stepped forward, feeling his way into the space. He expected to collide with a wall, or receive another stinging slap or slash from a blade, but he was so close now. Heather's ragged voice echoed around the room. He was blind and couldn't call out, but he fumbled toward her in the darkness.

Then the light flared again. This time from a lantern on a folding table. Blye switched on another, and the nimbus of light expanded, revealing more of the cavernous room.

It was like being in the hold of a great ship. There was a ceiling several stories overhead, but Cal could not see it or the full contours of the space around them. Finally, as Blye lit more lanterns, the light reached the center of the room.

And revealed Heather.

He had braced himself to see her in pain, in distress, but he couldn't prepare himself for this.

Her chair sat in the center of the hold, surrounded by massive steam-driven turbines, now dormant. They were like sleeping automatons, standing sentry over her. Her feet were shackled together and attached to a chain that ran to a grate in the floor. Her face and arms and clothes were streaked with coal dust—it was clear she hadn't let the chains stop her. She had crawled along the sooty floor as far as the chains would allow before returning to the relative safety of her chair.

How long had she been alone in the dark? Blye must have snatched her sometime after slitting Cal's throat, but when exactly? Her eyes were red and puffy and filled with both fury and terror as she watched Jason turn on his lanterns. When her eyes finally fell on him, she screamed, "Cal!"

Or rather she tried to. Her voice was hoarse. Blye had hidden her so deeply, so far down in the dark that he hadn't bothered to gag her.

Cal sprinted for her. Had he been closer to Blye, he would have fallen upon the killer and torn him limb from limb on the spot. But Blye had planned for that too. He had positioned himself several feet away, with Heather between them, watching with satisfaction as a helpless Cal rushed to her and dropped to his knees in front of her chair. He buried his face in her lap and wrapped his arms around her as she keened. The sound pierced his heart, but he fought to keep his emotions in check. If he was to save them both, he needed to focus on the threat, not Heather.

Just like the Very Hot Day.

I will kill you for this, Blye. I will kill you, Jason.

"Get me out of here, Cal," she wept. "Kill this fucking psycho and get me out of here."

"Is there something you two want to tell me?" teased Blye. "Because I'm starting to think you have a thing for my girl, Cal."

He leveled the pistol at Heather's head and jutted his chin at Cal. *Back up.*

Cal complied, holding his hands up in acquiescence. *Don't shoot.*

Cal took in what he could. Remnants of the plant's old life cluttered the cold floor—rusted tools, valves, cables, and other leavings of the boilers and turbines that once populated the hold. There were food wrappers and water bottles scattered around Heather—the bastard had even left a bucket—and Cal surmised she'd been here since last night. With the chains, she had a small radius. He didn't care if she crawled a little or screamed a lot. It was the illusion of freedom. Salvation just out of reach.

Cal looked around. He rubbed his fingers together, then looked at Blye. He pantomimed holding a phone, texting.

"Oh," laughed Blye. "You want to talk, do you?"

Cal held his hands out. *Come on.*

He needed to keep Blye engaged, not concentrating on Heather. He needed to buy time.

Blye thought about it for a moment, then one side of his mouth curled up in a wary grin. "I'm happy to chat for a minute, but only because I've been absolutely dying to, not because you're outsmarting me. Not on your best day, sport. Try calling 911 or anything stupid?"

He stepped forward and pressed the Glock's barrel to Heather's temple. Cal watched her pinch her eyes shut and clench her teeth.

"I wouldn't advise it. Besides, you'd never know *why*, Cal."

Blye pulled the burner phone from his pocket and pitched it to Cal.

Cal's thumbs flew across the screen. He held the phone out for Blye.

"Nice try," said the killer. "Behind that."

He gestured to the folding table where a lantern stood. Cal went around behind it at Blye's order, keeping the table and its lanterns between them. He set the phone down and backed a step. Blye moved cautiously to the table and glared at the screen, reading Cal's message.

After a moment, Blye burst out laughing. He doubled over, his cackle filling the dark overhead and bouncing off the walls. Each peal was like the wings of a bat flapping at Cal. When Blye straightened, he stared at the screen.

"Why, Jason? What's the ducking point?"

He wiped his eyes and held the phone in front of Heather's face.

"Ducking! Can you believe it? I said it the day we met, you're a gift from the gods, Cal. And you just keep on giving. 'Ducking' is so perfect, it absolutely typifies you. You try *so hard* to do a thing, but you can't help but come up short. Always. Oblivious and totally ineffectual. Swept along by currents stronger than you. Like me. Or autocorrect."

Cal held out his hand for the phone. Blye pitched it back to him.

Cal took a long look at Heather, then began to type. Blye was right: He was stalling, but his boiling anger was genuine. When he was finished, he flung it back at Jason, hard. Cal saw Blye's eyes narrow in the glow of the small screen. The killer read the message out loud for Heather to hear.

"How long were you working with Milton?"

77

B LYE'S CHEEKS PEELED upward in a warm smile.

Jason always had a handsome, charming smile, with just a hint of the rake in it. It was conspiratorial, letting you in on a wicked joke. The kind that made old ladies blush and titter instead of scold. But lit by the campfire lanterns, throwing jagged shadows across the planes of Blye's face, Cal saw it now for what it really was: the most terrible thing he had ever seen that didn't have blood on it.

"Well," said Blye, "look who finally caught up. How did you figure it out?"

Cal hadn't figured it out, not entirely, but it was a hunch. One he had plenty of time to think about while strapped to a bed and evading along the trails. Two killers who worked in IT and used the phrase "game over" might be a coincidence, but both with a connection to Heather?

Cal shrugged.

Blye nodded, his lips tugging down at the corners in an impressed expression. "Fair play to you, Detective."

"What?" sputtered Heather. Her voice had no strength left.

"I'm sorry, sweetie. You were supposed to die that day. But as the song goes, you can't always get what you want . . . And the thing of it is, I really wanted you, Heather. Once upon a time.

But I was always the runner-up. The guy you'd cry to when some-one else let you down or broke your heart. Remember that office holiday party a couple of years ago? You were between guys, so I got the call. Jason, the perpetual, platonic Plus One. But hey, why not? Get all dressed up, free booze . . . I figured, for the hundredth time, *maybe this will be the night.* But you ran off to the dance floor with your girlfriends the first chance you got. And I stood in the corner. With the guys talking sports and the wallflowers and the weirdos. And James Allan Milton."

A trapdoor opened in Cal's stomach, revealing an even deeper reservoir of nausea.

"You want a good party trick? Ask a couple of questions about someone and just let 'em go. They'll do all the heavy conversa-tional lifting for you, because people just *love* to talk about them-selves. I mean, look at me, right?"

Blye laughed.

"Milton talked to me about computers and video games and it wasn't long before he told me how much he hated ATMA and its people. Oh, he was such an angry boy, I could tell that from the jump. And all the while, I'm looking over his shoulder at you. On the dance floor. You were under a disco ball, and I swear to God it was like shards of light were coming off of you. Whirling and glowing and laughing with your girlfriends. You were radiant that night, and I realized you were never going to be mine."

Blye looked at her. For a moment, it was an expression of sin-cere longing, then his face cracked into his cocksure grin again.

"So Plan B then. Milton became my pet project. I pretended to give a shit about him. We became online *friends.*" Air quotes again. "We'd spend hours chatting online during first person shooter games. Or rather, I'd just listen to him fume while he blew away zombies or aliens or terrorist cells. All it took was a little push and he would just *go.* I'm talking epic fucking rants. But I knew he needed a bigger push, so I made an anonymous call to his supervisor Barry and let him know about Milton's online conduct as Vapor.

"After he was fired, he talked about shooting up the place. I was never judgmental. I was a shoulder to seethe on. And then I began to goad him . . . *I can see why you hate them . . . They were all assholes to me at the party . . . Heather only brought me there as a joke* . . . I laid it on a little thick, but let's face it, the guy was obviously not adept at picking up on social cues.

"Anyway, when the chats began to turn from *Wouldn't it be nice* to *If I were going to do it*, we took the conversation to the dark web. He was more comfortable there, so I just followed his lead.

"I mean this guy hated *everyone*. Women, immigrants, people of color, people without color. He even wrote a manifesto." Blye rolled his eyes. "The most important document of your life and you can't even bother with spellcheck? I convinced him to let me post it the minute the shooting started."

Blye made a jerking-off motion. "It went right in the trash."

He still had the gun pointed in Heather's direction. Cal didn't dare move. He looked at Heather. Her fists were clenched. Her head hung low, her long hair—dark with soot and drenched in perspiration—hid her face. That long-ago frayed rope swaying in the water again, of monsters in the deep, and the sense that he had gotten there too late. If he was reeling, he could only imagine the storm in her head.

"And then, on a beautiful summer's day, it finally happened. I honestly didn't know how I'd feel about it, but it felt . . . hollow. I mean, it was incredibly exciting at first, like a sugar rush, but I crashed. Sure, Milton did the heavy lifting. He pulled the trigger . . . but I pointed the gun. And no one would ever know. It was all so unsatisfying."

He looked at Heather.

"When I got word you were still alive, I was fucking gobsmacked. I got down to the hospital as soon as I could, and I was surrounded by this storm of activity. So many people were there, Heather. You have so many friends, but not a one of them knew what to do. They were utterly pathetic and sobbing on each other's shoulders . . . so I just took charge. Center stage. It felt good. Electric. I split people into shifts, organized food, acted the cheerleader. I was the guy."

"I started to get a new idea then. Deep down, you always thought you were out of my league. Now all of a sudden, the math had changed. Because I changed it. And wouldn't it be fun to see where it all led? I could play with you forever now. It would be like having a pet.

"And then . . . you," said Blye, locking eyes with Cal. "Blood still under your fingernails and the fucking need just radiating off of you. Everyone could see it. You were *perfect*. And I moved you around like a little action figure. *Go get donuts, Cal. Take this shift, Cal. Stand over here, Cal.* And you just did it. You were so fucking desperate to be of use.

"And then the damnedest thing happened. She fell for you. After everything I did for her, all the work I put in, I came in second again. I could see it in her eyes when she looked at you. *She fell for you.*"

Blye jabbed the air between them with the gun for emphasis. Cal held his breath. Then Blye laughed bitterly.

"Gotta admit, it was kind of infuriating. But now I had a new pet project, Cal. *You.* But this time, I'd have skin in the game. No more playing by remote control. Every night, I left Heather's and planned. Or went on my nightly errands. And in between, we'd all hang out, a bunch of pals, and I'd watch you two fucking idiots moon over each other, then rack yourselves with guilt about it. All the while, I had this secret knowledge. It was like walking around with a constant mental hard-on. It feels so good to get it all off my chest . . ."

Blye held out his free hand and spread his fingers wide. "Look, I'm shaking."

He blew out a deep breath.

"Here's the thing: Jack the Ripper is only Jack the Ripper because no one knows who he really is. If he was John Q. Schmuck, a consumptive chimney sweep or a drunken dock worker or even a syphilitic royal, who would care? He wouldn't be a legend. So I don't want everyone to know who I am. Just the two of you."

Blye smiled.

"So Cal escapes, kidnaps the two of us, and we're never seen again. They'll never find your bodies, I'll make sure of that. And I'll start fresh somewhere new, but I'll carry the looks on your faces with me for the rest of my life. You know what, though? Maybe I will pay Carly a visit on my way out of town. Or that pretty doctor. Or both. The perfect *digestif*."

He bent toward Heather and with his index finger, moved the hair from her stricken face and curled it behind her ear.

"Any last words?" He said it gently.

"Blye . . . ," said Cal.

His whisper was hoarse, dry as a grave. Blye's head snapped up.

"You talk too much."

78

Blye whirled the gun toward Cal. Hearing his raspy voice was something the killer hadn't anticipated, and by the stunned look on his face, he didn't like it.

He would like what came next even less.

Heather swung her fist out, with all the strength she had, connecting with Blye's thigh.

The killer dropped his gaze to his leg and saw the handle of the penknife. The penknife Cal usually carried in his pocket, but for several minutes, carried on his tongue. Until he fell to his knees in front of Heather and buried his head in her lap.

Blye drew in a breath to scream. Cal vaulted over the table, grabbing the nearest lantern in flight and brought it down in a wide, savage arc. The swinging threw tumbling shadows across the cavernous space as if the room itself was capsizing. The lantern connected with Jason's temple and exploded.

Jason reeled backward, getting a shot off. A blinding flash and deafening roar filled the dark hold. Someone jerked Cal from behind. A moment later, there was a high, bright sensation. A red-hot poker pressed into his upper left arm. He clamped it with his other hand, felt the blood flowing between his fingers.

Of course you've been shot, thought Cal. *You've been on borrowed time for months.*

The round knocked him back a foot or so, but he whirled back and pressed forward. He saw Blye's silhouette beyond the nimbus of light, scrabbling along the ground, trying to get to his feet. One leg bent and the other with the penknife kicked straight out, as if immobilized by a cast. He still clutched the gun. Cal charged forward, bringing his leg back to punt.

He was going to put Blye's head through the uprights.

Blye saw him coming and scrabbled to the side. The kick connected with the killer's stomach, not his head. The wind left him in a rush. The exhalation filled the hold, almost as loud as the gunshot. The kick lifted him off the ground and put him onto his side. The gun skittered away into the darkness.

Blye curled into a ball on the littered, coal-encrusted floor. Without thinking, Cal threw himself on the killer, raining frenzied blows on Blye's head and shoulders with his right fist. Too late, Cal realized Blye had drawn him in close.

Blye uncoiled and struck like a cobra. Cal tried to get his left arm up, but the wound prevented an effective block. He saw a ball valve swinging at his head, then the world rotated.

Cal came to on his back, staring into the hold's cavernous overhead. He touched his fingers to the side of his throbbing head and they came away sticky. It was Heather's screaming that snapped him out of his stupor.

"Cal!" she yelled. "Cal, get up!"

He sat up quickly and looked around. His vision wobbled, but he saw Heather in her chair, pointing. He heard the sound of grunting and heavy, arrhythmic footfalls receding. Cal spun, and when his vision caught up, he caught a glimpse of Blye—hobbling wildly across the vast hold—before the killer disappeared into the darkness, fleeing the way they had entered.

Cal staggered toward Heather. He dropped to one knee in front of her. She clutched him, digging her fingers into his wound without realizing. He gritted his teeth. The pain was sharp but it cleared the rest of his fog.

"You're bleeding," said Heather.

"I'm fine," croaked Cal. He suspected it was a through and through, but he was no doctor. All he knew for sure was his upper arm burned like hell.

He snatched another lantern from the table and returned to her chair to tug at her restraints.

"What the hell are you doing?" she asked.

He looked at her, incredulous.

From the moment they first met, they never needed words. Entire conversations passed between their eyes. Across crowded rooms, over Jason's shoulder, in stolen glances. Her eyes on that Very Hot Day said, "Don't go," all the while knowing he had to, so she sent him away with her badge, sacrificing herself and expecting nothing in return.

She had spent God knows how long in the coal-drenched darkness of that hold, yet this time her eyes said "Go."

Go go go.

He handed her the sole lantern and the burner phone Blye had dropped when the lantern collided with his face.

He turned to leave, but she called after him. "Cal!" Her quavering voice echoed through the shadows.

He faced her again. She was sitting in the middle of endless dark, clutching a single lantern in her lap. She looked as slight as a candle in that massive space, buried under an avalanche of shadow.

But she was in no danger of being blown out. In her eyes, he saw Heather wasn't a candle at all, but a laser—burning fine and blue—with an intensity that could punch through walls.

Come back this time, Cal. Come back, but kill him first. You owe me that.

"Promise me," she said, her voice quivering with rage.

He nodded and was gone.

CHAPTER

79

BLYE HAD MADE two things perfectly clear that night to Cal:
He was the smartest man in the room and he expected zero
resistance from the two of them. But like any bully, he wasn't
prepared for someone to fight back. His helpless conquest jammed
a knife into his leg and his perfect patsy gave him a couple of
solid blows to think about. Blye's painstakingly detailed plans had
turned to shit in an instant.

So Blye ran and Cal followed. He rounded every corner wondering if Blye had recovered the gun on his way out. Cal didn't
think so. Blye would have come back to finish the job. But the difference between thinking and knowing was deadly. He rounded
every black corner wondering if he was going to get shot.

Again.

Blye had purposely disoriented him on the way in, so he ran
down a few dead ends on the way to the exit. The corridors were
darker than dark. One lantern was smashed and Heather had the
other. But it was okay. A lantern would have made him a target
anyway. And after a few long moments in that blackness, his night
vision began to return. Just like the sea at night where, if you were
patient, the stars revealed themselves. The wave tops caressed the
ship. Shapes began to distinguish themselves—a hatch, a windlass, a lifeboat.

Cal was accustomed to stumbling in the dark, but he knew all things resolved in time.

Finally, Cal found the exit, moving sure-footed once more. He paused, grateful he had pitched the lock. Then he exploded from the doorway. He waited for the report of the Glock, to feel another round lance into him, but it was quiet.

He remained in the shadow of the power plant and closed his eyes. The echoing gunshot in the hold, the blood rushing in his ears, the pain at his shoulder, his throbbing head, his ragged breathing . . . it all created a cacophony in his head.

Ebb and flow . . . come and go . . .

The winds had picked up. It was as if the seasons had changed while he was in the dark hold. His heartbeat slowed. The night sounds rose along the trail.

Blye wanted Cal to believe that he was some mastermind—and he was—but he had a knife in his leg and was bleeding from his head. He had expected to kill them and he hadn't, so he needed to get away. *Fast.* That left only one option. Blye had to return the way they came, back to his vehicle.

Cal ran south along the trail to make up ground. From his morning runs, he knew every bend in the trail. With just enough moonlight and his night vision now wide open, he sprinted without fear of his surroundings. When he felt he must be catching up to Blye, he abandoned the trail for the strip of woods alongside it.

There was still a good chance Blye was lying in wait. A better than good chance. He was getting closer to the avenue where they had left Blye's car. Cal just wanted to charge for it, but he needed to stay alive. If Blye was drawing him closer again, if he killed Cal, he'd go back for Heather. She would die in that dark hold, and Blye would get away and start all over again somewhere else.

Cal moved silently through the trees now. He followed a small gulley parallel to the trail and darted from one copse to the next, listening. He approached a large oak. Blye whirled from behind it, screaming. He swung a heavy branch. Cal ducked his head but took the blow square on his lanced upper arm. The pain was dazzling. His knees buckled. Blye advanced, the branch held high over his head. Cal fell backward but threw a quick backstep jab into Blye's injured thigh. The killer howled and dropped the branch as Cal tumbled into the gulley.

When Cal got to his feet and climbed out of the gulley, he heard the heavy breathing and the halting gait of a limping run. There was a break in the trees on the river side of the trail. The distant lights of the Maryland side of the Potomac outlined Blye's silhouette, hunched and flinging himself forward to the safety of the streetlamps.

Cal broke from the trees and went straight for him.

Blye may have been a mastermind, but he was much diminished, and no longer armed. If Blye had the gun, he wouldn't have bothered with the branch.

Knowing Cal was closing, Blye changed course. He turned off the trail again, putting the river behind him to lose Cal in the trees once more.

It was a bad idea. Blye shuffled through the brush over uneven terrain, stumbling over tree roots. Cal followed. He was close enough to hear the killer's ragged breathing across the quiet patch of woods. From the racket, Blye was in a full panic now.

How does it feel? wondered Cal.

Blye was scared, tired, and losing blood, but there was a wide swath of grass that led right to the lip of the George Washington Parkway. He ran for the parkway flat out. He waved his arms frantically. Cars rushed by. Cal had to hand it to him; it was a decent gambit. Even in this instant, he was still making Cal look like the villain. A relentless horror film boogeyman, emerging from the woods. Silent and inexorable. In slow, chilling pursuit of a poor, frantic man limping for safety. Cal may as well have been wearing a hockey mask.

But Blye's plan worked too well. Not a single car stopped.

Haven't you heard, Jason? There's a killer on the loose in Alexandria. Some real Jack the Ripper shit.

"Help!" shrieked Blye. He flung his arms over his head. The cars may as well have been passing ships on the horizon. "Help me, you motherfuckers!"

Cal stopped running. There was no need to. Blye wasn't going anywhere.

Cal grabbed Blye by the shoulder and spun him around. The lantern had opened a gash on Blye's scalp. Up close, his face was a mask of blood and soot. It was jarring enough that Cal didn't notice the penknife in his hand.

Blye thrust it into Cal's middle, trying to gut him, but the handle was slippery and it raked across Cal's stomach. Cal felt the burning trail of it, the fresh blood, but the blade tangled in his shirt, and fell into the grass.

It only fed his rage.

Cal hauled back. Not to punch Blye's face, but to punch through it. He heard a crunch, felt teeth and cartilage give. He'd never hit anything like that before.

It felt good.

Blye's head snapped back and he went sprawling on the grass, just shy of the road. Cal pressed on. He was vaguely aware that his throat itched and pulsed. His shoulder burned and his head pounded and his stomach stung. But those sensations were remote. What he felt most were his fingernails biting into his palms, the blood throbbing in his fists, his teeth clenched so hard they threatened to shatter in his head. He was ready to beat Jason Blye to death.

Blye got up to all fours. He held a shaky hand out to stop Cal's advance. He staggered to his feet. They faced each other, intermittently illuminated by the headlights of the passing cars that wanted no part of their fight. Blye swayed on his feet as if with fever. His nose was a fount of blood. One pant leg was darker than the other. He was a bucket full of holes, any remaining blood pouring out of him.

It would take no effort at all to kill him. He wanted nothing more in his whole life.

With great pain, Cal said, "You're under arrest."

Blye began gurgling. The sound soared to a terrible keening. Cal realized it was a laugh, an unhinged bleat of pain and fear. But mostly it was rage. The sound of frustration, of being thwarted at the last possible moment. It didn't even sound human. He supposed it wasn't.

Cal stepped forward. Blye crouched again, then arched his back. He looked like he'd stepped on a live wire. Cal ran for him, but it was too late. Blye pitched himself backward onto the parkway.

There was the sound of crushing impact—crumpled metal and breaking glass—quickly drowned out by the screeching of rubber. A handful of cars slowed to a halt. The section of road was suddenly awash in headlights. Car doors opened. A woman shouted, *"Oh my God! Oh my God!"*

Cal turned his back on all of it and walked back into the dark woods.

80

IN HIS DREAMS, he carried Heather out of the coal plant in his arms.

She rested her head on his shoulder. Rather than taking the dark trail, he opted for the river side of the building. Somehow, he made his way down the bluff cradling her in his arms, like he had that day by the car and again on his porch. There was a small boat waiting for them, the kind his ship used for boardings in the Navy. He placed Heather in the bow and they set off, toward the string of lights on the other side of the river. He got the boat up to speed and the bow lifted free of the water and they planed across the Potomac, the relative wind blowing away the sweat and stench of that dark, coal-drenched hold. It was as close as they could get to flying. He steered and watched her from behind the open console. The lights along the shore twinkled ahead of her. She was dressed in one of her sundresses he loved so. Her hair flew back like red streamers. She looked back and smiled wide, like it was just another date. She reached back toward him to take his hand.

"The mayor will see you now," said the secretary. Cal rose to his feet in the anteroom. Unfolding himself from the chair activated his wounds and brought him back to the present. The healing penknife slice at his stomach flared. His necktie tugged at the lighter bandage that covered his almost healed throat. Striding toward the mayor's door, his sleeve scraped his upper arm where Blye's bullet had grazed him. His cuffs buttoned over the faded bruises where he had struggled against the hospital restraints, and later where handcuffs bit into his flesh. He welcomed the pain. Pain was knowledge, and the knowledge kept him grounded.

He had been here before. Not just the mayor's office, but *dazed* in the mayor's office, stuck between reality and the never-ending loop of *what might have been.*

His daydreams were sweet, if sophomoric, but his dreams at night were not. Most times Cal and Heather never left the hold. If he did escape to pursue Blye, he didn't make it back to get her. And if he somehow managed to return, she was always gone. Only swirling hair left behind.

It almost made him long for the nightmares from the Very Hot Day. Almost.

Cal walked into the mayor's office. Arrayed around the table was a tight knot of familiar faces. It gave him a feeling of déjà vu. He felt unstuck in time. Mayor Schleicher sat at the head of the table, but rose when Cal entered the suite. Everyone else followed: Chief of Police Ravelle, a couple of city councilmen, and the ever-present PR flack, Conway. It was surprisingly deferential, yet the mayor looked like he had a sour taste in his mouth when he shook Cal's hand.

Cal took a seat at the table to the mayor's left. He felt surrounded. At the end of the table was Deputy Chief Simbulan. If anyone in the room had his back, it would be Simbulan, but if the mayor looked like he had a sour taste in his mouth, then his deputy chief looked like he'd swallowed a hot coal.

That didn't bode well.

Cal needed to clear his head, but fought from giving it a shake in front of the City of Alexandria's leadership. Instead, beneath the table, he squeezed his fists, pressing his nails into the cut grooves there—still healing—from that night. He came round as the mayor began to speak.

"On behalf of the city, I want to apologize—" he said, glancing toward one of the suits—a lawyer—who gave his head a tiny, nearly imperceptible shake. The mayor adjusted course. "I want to *thank* you for stopping Mr. Blye's rampage. I think we can all admit that it was a rapidly evolving situation and very confusing in the moment, and while certain actions were taken in the best interests of the city, some of those actions in retrospect were ultimately suboptimal . . ."

Cal nodded, but said nothing.

The mayor cleared his throat to continue.

"So, thank you. We wanted to bring you over to show our gratitude . . ."

He stood, as did everyone else at the table. Once again, a photographer appeared.

Cal remained seated.

The occupants of the table loomed over him. Just as the jittery cops hovered over him on the trail that night.

From the hold, Heather managed to get a signal with the burner phone and called 911. Responders found and liberated her. While she was being sped to Inova Alexandria in the back of an ambulance, Cal was cuffed and seated on the trail, intercepted before he could reach her. Just out of earshot, he heard a knot of patrol officers trying to suss out just what the hell was going on. The only words he heard for sure were "Killer Callum."

And why not? All day long, they had been in search of Killer Callum, the bloodthirsty serial killer. A psycho who slit his own throat. He attacked Detective Stacy Porter, and word was no doubt circulating that he had murdered beloved Detective Adam Massey that very night. Cal overhead there were witnesses who reported Killer Callum threw a man into traffic who was now fighting for his life.

"Fuck, I wish he resisted," one of the uniforms had said.

Cal looked up and saw that it was Adelphia. He locked eyes with the officer.

Adelphia went quiet.

They were angry, but more than that, they were spooked as hell. The wind whipped around them. They were in the dark, at the center of something bigger than they understood, and they sensed it. Tonight would be one for the history books. Even with Heather proclaiming his innocence—and he didn't know at that moment if she had—the rumors of Cal as cop-killing boogeyman had a huge head start, and a hardheaded uniformed force had several months' practice at hating him.

But mostly, they were spooked.

He knew there was a good chance he'd be shot on sight—he couldn't even call out loudly enough to warn the knot of officers—so he simply materialized out of the darkness, around a bend in the trail, with his hands up and walking backward toward them. When they saw him and drew down, he got on his knees slowly and proned out without having to be told. Even with his compliance, his brothers in blue were less than gentle with him. The handcuffs bit into his wrists. It was something to focus on to keep his mind from his catalog of other wounds. Heather was safe. That was all that mattered. He practiced his breathing and looked through a break in the trees at the dark water of the Potomac and the string of pretty lights on the opposite shore. He didn't know how long he sat there like that. At some point, Sydnor arrived, a furious voice of reason, yelling like mad to release him.

Now Cal looked from face to face in the mayor's office. They hid it well, but the people standing around the table were just as spooked by him as the uniforms on the trail had been. They just had a bit more polish. In that instant, something Dr. Julia said flashed by like an arrow.

Not everyone here has your best interests at heart, Cal.

"No pictures," said Cal. The exhaustion in his voice was palpable.

Mayor Schleicher stared down at him for a moment. Cal caught the slightest hardening around the mayor's eyes, the barest glimpse of malice, but the smile never left his face. The mayor took his seat. One by one, everyone else did too.

"Why not, Farrell?" asked Chief Ravelle. "You've certainly earned some good press."

"But I didn't really last time, did I?" he said. "Maybe this'll balance the scales."

Chief Ravelle nodded. Deputy Chief Simbulan hid a smile. No one else met his eye.

But Cal wasn't here to have that conversation. Sometimes, overcoming impostor syndrome was realizing you were better than you believed. And sometimes it was realizing everyone else was just as fucked up as you.

Cal looked from person to person. The more uncomfortable they grew, the more at ease he felt.

"You know," he continued, "before he was killed, Detective Massey spoke about writing a memoir. About book tours and becoming a cable TV talking head. Cashing out."

"The department forbids—" began the chief.

"What are you going to do, strap me to a hospital bed?"

Cal laughed. He was the only one who did. It felt like the barometer dropped in the room, preceding an ugly storm.

"Relax. I'm not going to sue the department or the city. It wouldn't do any good—not for me and not for the people of Alexandria."

The mayor shifted in his seat. The lawyer leaned forward in his.

"I don't need the money," continued Cal. "But if I ever do, I have a pretty good story in my back pocket. For a rainy day."

Jason Blye was caught, he would stand trial if he survived his extensive injuries, and then he would go to jail. Cal would testify, of course, but that would be the end of it. No interviews, no photo ops, no award ceremonies. No dog and pony shows. Despite the inevitable rabid media coverage, he would not be the poster boy for Alexandria law enforcement. Not again.

Everyone was dismissed, but the mayor asked Cal to stay behind. Deputy Chief Simbulan exchanged a look with Cal, but Cal shrugged. Once the door closed behind Simbulan and the rest, it was just Mayor Schleicher and Chief Ravelle. The smile slid from the mayor's face.

"I don't appreciate threats, young man. Veiled or otherwise."

"Threats?"

Schleicher's grimace became a full-on sneer. "*The book.*"

Cal chuckled.

"I wouldn't worry about it, sir. I'm a terrible writer."

Chief Ravelle spoke up. "What the mayor is trying to say is, what is it you really want?"

Cal smiled.

81

IT WAS A very hot day. Cal stood on the pavement outside Alexandria Police Headquarters, squinting in the sun. She said she would stop by, but he wasn't sure, not until he saw her van coming down Wheeler Avenue. She pulled up to the curb and he walked around to the driver's side. Heather smiled at him. He forced himself to smile back. The van was loaded with everything from her apartment that hadn't already been shipped.

"Do you have time for lunch?" he asked, trying to sound breezy.

"I ate, thanks."

"Coffee then? It's a long drive . . ."

She pulled a large cup from the cup holder. "Already topped off. I want to get a jump on the day. Lot of road."

"Right," he said, nodding.

He was nodding a lot. He thought he must look like an idiot, so he stopped, desperately trying to figure out what to say next. To forestall the inevitable.

When they were finally reunited after that night, things had changed. Just like the weather. How could they not? She looked at him expectantly when they finally let him in to see her. Short of bringing her Blye's head, she wanted a look of confirmation that her tormentor was dead and gone.

He could not return her look.

Later, she told him her leaving had nothing to do with him, that she needed space. She was moving home to Portland. To be with family. And to be as far away from Alexandria as she could get. He had offered to come with. He would leave for her, he told her. He hadn't even thought about it, he just blurted it out. Once, she had given up her badge for him. He would happily do the same for her.

Go go go.

But she told him he *was* Alexandria. Like it or not, he would be a daily reminder of what had been done to her.

Blye wins, he thought ruefully.

Now they were face to face under the hot sun. Her air conditioning was blasting through the window. He wanted to be inside the cool, air-conditioned van with her, heading west. Or to draw her out, to somewhere shady and quiet, where he could continue to plead his case.

But she had an iron will and the van was idling.

That day in bed with her, he was thinking about a ring. Now she was leaving and there was nothing he could do to stop it. He was suddenly grateful for his hand on the windowsill, for something solid. His legs felt weak, like he had a fever. The world was spinning too quickly. In moments, she would be gone.

He knew what he wanted to say. He just needed to say it.

"I just need to tell you—"

She cut him off.

"No, Cal. Please no. I'm tired of what men need. What they need to tell me, what they need from me or need me to be. Projecting whatever bullshit . . ."

She made a frustrated growl, so different now than the kind she used to make when she'd hugged him. She trailed off.

"I'm just tired," she said. "I'm going home."

"Right." Cal nodded, swallowed it. He tried another smile. "I just wanted the city's last words to be kind ones."

She raised her eyebrow and gave him a crooked smile. "So you speak for Alexandria now? It's yours?"

He met her eye. "Yeah. I believe I do."

She nodded toward headquarters. "What about them?"

"I'm in the CAP Section now." *Crimes Against Persons.* Where he had once dreamed about being before his life's trajectory was knocked off course last summer. Blye had been right about one thing: he had been pushed and pulled by stronger currents, but no more. From now on, he would be the rock in the river. He had wanted CAP once upon a time, and when he saw his opportunity, he took it.

"Steering into the skid, aren't you?" she asked.

He thought about that moment in the museum, looking up at the boat, seeing the knots—really seeing them—just before the blade. That sensation of figuring things out. Like finding the word on the tip of your tongue. If he couldn't have her, he would have that.

"I belong there."

"About damn time, Detective. Come here."

He bent and leaned into the car window. She kissed him. It was long and sweet and their last. He didn't want it to end, but he pulled away first. She was still holding onto his tie.

"Take care, Heather."

"One second," she said. He thought she was going to pull him in for another kiss, but instead, she loosened his tie and undid the top two buttons of his dress shirt, revealing the long, thin scar that ran across his throat. It curved upward on either side of his neck, like a second smile. She traced her fingers over it.

"Don't hide it, Cal. I'm proud of mine. Be proud of yours."

He nodded, could not speak.

"Besides," she added, putting the van in gear and smiling her megawatt smile. "Chicks dig scars."

He watched her pull away, back up Wheeler Avenue toward Duke Street, and the highways that would take her west, as far away from Alexandria as possible. She rounded the bend and was gone.

"I just needed to tell you that I love you," he said.

He turned on his heel toward headquarters, slipping his tie off altogether as he walked back across the green plaza. He noted the large, replica Alexandria Police Department badge on the building's façade that normally elicited a grin. He wasn't in a smiling mood today, but he was excited about his new desk in CAP. Thanks to Heather, he had been fully exonerated, and one of Sydnor's buddies in the Electronics Investigations Section had cracked Blye's computer. He was still Killer Callum to some, but the truth was out there and gaining ground. People were coming around. A few officers and detectives by the entrance said hello as he passed by. Cal noticed that one of them was Maddox, Adelphia's pal. Maddox nodded.

Cal stood a little taller and nodded back.

He would own his scar. He would own being a detective. And maybe narrow the gap to his best self. It would take time, but if there was one thing he was certain of, all things resolved in time. For today, he would pray for a quiet afternoon, finish some reports, then go home and rest.

He passed into the air-conditioned lobby. The feeling that someone was watching him snapped him out of his funk. He looked up and saw Julia leaning on the railing of the atrium's lounge, looking down at him with a smile and two cups of coffee.

He stared up into the bright atrium, contemplating her with a hard look. She'd shared his files with the brass, but he supposed she had no choice. Plus, if she hadn't set him free . . .

Still, he was exhausted and in a mood. He held up his hand and made a face that said *Maybe later.*

Julia pulled an exaggerated frown, puffing out her lower lip until Cal couldn't help but laugh. She shook one of the coffee cups and raised an eyebrow.

Cal sighed and took the stairs to her.

ACKNOWLEDGMENTS

I F YOU'VE MADE it this far, dear reader, I'd like to thank you for taking this nasty little journey with me. This was by far the darkest book I've written, and most of my novels are horror. But when it comes to sheer terror, supernatural creatures pale in comparison to someone walking into a building with an AR-15.

During the day job, there was a period when active shooter events were in my portfolio. Full disclosure: I am no first responder, I never had to run toward the sound of gunfire, and the deadliest weapon in my work arsenal is PowerPoint. But for a time, I had to stay abreast of every mass shooting in the country—the who, what, when, why, where, and how. The worst part? How *busy* I was. And the debate continues to rage: *Is it a gun crisis or a mental health crisis?* The answer is yes. We're evolved beings, made of star stuff and electricity and capable of holding two competing thoughts in our heads at once, so let's figure things out together, yeah? Because if we can't manage this, we'll never sort out jetpacks. We were promised jetpacks. Seriously, they should be everywhere by now.

When I'm not shaking my fist at the jetpackless sky, I'm incredibly grateful for everyone who helped me write this book and get it to you. First, thanks to my wondrous wife Kate. She doesn't just put up with my madness, she encourages it. More than that, she made this a stronger story with her keen eye and by patiently nudging me toward breakthroughs I didn't even realize I needed. She is "all of the above" and inspires me daily. Thanks to my daughter Sidney, who astonishes me every day with her wide-open heart and resilience. Navigating middle school is tough enough without a global pandemic, and I'm so very proud of her. Time spent at the keyboard or stuck in my head is time away from my radiant ladies, so I deeply appreciate their patience, love, and support.

Thanks to my mother Linda Schweigart and sister Jaclin Madarang for their fierce love and encouragement, Jersey-style.

Thanks to Betzy and Larry Hansen, my incredible in-laws, for their endless generosity.

I'm incredibly fortunate to have my very own Author Avengers on speed dial. Thanks to Nick Petrie, author of the superb Peter Ash series and a fount of writing wisdom to many. He helped me turn a first draft into a novel with his deep insight and spot-on suggestions. Thanks to Don Bentley—author of the sensational Matt Drake *and* Tom Clancy Jack Ryan Jr. series—for similarly helping me crack the maddening challenge of the upcoming *Women and Children First*. His hustle astounds me. And thanks to Graham Brown, author of the Hawker and Laidlaw series and the NUMA Files series with Clive Cussler, for being Graham Brown, the most interesting man in the world. I'm in awe of these guys and blessed to call them friends.

Thanks to my indomitable agent, Barbara Poelle, for finding *The Guilty One* a home. She is actually a tiger shark in a trench coat, equal parts funny and ferocious.

Thanks to Terri Bischoff for taking a chance on this dark story and making it better. For every book you read, there's an assembly line of awesome professionals behind the scenes banging it into shape, polishing it, and rolling it out, and none are better than the Crooked Lane team. Thanks to Rebecca Nelson, Melissa Rechter, Madeline Rathle, Dulce Botello, David Heath, and Nicole Lecht.

Thanks to Sean Cameron for his signal boosting. I love it when Twitter friends become real friends. Sean and his gleefully unhinged partners, Chris Albanese and Mike Houtz, host the *Crew Reviews* podcast, where you can find a treasure trove of creator interviews. It's a spoonful of sugar to make the writing medicine go down. In this case, the sugar is bourbon. The medicine? Also bourbon.

Thanks to Adam Plantinga, author of *400 Things Cops Know*, an essential—and hilarious—resource. Also, a great follow on Twitter.

Thanks to Captain Jamie Bridgeman for being so generous with his time and answering questions about the Alexandria Police Department. Any details that ring true are due to him and any inaccuracies are mine alone. And thanks to Melissa Riddy for hooking us up.

In the Radiant Exemplar category, thanks to Greg Ferry, my unpaid and unofficial life coach, for motivating me for nearly twenty-five years. If you bottled this man's energy, it could power the Eastern Seaboard. He's my kind of crazy.

Thanks to my CISA colleagues, past and present, for always keeping a weather eye out. Thanks to Andrea Schultz, architect and champion of the first ever federal active shooter training materials. Thanks to Shannon Brown for always letting me vent—I miss our daily coffees. And thanks to Wade "Easy Day" Townsend, Stoic brother and all around magic skeleton.

In the Appreciate You from Afar category, thanks to Brian Johnson and the team at Heroic for helping me optimize energy, work, and love. And thanks to Brian Michael Bendis, Kelly Sue DeConnick, and Matt Fraction for the inspirational virtual meal. Face time with my heroes was a gleaming bright spot in those dark, early days of the pandemic.

Thanks to this man's best friend, the Mighty Bear, for helping me break story on our walks. And thanks to Ginger, Cinnamon, Pumpkin, and Ripley for the daily cuddles.

And once more with feeling, thank you, dear reader. I sincerely appreciate you giving *The Guilty One* a chance. Wishing you love and jetpacks.